And Justice Will Be Done

Morgan Currier

Hog City Books

ISBN-13: 9781953164018

Cover design by: Jessica Maisonet
Published by: Hog City Books

To my husband Tracy. Because you've always told me I could.

ACKNOWLEDGMENTS

Thank you to my team of beta readers and editors: Lisa Newton, Tracy Standafer, Sarah Kaufmann, Bob Sirrine, and Jessica Shevock-Johnson.

A big thank you to Jessica Maisonet for her beautiful cover work.

Thank you, Anna and Nat, for harassing me to get this one finished.

And most of all, thank you to Tracy Currier, my wonderful husband, for putting up with the late-night writing, plotting, editing discussions, and me. I love you.

CHAPTER ONE

"This guy has beautiful hands."

"For a dead guy, you mean?" Detective Berlin Redding stopped writing in her notebook and looked at their loaner medical examiner kneeling next to Charles Bryant.

"For any guy," the ME said. She was holding the dead hand in question. "I mean, look at these." Her thumb rubbed the nail of his index finger. "His nails are spotless. Not a ding or a scratch. No imperfections." She leaned closer to the hand. "Everything is healthy and pink. And look at the tips. He must get regular manicures to get that perfect of an edge." She looked at Berlin. "I don't know many women whose nails are this nice."

Berlin moved across the basement floor and crouched beside the ME. "You're right. He has nice nails." She took the hand and examined the skin on the back of it and then the palm.

"His skin looks fantastic, too. If his hands are

anything to go by, he's never done a minute of physical labor in his life. I don't see any marks or scratches. No sign he's ever even had a callus. Jesus, even his wedding ring looks brand new." Berlin returned the hand to the ME and tried to think of the woman's name. Something that started with R?

The ME grinned. "I don't think we needed to look at his hands to know he wasn't your typical DIYer." She nodded toward the gaping holes in the drywall above their heads. "Do you think he knew how to check for studs?"

Berlin studied the mess of paint cans, boxes, random tools, miscellaneous junk, and the expensive wooden shelf piled on top of Charles Bryant's head. "I think he skipped that part of the instruction video."

"Detective Redding?" The question came from outside the storage room.

Berlin pulled off her gloves as she stood. "In here."

One of the rookie officers entered the room. He was fresh-faced, bright-eyed and reminded her of an eager puppy. He didn't look much older than sixteen, but she knew that had more to do with her age than his.

"What's up, Officer Chase?"

"Detective Lewis is ready for you, as soon as you're done here, ma'am."

She winced at the *ma'am* but smiled at Chase. "Thank you. I'll follow you upstairs." Berlin turned back to the ME. "Unless you need anything else from me?"

"Nope."

Berlin nodded. "After you, Officer Chase."

He grinned at the ME. "Bye, Doc Anderson."

"See you later, Sam." The ME smiled at Chase and then turned her attention back to the body.

Anderson, huh? Guess it wasn't an R.

Berlin followed Chase out of the storage room and back through the twenty-seat home theater. They exited the theater and entered a long hallway and finally reached the stairs leading to the main floor.

At the top of the stairs was another hallway with several options for doors. They went through the second one and entered a large, formal sitting room. Straight-backed chairs, a firm-looking couch, dark wood side tables, and a simple Persian rug were the sparse furnishings. None of it said, "sit back and relax".

As they walked through the room, Berlin noticed pictures in heavy silver frames on one wall. She slowed her steps to look at them, and then finally stopped. She stared at them, trying to tie the images behind the spotless glass to the one of Charles Bryant's head smashed in by cans of expensive paint.

The pictures were arranged in chronological order: Charles Bryant and his wife Kay at their wedding, dressed in designer outfits. A picture of the perfectly tanned and toned couple on a white sandy beach, holding a "Just Married" sign, enormous grins on their faces. A little girl started to appear in the pictures, chubby and cute when she was young, but soon Berlin could see the perfect blend of Charles and Kay in the pretty blond girl's face. Then an older Charles and Kay golfing, scuba diving, sitting in a bright red sports car.

Chase looked back to see what was keeping her. When she didn't move, he returned to her side and studied the wall with her. After a couple of minutes, he said, "My family puts pictures up on the refrigerator.

Mom pulls 'em down every few years and starts over with updated ones."

Berlin nodded. "My parents have pictures in those multi-frames. You know, the ones that have twenty-four spots?"

Chase nodded.

"Everything is probably ten years out-of-date."

"Weird where people put their priorities, isn't it?" Chase said.

"What do you mean?" Berlin turned toward him. His face was serious as he studied the photos. The young, eager boy was gone, and a police officer stood in his place.

"The pictures all updated, carefully maintained. Maybe they only want to show the world the cleanest version of their lives?" He looked at Berlin. "Not necessarily the real one."

Berlin frowned. "Just because they have updated picture frames doesn't mean it's not their actual life. Nothing on this property tells me they're not the well-off, well-established family we see here." She nodded toward the pictures.

Chase shook his head. "That's what I mean. Just look at this room. At this entire house. Nothing in this place looks genuine. It's like they want to prove to everyone who comes here what a wonderful family they are. Nobody is this perfect in real life."

Berlin raised her eyebrows. "It's sad that one so young is such a cynic."

The big grin was back, and just like that, Chase was a goofy rookie again.

"Detective Redding, you have questions for Mrs. Bryant?"

Berlin stepped around Chase and moved in the direction of her partner's voice. "Excuse me, Chase. The boss has summoned."

She finished crossing the sizeable room, walked down a short hallway and into the elaborate kitchen. Everything there looked heavy, sterile, expensive and brand new. Except her partner. Berlin fought back her grin when she saw him.

Detective Peter Lewis perched on a dainty wooden chair at an elegantly useless table. He looked as comfortable as a bull in a lingerie shop. His yellow legal pad, filled with scribbled notes, was in front of him and looked equally out of place against the gold and black marble. Another officer leaned against the contrasting white marble countertop across the room, picking at his nails. The only person who belonged in the room was Kay Bryant.

Even with the added years since her wedding picture and the reddened puffiness from crying, Kay Bryant was a handsome woman. Her body had the athletic composition often seen in golf or tennis players and she had a strong facial structure that was handling age well. Her blond hair was expertly cut to look both sophisticated and cute, her makeup applied so it was barely noticeable, and her skin showed enough lines from aging to make it believable she had had no work done. She dabbed at her eyes with a white linen handkerchief that probably cost more than the nicest dress in Berlin's closet.

Berlin joined Pete and Kay at the table, careful not to bump the intricately carved legs. Aiming for a sympathetic tone, she said, "Thank you for answering our questions, Mrs. Bryant. We understand this is a difficult time for you and your family and I know you've given Detective Lewis a great deal of information. But if you think you could go through things with me, I might ask something differently, or hear you say something that might help us piece together what happened…"

Kay nodded her head, straightened in her chair, and said, "Yes, of course. Go ahead and ask your questions."

Berlin smiled at her encouragingly. "What time did you come home today?"

"It was maybe around six this evening. I left the volunteer center just after five-thirty. Charles had a meeting until six-thirty. I thought I would have time to get home and get ready for dinner. But his car was in the driveway when I got home."

Looking at her notes, Berlin found the description of the cars on the property. "Did your husband drive the silver Lexus or the red Mercedes?"

"The Lexus."

Berlin made the correction to her notes and then asked, "Did you hear from him today? A call or text letting you know he'd be home early? Maybe the meeting was cancelled, or he wasn't feeling well and planned to skip?"

Kay shook her head. "No, nothing. We rarely talk during the day. Charles spends his time with clients, or the partners and he requested years ago that I didn't distract or bother him at work." She dabbed her eyes again.

Berlin gave her a moment and thought, *sounds like a great guy*. Maybe Chase wasn't that far off. When Kay looked ready, she asked, "Do you have any idea why he was in the basement? Was he starting a project? Painting? Fixing something? Hanging a new photograph?"

Kay's lips tightened in a frown. "I have no idea. Charles insisted on putting the shelf up a few months ago and then stuff just accumulated on it." The disapproval was obvious. "It should have been thrown away, not kept in the house. And I don't know why he was down there today. He shouldn't have been home!"

Berlin looked over at Pete. He made a rolling motion with his hand. *Wrap it up*. "Mrs. Bryant, did anyone else have access to the house? A gardener or a handyman? Anyone you can think of?"

Kay drew a deep, quivering breath and shook her head. "No, Charles never gave keys to people like that."

Berlin felt her smile tighten at Kay's words but said nothing.

Kay continued. "Our daughter has one. And our parents. We give a spare to the neighbors when we're going away, but we have that key here in the house."

"Would any of them have had a reason to enter the house today?"

"No. And the alarm was set to our private code, so I know no one came in."

Unless someone else had the family's private code. Berlin filed the thought for later. She smiled at Kay again, and said, "Okay, thank you. That's all I have for right now. Would it be all right to come back if I have more questions?"

Kay nodded and gave a slight smile. "Yes, of course."

Berlin slipped a card with her contact

information across the table to Kay. “Please, contact me or Detective Lewis if you have questions or if you think of anything that might help.”

As they walked through the house on their way out, Pete said, “Their daughter is away at a boarding school. The wife’s sister is heading over to pick her up, and then she’ll stay here with them.”

Berlin nodded. They walked past the photos of smiling people and she said, “We need to contact Charles Bryant’s office and find out what time he left and see if they canceled the meeting.”

They exited the double doors at the front of the house and walked down the flagstone path to the car. It was raining, but people milled around in small, tight groups. Berlin asked, “Has anyone talked to the neighbors?”

“Teddy and Martinez took statements from anyone willing to talk. No one noticed what time his car showed up in the driveway. The earliest it was noticed was around four o’clock. We’ll get a tighter timeline once we talk to his office.”

A dark blue BMW traveling too fast pulled onto the street and came to a screeching halt just before the Bryant’s driveway. The driver’s side door opened, and a small, curvy blond woman rushed out. She looked at the police cars and then around her. When she saw Berlin and Pete, she slammed her door shut and half-ran over to them.

“Where’s Kay? Did something happen to Kay? Or Cassie?” Her voice was tight and demanding, but her skin looked bloodless. Berlin wondered briefly if they’d be dealing with a panic attack.

“Ma’am, take a deep breath and calm down.”

Pete's voice was hard and equally demanding. Instead of having a calming effect, the woman looked like she wanted to punch him.

Berlin said, "Please give us your name and how you're related to the Bryant family." From the woman's looks, she could be Kay's curvier, deranged sister.

The blond woman looked at her. "I'm Nichole Kellner. I'm a friend of Kays." Her voice lost the demanding edge when she said, "Please, is she okay?"

"Kay is fine. Were you home at any point this afternoon?"

Nichole Kellner shook her head, her tight curls bouncing. "No, I'm just getting home now. I saw the police lights from down the road. All I could think was something happened to Kay or Cassie."

"Cassie is the daughter?" Pete asked.

"Yes. Their only child."

"Cassie and Kay are fine, Ms. Kellner," Pete said. "Unfortunately, Mr. Bryant had an accident. Are you and Kay close?"

"She's one of my best friends." Nichole told them.

"Kay needs all the support she can get," Berlin said. "Perhaps you could go stay with her until her sister arrives?"

"Oh God, of course!" She started towards the house without another word.

Watching her go, Pete said, "That woman has a fine, round ass."

Berlin rolled her eyes and opened the driver's door. "Great Pete. Real helpful." But she didn't argue with him.

CHAPTER TWO

Lost in thought, Berlin drove back to the Moultonborough office of the Lakes Region Police Department. She half listened to Pete's commentary on a movie he'd watched the night before, inserting noises of interest when she thought they might be appropriate. When he was quiet for more than a minute, she glanced over and caught him staring at her.

"What?"

"That's what I should be asking."

"What are you talking about?" She stopped at a yellow light and watched as the driver behind her threw his hands into the air.

"You agreed to stop at Artie's for lunch and then drove right past it. Something's bothering you, Redding. What is it?"

Drumming her fingers on the steering wheel, Berlin considered his question. The light changed to green, and she accelerated slower than she usually did. The driver was making *go* motions, so she slowed even more. "You still think this was an accident?"

"Bryant's death?" Pete asked.

She nodded.

"Yeah. I don't see how it could be anything else." He looked pointedly at her. "You're an officer of the law, Redding. Stop pissing off the civilians."

Berlin smiled but sped up to the posted speed limit. "You found nothing odd about how Bryant was dressed? Or that he's not the type to clean off a shelf, much less put one up?"

Pete huffed out air. "You're letting your prejudices get the better of you."

"What?" Berlin looked at him in amazement. "I am not prejudiced."

"Everyone has a prejudice against someone."

"Really. And who am I prejudiced against?"

Pete smiled at her, creating the crinkles at the corners of his eyes she loved. "Rich people."

"Jesus, Pete." She shook her head. "You're so full of shit."

"It's true. You don't think rich people can do things on their own. You went into that house, saw old man Bryant, saw his clothes, saw his wife. And you instantly assumed he wouldn't do home projects. Just because he has money."

"And you think I'm wrong?" Berlin asked.

"Nope. I think you're right. Mostly. But I also have a dick. So, I have to take into consideration that old Charlie may have been feeling unmasculine and decided hanging up shelves might do it for his wife and get him laid. So, he hung the shelves, but did a shitty job because he didn't know what he was doing."

"Please," Berlin said, motioning forward, "don't stop now. Share more of your manly knowledge with me. What was he doing in the basement this afternoon?"

Pete shrugged. "He probably wanted to get laid again, so he found another project. Patch a hole. Touch up scraped paint. Mend a tile. You can find that shit on YouTube and they make it look easy."

Berlin shook her head. "You're amazing."

"I know," Pete said. He waved at a redhead in a yellow truck and then turned back to Berlin. "Okay, your turn. Why are you so hung up on this?"

She started with the most obvious. "He was still in his office clothes. Everything in that house is top of the line and high-end. I doubt he skimped on his clothing, either. I can't see crawling around in a basement, even a nice basement, in Armani just to get laid."

Pete considered. "Okay, fair point. What else?"

"Did you notice his hands?"

At his look, Berlin said, "Seriously. The ME, Doctor Anderson, pointed it out to me. His nails were perfect."

"Oh, come on Redding ...."

"And the skin on his hands! No scratches, no scars. Nothing."

"While you and Liz were admiring the corpse's hands, I don't suppose she mentioned me?"

"Grow up, Pete."

"Fine. He took care of his hands. That's not

enough to build a case from."

Berlin thought about the scene more, her fingers drumming once again on the steering wheel. "Everything was nice in that house. Perfect. Did you see anything that needed mending?" She pulled into the parking lot of the police department and put the car into park. Turning toward Pete, she said, "Kay wasn't expecting him home until later. So why was he there so early? Especially if he was so anal about being disturbed at the office. I mean, really? She couldn't text him when he was at work?" Berlin shook her head. "Nope, something specific brought him home and put him in that basement."

Pete shrugged. "Even if that's the case, that doesn't mean his death wasn't an accident."

Berlin couldn't argue with Pete's reasoning. She shut off the car and stared at the dated brick wall of the building. She shook her head again. "I don't know. Something doesn't feel right."

"We'll make some calls and see if we can get an idea why he left work, and when. We'll look at his phone records, see if he called anyone. But I'll be honest with you, Redding. When the boss asks, I'll tell him it looks like an accident."

They both got out of the car. "Fair enough," Berlin said. "But I'll still tell him I think we need to look into it more."

"Let me know how that goes for you," Pete said.

*****

It didn't go well.

Captain Luke Phillips was an officer other men admired and respected, and women wanted to jump. Armed with two degrees and several years of working Boston's streets, he was tall and dark with a well-toned body maintained through dedicated workouts. He'd become the department's poster boy early in his career and it was a spot he worked hard to keep. When he was told the average number of years on the job for making captain was fourteen, Phillips did it in thirteen. He cleared a record number of cases in his department, forced a couple of low-energy old-timers to retire, brought in fresh blood, and managed everyone with a strict hand.

While a few officers and staff members originally bucked under the tighter rule, eventually the department embraced the changes. In return, the department enjoyed being left alone by the county and a city appreciative of their hard work.

Then, just shy of four years as the department's lead man, Phillips announced he was making a run for County Sheriff and since then he'd had no qualms letting his officers know it was his top priority.

Berlin and Pete found Phillips in his office with his weaselly campaign manager. The Weasel handed Phillips a folder as they entered, and Phillips opened it. He nodded to Pete and said, "Begin, Detective Lewis," and then started scanning the document from the folder.

Berlin watched Phillips as Pete recited the details of the case, hoping to get some indication of how Phillips would take her murder proposal. He frowned as Pete gave the basic information on the victim, but then pointed to something on the document and looked at the Weasel. When the Weasel shook his head, Phillips went back to reading. Other than occasionally nodding while Pete talked, Phillips gave little sign he was even listening.

When Pete finished, Phillips signed the document at the bottom, handed it back to the Weasel, and said to Pete, "Good. Get it wrapped up and filed." Another document appeared in front of him and he turned his attention to it, dismissing Berlin and Pete.

Here goes nothing... "If I may, sir."

Phillips didn't look up from the papers. "What, Redding?"

Berlin ignored Pete's eye rolling. "Detective Lewis believes Charles Bryant's death was an accident, but it's worth considering it may-"

"He died in his basement when a bunch of shit fell off a shelf and crushed his head. Correct?"

"Yes, sir. But-"

"The shelf failed. Correct?"

The Weasel gave her an irritated look.

Straightening her back, Berlin said, "We can't say that for certain. We're waiting to hear from-"

Phillips interrupted again, still looking at the papers. "Is there any evidence there was someone in the house with him? Someone who may have held him down while piling that shit on top of him? Maybe taking the time to hit him a few times with a paint can, just to make sure he was dead?"

Berlin could feel the red creeping over her face. She drew a deep breath. "No, sir."

He finally looked up. “Then file it as an accident and stop trying to make everything into a major investigation. We are not New York, Redding. If you want more excitement than some idiot killing himself by doing home repairs he wasn’t capable of doing, by all means, go somewhere else.” He went back to reading.

Berlin wanted to punch someone. She turned and looked at Pete. He stepped back from the look on her face, mouthed, “Let it go,” and backed his way out of the office.

She looked back over at Phillips, now in deep discussion about the upcoming election and ignoring her. She walked out after Pete, trying to figure out why she couldn’t let it go. It wasn’t a matter of being right; it was a matter of making sure she wasn’t right. Berlin took a few deep breaths and then went to find Pete. He was sitting at his desk, headphones on.

“It’s not about being right, you know.”

He ignored her; his music probably way too loud. Berlin sighed and hung up her grey jacket and sat at her computer. As soon as the search engine came up, she logged into the department’s database and typed in the name Charles Bryant. There was nothing there. Not even a parking ticket. She opened a second window and entered his name again, coupling it with lawyer. She scrolled through the typical pop ups, including white page advertisements, obituaries, and classmate finder suggestions. Halfway down the page she had a hit with an article from three years prior announcing Bryant’s promotion to partner in his law firm. There was a summary of his accomplishments in the firm, a brief mention that his wife's name was Kay, and their daughter's attendance of a private school on Lake Kanasatka.

Berlin marked the article and went back to her search. She scrolled through a few more pages but found nothing of interest. Adding Kay's name, his daughter's, the academy, and Moultonborough made little difference. She learned he had coached sports over the years, had donated money to the local library, and volunteered at his daughter's school, but nothing substantial to his death or her case. Berlin sat back, drumming her fingers on her desk, her mind blank.

The Imperial Death March coming from her cell phone startled her from her daze. She sighed and hit the green button.

"Hi mom."

"You're coming to dinner tonight, correct?"

Shit! "Umm, I don't know if I can make it tonight. I have a case I'm working on-"

"Peter said it was an accidental death."

"What?" Berlin whipped around and glared daggers into Pete's head. He was typing furiously. "When did you talk to Pete?"

"I texted him to ask him to dinner, and he said you'd both be here. He said you went to a scene today, but it was an accident so there was no reason to skip our family dinner night."

Berlin closed her eyes, asking whatever Gods were out there for the patience not to kill her partner. "Mom, just because Pete thinks it was an accident doesn't mean we don't have an obligation to look into it further."

"Good, then bring your notes and you can run them by your father. It'll give him something new to think about. Dinner is at five-thirty." She hung up.

"Damn it, Pete!" Berlin looked back at his desk, but he was gone. There was a scrap piece of paper on his keyboard with the words *see you at dinner* scribbled across it. "Bastard." She went back to work.

*****

Berlin left the department late just to be contrary. Then she stopped at the liquor store and picked up two bottles of Flag Hill wine as an apology to her mother, since it was really Pete she was irritated with. His car was parked outside her parent's farmhouse, the hood cold when she felt it on her way up the driveway. He'd probably arrived early so he could report to her mother about her spat with Phillips.

Her parents still lived in the house she'd spent the latter part of her childhood in. Berlin's heart tightened every time she started up the wheelchair ramp installed three years prior or saw the new pill bottles added to the overflowing tray that took up half the counter by the phone.

The wine bag in one hand, she grabbed the door handle with the other, forced a smile on her face and walked into the kitchen. "Where's that rat-bastard partner of mine?"

He was sitting on a stool at the kitchen island,

talking to her mother and drinking a bottle of Pig's Ear ale. Pete grinned at her and stole a piece of fried chicken from the plate her mother was filling. "You know I can't pass up your mom's chicken," he said, his mouth full.

"You're not forgiven." Berlin bumped into him hard enough his arm knocked into his bottle. He caught it before it toppled over. She kissed him on top of his head, kissed her mom's cheek, deposited the wine on the counter, and continued across the kitchen. "I'm going to say hi to dad before dinner."

Her father's room was on the main floor, down a short hallway off of the kitchen. Her mother slept next door to him. Close enough she could be with him in two seconds, but she could still read or watch TV in her own room without disturbing him.

Tom Redding was sitting in an old leather recliner, staring out into the darkening evening. He didn't turn to see who had entered the room.

"Hey daddy. You're looking good tonight." Berlin knelt by the chair and pulled the red and blue wool throw higher on his lap, ignoring how his hands clenched at the arms of the chair. She covered his hand with her own and felt the shaking that never seemed to end.

The slight tremors started a year after he retired from the police force. Something her father had considered a blessing, but Berlin thought was cruel. He and her mother had gotten such a brief time to enjoy retired life together before having to focus on the Parkinson's. Tom handled it well at first. When the tremors were controllable with the medication, before his speech became slurred, and before he started to lose his train of thought in the middle of a sentence. Then, because fate was a truly cruel bitch, he had a stroke. His speech and ability to hold on to his thoughts worsened tenfold. Depression set in and he stopped talking before the second year of dealing with the disease was complete.

"We need to have a pow-wow after dinner. Mom thinks I should talk over our recent case with you so you can tell me it was an accident. Not a murder." She stood up, kissed his cheek, and squeezed his hand. He clenched her hand in return. Berlin knew it was most likely a tremor but still couldn't fight the brief smile that flitted across her mouth. "Yeah, thought you might like that."

She left his room and reentered the kitchen. Her brother had arrived with his eight-month pregnant wife and two children; five-year-old Lynn and fourteen-month-old Thomas. James and Ellen were arguing about changing the baby.

Berlin stepped in, took Tommy from his mother's arms and deposited him in Pete's lap. Pete grabbed the squirming boy on reflex but handled him easily.

"What am I supposed to do with him?"

Berlin tucked a diaper and a travel pack of wipes pulled from the diaper bag under his arm. "Go change him." She gave him a big smile.

Pete gave a dramatic sigh, breathing loudly on the baby. Tommy smiled in response. "The things I do for your aunt." Pete got up from the chair and carried the baby to the kitchen table.

Christine Redding didn't even look up from smashing the potatoes. "Not on the table, Peter.

Take him into Tom's room to change him. His grandfather hasn't said hello to him yet."

"Yes, ma'am." And away he went with the baby.

Berlin pulled plates out of the cabinet and walked the stack over to her brother. "Stop annoying your wife and help set the table. I don't think any of us want her in labor until after dessert."

James kept his arms crossed across his chest and glared at Ellen.

Berlin looked between the two of them and shoved the plates into his stomach. He finally looked at her and took the plates. Ellen's lips were drawn tight, doing nothing to ruin her prettiness. There was something going on between the two of them, hopefully just the stress of the upcoming birth.

Berlin tried to catch her mother's eye as James put the plates on the table with more force than needed, but Christine was focused on punishing the potatoes.

Pete came out of her father's room with Tommy, zooming him around like a rocket ship. Tommy looked unsure if he should laugh or scream.

"If he throws up, you're cleaning it up," Berlin said while putting out the forks and knives.

The zooming stopped. Pete looked at Ellen. "Where do you want him?"

She looked at her husband, who was definitely ignoring her. "I'll take him. Thanks, Pete."

Berlin sided up to her mother and handed her a serving bowl. "I think they're dead, mom. Put 'em in the bowl before they transform into something inedible."

Christine stopped pulverizing the potatoes and glopped them into the bowl and handed the bowl back to Berlin. She looked as stressed as Ellen did.

Lowering her voice, Berlin asked, "What's going on with Jamie and Len?"

Her mother shook her head, grabbed the platter of chicken and a smaller bowl of green beans. She nodded her head at the bowl of squash and Berlin picked it up and followed her mother to the table. "Jamie, please get your father. Everyone else, let's sit. Peter, grab the rolls on your way, please."

By the time they had situated Tommy and Lynn in a highchair and booster between their parent's chairs, James returned to the room with Tom in a wheelchair. He wheeled his father up to the table next to Christine and then took his own place.

Christine started handing around the food. "So, how was everyone's week?" She spooned a small helping of potatoes on Tom's plate. He didn't eat with them anymore, but she liked him to be part of the family routine.

Lynn was smashing her chicken and potatoes together in a good enough imitation of her grandmother that Berlin couldn't help but grin. "We made dough in school," she told her older relatives while smashing.

"Dough?" Berlin asked. "For cooking?"

"It was purple."

Christine looked at James and Ellen for clarification. Ellen was feeding Tommy squash with a baby spoon. "It was play-dough. She got it all over the floor and in the carpet."

"Maybe she shouldn't have had it in the living room," James said in the condescending tone Berlin had hated growing up.

"Maybe someone should have been watching her instead of playing on his phone," Ellen suggested while smiling at Tommy. Her voice equally condescending.

Uh-oh. Berlin looked over at Pete, who was as focused on his chicken as possible. She kicked him.

He looked up from his plate, saw Berlin's face, and said, "We found a dead guy in one of the ritzy lake houses today. His head was bashed in by paint cans."

"What does bashed mean?" Lynn asked. Her potatoes and chicken had become an impressive mini mountain in the middle of her plate. Orange squash decorated the outside, making it appear as though lava was coming down the sides. She was sticking green beans into it, giving it multiple arms.

"Not appropriate, Peter." Berlin said.

"It's the same thing as smashing, sweetie," Christine told her granddaughter before turning her focus on Berlin and Pete. "An accident you said, Peter?"

He nodded. "Yup, looks that way." He grabbed another piece of chicken off the platter.

"Well, Pete thinks it looks that way. Not everyone at the scene agreed with his assessment."

"Who besides you didn't think it was an accident?" Pete asked her.

"If I have my doubts, it's probable other people do, too."

He snorted.

"So, what happened?" Ellen asked, finally looked interested instead of stressed. She'd stopped the spoon just outside of Tommy's reach. He leaned forward in his seat, opening and shutting his mouth like a fish.

"We found him under a shelf, buried by the crap they had on it. It wasn't mounted properly, and they had too much weight on it, anyway," Pete said.

"Pete's convinced the victim put the shelf up to impress his wife," Berlin added.

"Why?" Christine asked.

Berlin raised her eyebrows and smiled, turning to her partner. "Yes, Pete. Why?" She was delighted with how uncomfortable he suddenly looked. *Ha, he has no problem spouting that shit off at me. Let's hear him explain it to someone else.*

Pete shifted in his chair. "Well, I just suggested it was maybe a way he was trying to get, uh, *adult time* with his wife."

Christine took Lynn's sculpture away and gave her the last piece of chicken. "I think I'm missing something, Peter. Why would this person put up a shelf to get time with his wife?"

Berlin sipped from her glass of wine and watched Pete squirm.

"You know, Christine. Sometimes a man has to do things to impress his wife. To get her attention. In the bedroom?"

A smile slowly spread across her mother's face, making the whole thing that much better. Her mother didn't smile very much anymore.

"Is that what I should have done?" James was looking at Ellen.

"This isn't the time, Jamie," Ellen said, wiping dried potato and squash off Tommy's chubby cheeks.

"Put up some shitty piece of wood so you'd pay attention to me again?" His usual happy-go-lucky expression was gone, and a bitter person was sitting in Berlin's brother's place.

Ellen threw the cloth on the table and looked at her husband. "I don't know, James. But screwing your secretary certainly got my attention. So, either way, I guess you got what you wanted."

There was complete silence at the table while James and Ellen just looked at each other. Ellen finally pushed away from the table and collected Tommy from his highchair. "Please excuse me, Christine." She moved towards the kitchen and Tom's room.

Berlin stared at her brother. "Please tell me you didn't cheat on your wife, Jamie."

He looked at his plate, fiddling with his fork.

"What the hell is wrong with you? She's the best thing that ever happened to you and you just threw it away? On who? Some bimbo?"

"Shut up, Berlin. You don't know what's been happening, okay?"

Berlin sat back in her chair. "Well, whatever it is, I'm sure it warranted you fooling around."

She felt a nudge under the table. She ignored it and the warning on Pete's face.

Lynn looked back and forth between her father and her aunt. Her little round faced was scrunched up and her lower lip was quivering. Christine patted her hand. "It's ok, pumpkin, auntie and daddy are just having a little disagreement. But they're done now." She glared at her two children.

Berlin shrugged. "I just think I wouldn't have-"

James threw the fork on the table. It went skittering across the tablecloth and ended by their father's place. Tom didn't twitch.

"Yeah, please tell me what I should or shouldn't have done. How's that worked out so far, Berlin? You telling people what they should or shouldn't do? If memory serves, not so fucking great for the people who listened to you."

"James Thomas!" Christine was half out of her chair.

Berlin pushed her chair back and got up. She collected her dishes and took them into the kitchen. She placed them next to the sink, grabbed the unopened bottle of wine and her coat and walked out of the house.

*****

She drove without thinking. Berlin couldn't believe her brother was stupid enough, or ballsy enough, to screw around on Ellen. They'd been together since college and he'd begged her for months before she took pity on him and agreed to a date.

Berlin knew she should have kept her mouth shut, because it wasn't any of her business. But he was the one who had brought up the whole cheating thing, anyway. And he knew better than to think she'd keep quiet about something like that.

She could admit to herself it was anger and fear

that had caused him to lash out at her. And given Ellen's temper, he had every right to be afraid. Berlin sighed and let go of her anger at her brother. She could also admit that he wasn't the one she was mad at. His comment was an unneeded reminder of her habit of butting into other people's business and giving advice that wasn't always wanted.

Was that what she was doing with the Bryant case? Trying to create an issue where there wasn't one so she could feel like she was helping someone? Berlin frowned and considered what she knew about the case.

She wove through the streets while she made the mental list. It took half a block.

Bryant was still dressed in expensive clothes and had come home unexpectedly. Berlin originally included he wasn't the fix-it type but removed it because of Pete's earlier comment on her prejudice against rich people. The entire case was incredibly weak.

Without paying attention to where she was, Berlin found herself in the Bryant's neighborhood. The houses all sat on gigantic lots set against the lake. She couldn't imagine having enough money to even dream of owning a house like these. Since she was so close, she continued along the street until she was parked outside the Bryant's house.

The house looked empty, no lights on in the inside, no shadowy movement in the massive bay windows. Yellow police tape still decorated the front door, warning everyone to stay out. Once the police filed the official report marking it as an accident, Kay would be free to remove it.

Berlin wondered if she'd sell the house and move to a new area. Most people did; not wanting to deal with the memories of their deceased loved one. Looking at the gorgeous structure, Berlin didn't know if she would let memories chase her out of that particular house.

A knock on her side window made Berlin jump in her seat and put her hand on the pistol on her hip. A woman was standing outside her door, leaning over and motioning for Berlin to roll down the window. It took a moment and then Berlin realized it was the woman who said she was Kay's friend. She rolled down her window.

"Is everything okay?" the woman asked, concern on her pretty face.

"Yes, everything's fine. Mrs. Kellner, isn't it?" Berlin asked.

The woman smiled, flashing dimples. "It's Ms. But just call me Nichole." She looked over her shoulder at the Bryant's house. "Are you looking for Kay?"

Berlin shook her head, looking towards the dark house, too. "No. I came back to see if anything jogged my memory." She looked back at Nichole. "How is Mrs. Bryant doing?"

"As well as expected. Kay and I picked up Cassie after the police left this afternoon and I took them to my house. Her sister had to wait until tonight to drive up from New York. She'll get in tomorrow morning."

"I'm sure they appreciate having a friend to turn to, especially now." Berlin said.

Nichole shrugged and tucked blond curls behind

her ear. “It’s the least I can do. I can’t imagine what Kay is going through. I didn’t think she should be alone. And she’s in no condition to look after Cassie. Such a horrible accident.”

Berlin nodded. “You told us earlier that you and Kay have been friends for a few years. Were you close with Charles?”

Nichole shook her head. “Not really. He was always busy with work and Kay was alone a lot. Especially after Cassie went away to the boarding school. It was sort of like Kay was single, and since it’s just me, we fell in together.”

“She’s lucky to have you to lean on.”

The dimples flashed again. “It’s always good to have friends. You should let me know if you ever want a new one.”

Berlin didn’t know how to respond. She thought Nichole was flirting with her, but it had been so long since anyone had flirted with her, she knew she could be reading it wrong.

Playing it safe, Berlin said, “I’ll do that. Thank you.” Before she could think better of it, she pulled a card and a pen from the middle console and wrote her cell phone number on the back of it. She handed it to Nichole. “In case you or Kay need anything.”

Nichole looked at the card and ran her thumb over the upraised lettering of Berlin’s name. Her smile turned into a grin as she stepped back. “Guess I should get back and see if Kay’s okay.”

At her comment, Berlin looked around and then closer at Nichole. “I didn’t even think to ask. What brings you out here?”

Nichole picked up a duffle bag and held it for

Berlin to see. "Cassie wanted some things from the house. Comfort things, I think. An old sweatshirt, a pair of worn out socks." She shrugged. "Kay said she'd bring her over to get what she needed but I could tell neither one was up for it, so I offered."

At Berlin's look, Nichole said, "The officers said it would be okay if she went in. Don't worry, Detective Redding. I didn't go in the basement and mess up your crime scene."

Silently cursing whoever had given Kay permission, Berlin gave a brief shake of her head. "Do you need a ride? I know it's not far, but it's late."

Nichole slung the bag over her shoulder. "Nah, I like walking. But thank you for the offer." She smiled. "Now, you have a good night, Detective. I'm sure I'll be talking to you again." She started down the side of the road.

Berlin watched until Nichole turned up her own driveway and then made a U-turn in the road and headed back the way she had come.

Her house was dark when Berlin pulled into the driveway. Not that she expected anything different. She unlocked the door and opened it, listening for any sounds before entering the bare entryway. Nothing. She flipped on the light, threw her keys in a clay bowl on the counter, and locked the deadbolt. It wasn't even eight o'clock, and all she wanted to do was sleep. Berlin considered watching TV for a while but couldn't think of anything she wanted to watch.

"Screw it." She walked through the kitchen, turning off the light as she exited the room on her way to her bedroom.

After showering and brushing her teeth, Berlin studied herself in the mirror. Dark brown eyes framed by thick, long lashes stared back at her. They were the only pretty thing about her. Straight brown hair hung loose around her broad shoulders. She was too small to look Amazonish, but too big to be feminine. It was hard to believe someone as pretty and delicate as Nichole Kellner would be interested in her.

Berlin finished in the bathroom and turned off the light in her bedroom. She lay in bed and thought about Jamie and Ellen and the kids, wondering what would happen to them. She wondered if her sister would have had children by now, and if Laurel having kids would have made Berlin want kids. She wondered what Laurel would tell her about Nichole, and if she would consider what Nichole had said to be a flirtatious invitation. Berlin rolled to her side, hugging her pillow. As she did every night, she thought about Laurel and how much she missed her. But before she drifted off to sleep, Berlin also found herself wondering about Nichole Kellner.

CHAPTER THREE

"Seems you were right to be suspicious about Bryant." A folder came flying from Berlin's left and landed on her desk in front of her. Pete threw himself down on the black rolling chair next to her desk. Berlin eyeballed him but picked up the folder and opened it. She paged through the report, quickly scanning the pages, and then went back and read the first one more carefully.

"He had sex just before he died?" Berlin looked at Pete.

"It looks that way." Pete leaned back in the chair, putting his hands behind his head. "And if what his wife said is true about not seeing him after he left for work, Ol' Charlie boy was having sex with someone other than her."

Berlin set the report and folder back on her desk and stared at her computer screen. "And why would Kay lie about seeing him after he left for work in the morning? That wouldn't make any sense." She picked up a pen so she could tap it on the desktop. "So, he was sleeping with someone else." She looked back at Pete and found him watching her. "If Kay knew about Charles messing around, that would give her a motive."

Pete nodded, smiling. "Yup. Or whoever he was screwing around with could have gotten pissed off at him and knocked him off."

Leaning forward in her chair, Berlin scanned the first page again. She asked, "Nothing in on the DNA from the other person?"

"Nah. They got spermicide and residue from a condom with trace amounts of DNA from whoever he had sex with. But nothing popped up in the system. Could be there wasn't enough to make a match, or whoever it was isn't in our system." He sat up and picked up a sloth-shaped stress ball from the desk. He tossed it in the air and caught it when it came back down. He did it again.

"Do we have his phone records back?"

His focus still on the sloth, Pete said, "There were a few numbers that cropped up more than others. Three were legit business-related numbers." The sloth continued its journey to the ceiling and back to Pete's hands.

"And?"

"And what?" He glanced at Berlin and missed the sloth.

"You said three were legit. What about the ones that weren't legit?"

"Just one. And it's a burner phone."

Berlin watched him for a bit, then picked the report back up and sat back in her chair as she read. There was nothing else particularly exciting from the autopsy report. Paging through, she asked in a casual tone, “So, did you let Phillips know yet?”

The sloth hit her in the middle of her forehead. “What the hell, Pete?”

“I knew you wouldn’t last more than five minutes without asking.”

She rubbed her forehead. “Asking what?”

“Don’t even try to pretend, Redding. I knew you’d want to gloat a little. I figured we’d swing by his office on our way out.”

Berlin shot out of her chair, stuffed the report in her top drawer, and slammed it shut. She grabbed her coat and stared at Pete. She was practically bouncing in place. “Well?”

Rolling his eyes, Pete slowly got out of his chair. “Gloating isn’t ladylike, you know.”

Berlin pushed him along the hallway of cubicles. “Lucky for me, I’m not worried about being a lady.”

Phillips was sitting at his desk, frowning at his computer. For once, he was alone. Pete gave one sharp knock on the doorframe and Berlin elbowed her way into the office before him.

Phillips looked up. “What?”

Berlin said, “Charles Bryant was having an affair, giving his wife and the person he was sleeping with a potential motive for killing him.”

“I thought you closed this thing last week.” Phillips did not look impressed.

Pete side-eyed Berlin. “We were waiting on the autopsy to come back. This came up in the report, so we’re just tying up ends. We’ll head over to talk to his wife, see what she has to say about it.”

Phillips stared at them both, the displeasure clear

on his face. "I have less than a month before the general election. Today's polls show that Adrian Greeley is breathing down my neck. The last thing I need you to do is turn a simple accidental death into some wild goose chase and have the press all over it." He looked at Pete. "Just because this guy was banging someone else doesn't mean he was murdered. Got it?"

Pete nodded. "Yes, Sir. We'll get it wrapped up. But we also want to make sure we don't miss something that might make the department look bad."

Phillips folded his arms over his chest and sat back. "What are you talking about, Lewis?"

Pete turned to Berlin. "Wasn't it Jan Thompson who lost an election a few years ago for missing evidence during an investigation?"

It took her about fifteen seconds to catch on. "I think it was back in 2014. Maybe the election before that?"

Pete shrugged. "It's your call, Captain. I'll sign the report now if you want me to."

Phillips turned back to his computer and began typing. "I want the report filed and the certificate turned over in forty-eight hours." He looked up again. "Good job, Lewis. Dismissed."

Berlin didn't say anything as they left the department or after they got in the car.

Pete waited a few minutes after they were on their way before speaking. "It's just because I'm senior."

Berlin nodded. "I'm sure that's what it is."

Pete smacked her in the arm. "Come on, Redding. You know it doesn't make any difference to me."

She looked at him. "I know. And I know you recognize what I bring to the table during these investigations. But that doesn't help me with Phillips. If I had a dick, he'd maybe take me seriously. But since I don't, nothing I do is good enough." She turned to look out her window.

Pete was quiet for a few more minutes. Then he said, "I'll let you hold my dick."

She ignored him. "You aren't concerned he seems more worried about the election right now than his officers doing their job? I mean, he was all ready to force us to close this before we had time to finish the investigation. If you hadn't mentioned that it would look even worse if we missed something with the death, I think he would have made us close it right there in his office."

"There's nothing wrong with ambition, Redding. And I don't know what you're being so pissy about, anyway. If Phillips wins the election, he's out of the department and out of your hair. I thought you'd be thrilled."

Berlin looked out the window and just shook her head. "I don't like that he suddenly has this hidden agenda."

"Don't kid yourself, Redding. Everyone has an agenda."

*****

They pulled up to the Bryant's house and got out of the car. Berlin studied the house, but it seemed as abandoned as it had the night she'd stopped. She glanced up the road toward Nichole's driveway. There was nothing.

"Kay and her daughter Cassie stayed with the neighbor, Nichole Kellner, the night of the accident. Ms. Kellner told me that Kay's sister would arrive the following morning."

Pete raised his eyebrows. "And when did you pick up this bit of information?"

"The night Bryant died. I stopped by on my way home from mom and dad's and ended up talking to Ms. Kellner again. She's the lady who drove in as we were leaving."

"The one with the nice ass, you mean," Pete said.

Refusing to take the bait, Berlin started up the walk to the Bryant's front door. "I suppose Kay could have gone back to New York with her sister, but at some point, Cassie will have to return to school."

She rang the bell and they waited. There was no sound or movement from inside the house. After another minute, she knocked on the door and called, "Mrs. Bryant, It's Detectives Redding and Lewis." Nothing.

Pete backed away and stepped off the stoop. "Let's try the friend's house," he said.

They walked down the driveway and along the road and up Nichole Kellner's driveway. It wasn't nearly as grand as the Bryant's house. It looked more cookie-cutter and fairly bland, but it still wasn't anything Berlin could afford.

Berlin rang the bell and knocked, but there was no response.

They left Nichole's property and stopped on the road, midway between the two houses. Pete looked back at Nichole's house, and then at Kay's. "I'll have someone come by later today and see if there's any movement at either place." He looked down at Berlin. "What's our next move?"

Berlin started walking back to their car and Pete followed. She thought as they walked. "Bryant volunteered at his daughter's school. It's possible he was messing around with someone there." She unlocked the car and got in on the driver's side.

"Also possible that it was someone at work," Pete said, buckling his seatbelt.

"Harder to get away with it if both of you are absent from work," Berlin said.

"True. Let's start with the school and then the law firm."

CHAPTER FOUR

Lake Kanasatka Academy was enormous. It looked more like a college campus than a high school. Immaculate landscaping showcasing large maple trees and evergreens helped highlight the beautiful brickwork on the buildings scattered across the campus. Granite paths crisscrossed over the lawns between the buildings and at every third intersection, there was a group of trees with several granite benches. To top it all off, everything was set against the lake.

"You sure this is a high school?" Pete asked.

"According to their website they are a coeducational preparatory institute for individual thinkers." Berlin nodded to a centrally located sign proclaiming Administrative Office that pointed them towards one of the larger buildings.

They took the path that led to the office. "What's that supposed to mean?"

Berlin nodded at an older woman heading the opposite way and didn't receive so much as a smile.

"I'm pretty sure it means these are not our people."

They entered the building and walked down the hallway, their steps echoing off the cream walls. "This is nothing like where I went to school," Berlin said.

"Me neither," Pete agreed. He was staring at the framed paintings and graphic prints on the walls. "Jesus, this is nicer than where I live."

They found the administrative office and went through the raw oak door to find an attractive, older woman wearing a pastel green silk blouse with pink polka dots and a large floppy bow sitting behind a big desk. She looked up from her computer and said, "Can I help you?"

Berlin ignored the polka dots and bow and smiled politely. "Yes, ma'am. I'm Detective Redding and this is Detective Lewis. We're with the Lakes Region Police Department, and we're looking into the death of Charles Bryant. We know his daughter Cassie is a student here, and we were curious about other ties he might have had to the school."

The older woman's face fell at the mention of Charles's name. She grabbed a tissue from a porcelain box decorated with lilacs on her desk and dabbed at her face, displacing her glasses as she did so. She sniffed dramatically. "I couldn't believe it when I heard the news. He was such a wonderful man. I don't know what Kay and Cassie will do without him." She blew her nose.

"Was he at the school often?" Berlin asked.

The woman nodded. "Oh my, yes. He'd been an assistant coach for several of our teams over the years. Cassie is very active in our sports program and Charlie liked to support her."

Berlin caught the twitch of Pete's mouth at the nickname but kept her focus on the secretary who finished with an emotional, "He came for every practice and every game."

"Was there anyone here he was close with?" Pete asked.

She shrugged. "The other coaches. Some of the teachers. The students he coached just loved him." She thought a moment and then added. "He was also close with some members of the school education board." She leaned forward and quietly added, "The Bryants made fairly sizable donations to the school through the years."

Berlin smiled and nodded encouragingly. "Can you think of anyone we should speak with? Someone who might have more information, or may have heard from him the day he died?"

"Well, Alex Johnson is the head coach for the girls' basketball team. She also teaches here at the school." She sniffed again, this time with what almost seemed like disapproval.

Because of the woman herself, or their relationship? "If we wanted to speak with Ms. Johnson, where would we find her?" Berlin asked.

"If she isn't teaching, she'll most likely be in her office. Or possibly the basketball court." She bent down and opened a file drawer and eventually pulled out a piece of paper and gave it to them. It was a map of the campus. She pointed to one of the rectangles. "We're here. Just go down two buildings and her office is on the third floor of Kennedy Hall. The basketball court is on the main floor."

"Thank you for your help," Berlin said, taking the map. "We appreciate it." She pulled a card from her breast pocket and handed it to the woman. "Here's my card, in case you have questions or think of anything else that might help."

The woman took the card. She looked at it for a moment and then looked up at Berlin and Pete. Leaning in again, she said, "This is a very prestigious school. Our families send their children here for a reason, and for their generous contributions, we try to maintain privacy and subtlety." She gave them a tight smile. "I'm sure you understand what I'm getting at?"

"Of course. We'll do our best to be… discreet." Berlin said, smiling the entire time. "Thank you again. Ms.?"

"Oh, where are my manners?" She gave a little laugh. "Lambert."

"Well, thank you Ms. Lambert." Berlin smiled again, and then she and Pete headed out of the office.

Walking back down the corridor, Berlin said to Pete, "Good thing we left the marching band at home."

"Your prejudice is showing again, Redding."

She took a deep breath and rolled her shoulders a few times. "You didn't find that demeaning?"

"No," Pete said. "I found her outfit demeaning, but not her attitude."

They were back outside. Berlin turned to answer Pete but stopped when she heard her name called from behind her. She turned to look and saw a petite figure with curly blond hair heading their way. "Ms. Kellner," Berlin said, surprised.

"Please, call me Nichole," Nichole said when she caught up to them. "Are you looking for Cassie? I don't think Kay's bringing her back to school until after next week."

Pete was looking at Berlin, an eyebrow raised. Berlin took the hint. "Nichole, I don't know if you remember my partner, Detective Peter Lewis."

"Of course," Nichole said, flashing a smile and offered her hand to Pete. "That wasn't a great day, so I don't think we introduced ourselves."

Berlin rolled her eyes as Pete pulled out his usual "this woman is attractive" smile. "Don't worry about it, Nichole. Most people are shaky during stressful situations like that. And I remember you being pretty helpful."

"Anything I can do to help Kay. And the police," she said, still smiling.

"We're actually going to go talk to one of the teachers," Berlin said, interrupting Pete's attempts at flirting. "How are Cassie and Kay holding up?"

Nichole turned back towards Berlin, a slight frown now decorating her face. "Not great, I'm afraid. Kay is beside herself with what to do. Cassie seems to feel guilty because she's not as sad as she thinks she should be…" She shook her head. "I don't mean that to sound like she doesn't care or miss her dad. She loved her dad. But she was at school so much, and he was at the office so often when she was home. She saw him the most when he was helping coach, so the upcoming basketball season will be hard on her. She's also focused on finals. It's just a lot for her to process."

She shook her head again and gave an embarrassed laugh. "Sorry, I didn't mean to just blurt all of that. Anyway, Kay is trying to figure out funeral arrangements and decide what she wants to do with the house. It's a bit of a mess."

Pete broke in, "So what brings you here, Nichole?

Since you already know Cassie isn't here, I'm assuming it wasn't to talk to her?"

"I'm actually a teacher here, Detective Lewis. I teach Spanish to the kids willing to look past my terrible accent."

Berlin was interested to note that Pete had lost the flirtatious note to his voice and was in full investigative mode.

"So, you were neighbors with the Bryants, and you also saw Charles at the school?" Pete asked.

"Neighbors, yes. But Charles volunteered his time with the sports program." She smiled again and motioned to her curvy figure. "As you can see, I'm not the most athletic person." She looked at Berlin again. "As I was telling Detective Redding the other night, I didn't know Charles very well. He worked a lot and left Kay on her own most of the time." She frowned again. "I'm sorry, I thought they finalized everything about the accident?"

"We're just tying up a few loose ends, getting a better picture of the events that day," Berlin said. "But we won't keep you any longer, Nichole. Again, please reach out if you think of anything else."

"I'll do that, Detective," Nichole said, smiling again. She nodded to Pete. "Detective Lewis." She walked past them, taking the sidewalk leading to a building on their left.

Berlin was about to continue to the athletic building when Nichole called her name again.

"Detective Redding?" She had turned back around and was heading towards Berlin again, her hand extended. Berlin took the white card Nichole held out. "In case you think of any other questions you might have for me."

Berlin didn't have a chance to respond before Nichole hurried away.

As they started back down the sidewalk Pete said, "Please tell me you're going to call her."

Berlin shoved the card into her pocket. "Why? You heard her say she didn't know Bryant very well. I can't think of any other questions I might have for her."

She stopped walking when she realized Pete was no longer beside her. She turned to find him standing a few steps away, a slightly pained expression on his face.

"What?"

"You aren't serious."

"What are you talking about?" Berlin folded her arms across her chest.

Pete coughed a laugh. "Jesus, Redding! She was coming on to you." Pete walked up to Berlin and she continued forward with him.

After a minute she said, "I wasn't sure. The other night she seemed a little flirtatious, but I wasn't certain. I'm bad at reading people."

He started laughing. "You're a riot, Redding. You know that?"

"Now what?" Why did he always have to sound so smug?

"You're one of the best cops in the department at reading people. That's why we don't invite you to poker nights."

Berlin didn't say anything.

Pete said it for her. "Guess you're just bad at trusting your instincts with your personal life."

*****

Alex Johnson was an athletic woman with shoulder-length blond hair. Berlin put her in her mid to later thirties, and someone who thought very little about her physical appearance. She was pretty, but more naturally than manufactured. She also looked less than pleased when they introduced themselves and explained they wanted to ask her about her assistant coach.

She frowned heavily; the lines etched deep on her face. Berlin wondered if she was older than she first appeared. She waved Berlin and Pete to two chairs in front of her desk. “Please, sit.”

“Thank you, Ms. Johnson. We appreciate you taking the time to talk to us,” Berlin said.

“Please, call me Coach Johnson. It’s what everyone around here calls me.”

Berlin ignored Pete’s raised eyebrows. “Okay. Coach Johnson, please tell us when you last spoke to Charles Bryant.”

The coach leaned forward in her chair and studied a calendar on her desk. She tapped a couple of the dates, finally keeping her finger on one. “I talked to Coach Bryant on the 12th.”

Berlin looked at Pete and then turned back to the other woman. “Are you sure?”

The coach looked at her calendar again and nodded. “I’m sure. He called so we could discuss one of our players who had to sit out the game that night.” She looked up at them. “She’d gotten hurt during practice and we were hoping she’d be okay for the game.” She sat back in her chair and crossed her arms over her chest. “Anyway, Coach Bryant and I discussed our options for the game line up.”

"What time did you talk to him?" Pete asked.

She consulted her calendar again. "Ten that morning."

"Was he at work when he called you?" Berlin asked.

Alex Johnson tilted her head and Berlin felt like a bug. A stupid bug. "I don't know, Detective Redding. I forgot to put the videoconference on." She paused, and when she answered again, the condescending tone was a little less evident. "I wasn't in the habit of asking Coach Bryant about his whereabouts. We discussed games, players, sports… our discussions rarely went past those topics."

Berlin made a couple of notes in her notebook and then said, "Had you coached together long?"

"A few years." Johnson shrugged. "He assisted the previous coach for a few years before I took over the position. I guess you could say I inherited Coach Bryant."

Her voice stayed cool, but Berlin still got the feeling she hadn't been thrilled about the inheritance.

Pete looked skeptical. "You coached together that long, but your conversations never went beyond the team or the sport? Nothing about family life? Spouses? Children?"

"Look, I got this job because I have a very good reputation and an excellent game record. I do that by not getting involved with the people I work with. Especially the men. Coach Bryant tried to be more personal when I was first hired, but I made it clear I wasn't interested in knowing him." She stood up. "Now, if you'll excuse me. I have students to get to."

Pete stood up. Berlin wanted to stay seated just

to be obstinate but stood up as well and put out her hand. "Thank you again, Coach Johnson." They shook hands and then Johnson showed them out of the room. She shut the door firmly behind them.

"Did you find any of that weird?" Berlin asked Pete as they walked down the hall towards the front entrance.

"Yeah. Even when you don't like someone, you pick up pieces of their personal shit. Especially if you're around them any amount of time." They went down the stairs. "And I think Johnson and Bryant spent a lot of time together over practices, games, traveling…" He shook his head. "I'm not buying they didn't have a relationship past the team."

Berlin nodded. "I agree. When someone is that adamant about not having a personal relationship with someone else it makes me wonder if something happened in their past."

Pete side-eyed her. "You're thinking they slept together?"

"Not necessarily," she said. "He may have attempted more of a relationship than she led us to believe. Or maybe she tried to have one with him and he brushed her off." Berlin shrugged. "We're just speculating at this point. But regardless, it feels like there's something there other than basketball." They exited the building and headed to the parking lot.

"Where do you want to go next?" Berlin asked.

"Lunch."

CHAPTER FIVE

They went to a divey diner that smelled like grease and butter and served great burgers and onion rings. The place had a handful of customers, mainly old men sitting at the small counter. They slurped soup and coffee and flirted with the waitress who had blue hair and false teeth.

Berlin and Pete sat at their usual booth in the back corner. Berlin smiled at the waitress. “Hey Cheryl. Looking hot today.”

Cheryl nodded. “Thanks kid,” and then called out, “Hey Stan, Redding and Lewis are here.”

A wall separated the dining room from the kitchen, but a small opening allowed customers to watch Stan work his magic with meat, potatoes, and grease. Without looking up from what he was doing he yelled, “Tell ‘em I’m on it.”

“Yeah, yeah,” she said, and went back to chatting with the men at the bar.

Berlin took off her jacket and put it on the

wooden bench beside her. "We need to talk to Kay again. Get a feeling if she knew Charles was seeing someone."

Pete nodded. "We can have Martinez get contact information for the sister, in case Kay's not answering her cell. We can have him find out where they're staying, too. Maybe have him stop by and ask if she needs anything, see if he can get a feel for how distraught she really is."

Berlin tapped her thumbs on the scarred tabletop. "She legitimately seemed upset that night. Shocked. Like she couldn't believe it was happening." She shrugged. "It didn't come across as fake or rehearsed to me."

Cheryl shuffled over and unceremoniously dumped their plates on the table, followed by two coffee mugs. She went back to the bar and grabbed the coffeepot, put it on the table and left again.

Berlin swiped a few of Pete's rings from across the scarred table and put them on her bacon cheeseburger while Pete poured their coffee. "Do you think she had anything to do with it?"

He shrugged and took a big bite of his burger. After swallowing, he said, "Probably not." He sipped carefully at his coffee and took another bite. "Honestly, it still looks like an accident. He was definitely screwing around, but that doesn't mean someone murdered him. Maybe it was just karma."

"I don't believe in karma," Berlin said and then bit into her burger. The onion rings were fabulous.

"Why not?"

She took another bite, tipped her head and thought for a few moments as she chewed. "I guess because we see too many assholes get away with shit they should be in jail for. And there are too many people who get hurt because they were in the wrong place at the wrong time. It seems like those are the people getting punished for playing by the rules while the evil ones get what they want by breaking them." She took another bite of her burger.

Pete threw the rest of his burger on his plate, a look of disgust on his face. "Thanks Redding. You're really a joy to have around, you know that? I was just bullshitting and then you have to get all serious on me."

"Sorry," she said, not at all sorry. "But you asked." She stole the last onion ring.

"You know what would help you?"

"Somehow I don't think I want to hear this." She wiped her hands on her napkin.

"That cute blond." Pete picked his burger back up and shoved half of it in his mouth.

"And I was right," Berlin said. She pulled some cash from her pocket and put it on the table. "Are you pitching in or am I getting this?"

Pete sucked down the rest of his coffee and placed the mug back on the table. "I'm a modern guy. I'll let you get it."

"Thanks." She grabbed her jacket and shrugged it on.

"Are you going to call her?"

"No. There's no point to it."

"You don't know that, Redding. She may have insight into the Bryant's relationship. She's friends with Kay. Maybe Kay has said something to her about ol' Charlie screwing around."

Berlin stood up. "You just told me you think his

death was an accident."

"Christ, work with me here, Redding. I'm trying to get you laid." He stood up and started walking towards the entrance.

"Really?" Berlin said. At his nod, she said, "As my superior, you're recommending that I sleep with a potential witness?"

Pete shrugged. "It's an accidental death, so what do I care. Plus, Phillips is the one that'll have to deal with you. Not me."

Berlin glared at him as she walked and bumped into a chair. "You're a real asshole, Pete. A real asshole."

He put his arm around her and steered her out the door. "And that's why you love me."

*****

Pete drove to Bryant's law firm as Berlin filled him in on Charles's status as a partner in the firm, along with the information she'd found on his accomplishments.

The firm was housed in a two-story brick building on the main street. There were several cars parked along the street, but otherwise the building appeared to be quiet.

"What type of law firm is this?" Pete asked.

"From what their website said, they mainly deal with businesses. Acquisitions and mergers, litigation, that sort of thing. It looks like they handle some criminal cases, but only non-violent financial stuff."

"Sounds exciting," said Pete, yawning.

"Mmm. Very lucrative though," Berlin said.

"The firm was started by one individual, Jack Brian Abrams Senior. He ran it alone for the first three years before bringing his son on. Over the next ten years he hired another eight lawyers. The last four were in the last two years."

Pete's eyebrows went up. "Damn, that seems like a quick build up."

Berlin nodded, studying the brick building. It didn't look like it held a company that pulled in the money that the law firm reported. "I thought so, too. They brought Bryant on as the second of the eight new lawyers."

"And he made partner when?"

"About three years ago, if I remember correctly."

Pete opened his door. "Well, let's go see what we can figure out."

They exited the car and Berlin led the way to the front door. While the exterior of the building was more suited for a small-time business, the inside of the building was decorated with the saying 'you get what you pay for' in mind. A short walk across what Berlin suspected was marble tile brought them to a gold and glass reception desk backed by a smoked glass wall.

A young, redheaded woman stood up from behind the desk and smiled at them. "Good afternoon. Do you have an appointment?"

Berlin showed the woman her badge. "Good afternoon. I'm Detective Berlin Redding and this is Detective Peter Lewis. We were hoping to talk to someone about Charles Bryant."

The receptionist's smile melted from her face. "Oh my God, I couldn't believe it when I heard Charlie was dead!"

Pete stepped forward. "Did you know Mr. Bryant well, Mrs…?" He gave her his full-wattage smile.

She flushed an unbecoming pink for a redhead and looked down at her bare left hand. "Miss. Katie Albert." She smiled again and focused fully on Pete. "I knew Mr. Bryant fairly well. He was here when I started, and he's been one of the top-producing lawyers." She flushed again, and then said, "Was."

Berlin broke in. "Do you know when he left the office on the 12th?"

Katie shook her head. "I'm here Mondays, Thursdays, and alternating Fridays. Andrea Butler is the other receptionist. She was working on the 12th."

"Do you know if they held the meeting scheduled for that afternoon?"

Katie shook her head, her smile less certain. "I'm sorry, what meeting?"

Berlin looked over at Pete and then back at the receptionist. "It was our understanding there was a big meeting scheduled for that day. In the afternoon."

Katie frowned and looked down at her desk. An elegant day planner was open to the current week. She flipped back several pages and ran her finger down the page, shaking her head. She looked up, the smile firmly back in place. "No, I'm sorry. You must have been misinformed."

"Thank you, Miss Albert. You've been very helpful," Pete said.

Her smiled widened, showing a good amount of her gums.

At least they look healthy and pink, thought

Berlin. Out loud she said, "If there's someone who worked that day and who knew Mr. Bryant well, it would be very helpful if we could talk to them."

"Let me find out who's available." Katie moved from behind the desk and over to the left side of the glass wall. She pushed gently and a section of the glass slid aside.

Berlin moved away from the desk and examined the reception room. Quality-framed artwork hung on tastefully painted soft gold walls. The tones were just different enough to be complimentary. One wall held formal headshots of ten men. The last picture in the top row was Charles Bryant's. The men were all of a similar age, and had the same well-groomed, arrogant look to them. The lawyers, Berlin guessed. A picture of the founder, J.B. Abrams, also hung on the wall. He was quite a bit older than the other men but gave her the same impression.

In the corner, set on a glass-topped end table, a display shelf held glossy pamphlets with information on the types of law cases the firm handled. Berlin scanned over them and saw it was mostly the same information posted on their website. A pamphlet caught her attention, and she picked one up. She walked back to the reception desk as the glass door slid open. Berlin handed it to Pete as Katie came out of the inner office.

Pete raised his eyebrows at the 'Sexual Harassment in the Workplace' pamphlet. "Thanks?"

Berlin smiled. "You're welcome." She turned her attention to Katie.

"Mr. Abrams would like to speak with you both," Katie said, her voice soft and very formal. "This way, please." She motioned them to a different door.

The inner office was decorated similarly as the waiting room. Soft golden walls gave off a warm and welcoming atmosphere. Walls to what Berlin assumed were private offices were created using the same smoked glass as the reception area.

"Are there additional offices on the second floor?" she asked Katie.

"Yes, and several conference rooms." Katie stopped at a closed door, knocked sharply, and at a muffled, "Come in," opened the door.

It was a massive office decorated in dark wood and cream tones; a pleasant change from the gold. The front portion of the room was arranged with a round, glass conference desk and ten black leather chairs evenly spaced around it. A beautiful, dark wood dry bar was set off to the side of the conference table. The back of the room was arranged as more of a traditional office space. Built-in bookshelves covered the back wall, with additional shelving artistically filled with framed pictures, awards, and pottery. The walls held more artwork, awards, and portraits of men who, Berlin assumed, were in the Abrams line. A wooden desk, large enough for at least three people to work at comfortably, was the major focus of the space. It was almost bare except for a phone, a closed laptop, a folder, and a baseball bat held lengthwise on a stand. While the desk was impressive, it was the man behind it who commanded attention.

Jack Abrams Junior stood when they entered the office. His dark grey suit hugged his frame tight enough Berlin could see he wasn't carrying extra weight. She placed him in his early fifties with salt and pepper hair cut tight to his scalp. His cleanly shaved face held an open intelligence that probably put clients at ease and encouraged them to trust him.

He waved them to the two chairs in front of his desk, sat back down, and dismissed his receptionist with, “Thank you Ms. Albert. Nothing else for now.”

Berlin waited until the door closed and then focused on the man in front of her. “Thank you for seeing us, Mr. Abrams. I’m Detective Redding, and this is my partner, Detective Lewis.”

“Please Detective, call me Jack. Mr. Abrams is my father.” He smiled at her, showing very white, straight teeth. They looked real.

Berlin nodded. “Thank you, Jack. We know this can’t be an easy time for your firm.”

Jack Abrams leaned back in his black leather chair, his fingers steepled together. “No. It certainly isn’t. Charles Bryant was a very good friend of mine. We grew up together and then went off to the same law school. I was best-man at his wedding.”

“We’re very sorry for your loss,” Berlin said. “It would be hard enough to lose an employee and partner. Even more so to lose a friend.”

“Was that why your father hired him into this firm?” Pete asked, leaning forward. He was peering at the baseball bat.

Berlin winced and closed her eyes. *Smooth Pete, real smooth*. But Abrams didn’t seem particularly upset by the question. He wore a small smile as he watched Pete eyeing the bat.

“It’s from the 1915 World Series. The Red Sox beat the Phillies four games to one.” He nodded to the bat. “It’s signed by all the Red Sox players.”

Pete let out a low whistle. “That’s impressive.”

He looked up at Abrams. "Bet it cost you a pretty penny."

"It was actually a gift. Well, a thank you, really. From a client who wanted to show his appreciation of our services."

Pete raised his eyebrows. "He must be well off, too, to get his hands on that and then to give it away." He sat up in his chair. "I don't suppose you'd be willing to say who? Maybe he needs another friend."

Abrams smiled. "He appreciates the discretion of this firm. Detective, all of our lawyers are very discreet and very good at their jobs. Abrams & Abrams demands it." He spread his arms out, palms up. "We've built an excellent reputation, and this firm is seen as a pillar in our community, and the surrounding communities. People expect professionalism, integrity, and discretion. And they get it. That's why my father hired Charlie into this firm. Charlie understood how to take care of and protect our clients." He laughed. "It didn't hurt that he was a hell of a litigator, either. Nothing scared that man."

"I'm sorry, I didn't think your firm handled criminal cases," Berlin said.

Jack nodded, looking almost pleased by her comment. "Businesses can be a lot more terrifying than a murderer, Detective Redding. Think of it. If someone kills you, you're dead. Nothing to worry about anymore. But if a company with billions of dollars behind them wants to ruin you, that's years of torture and stress ahead of you." He took a sip of water, and then realizing what he'd done, said, "I'm sorry. Where are my manners? Would either of you like something to drink?"

Before Pete could answer, Berlin said, "Thank you, no. We're fine."

Jack took another sip and then went on. "Charlie could go up against those businesses in the courtroom like a gladiator." He shook his head, smiling at the thought. "Christ, he was really something to see." He sighed and put his glass back on his desk. "These young guys have no idea. They're fearless but rather naïve, I'm afraid. I don't know what we'll do with Charlie gone."

Pete shifted in his chair. "Did Mr. Bryant handle any other types of law cases?"

"We all handle the usual business dealings. Buyouts, acquisitions, contract overviews."

"Was he well-liked in the office?" Berlin asked.

Abrams thought for a few seconds, his head tilted. "I would say so, yes. He made partner a few years ago, and there's always a few hard feelings from anyone who doesn't get picked. But my father and I are the only true partners in the firm. The other two partners are non-equity. So, no one took it too hard."

Pete looked at Berlin, but she shook her head. "Non-equity?" he asked.

Abrams sat forward. "It's really more of a title with a few perks. But no actual decision-making abilities, and no equity in the firm." He shrugged. "It's not the way I would necessarily run it, but my father is a traditionalist. He wants the Abrams family to retain full control."

"What are the perks?" asked Pete. "Other than shoving it in someone's face at a high school reunion."

The older man smiled. "Ahh, Detective Lewis. Sometimes that title is all that's really desired. Banks take you more seriously, business associates. You'd be surprised."

"I bet it even helps on applications to private schools," said Berlin.

He nodded in agreement but said nothing.

She thought another moment and then said, "It can't look bad on the firm's portfolio, either. Being able to brag about having multiple partners. Young, upcoming ones at that."

Pete caught on to her line of thinking. "I would hazard a guess the price goes up, too, if you want a partner to argue your case."

Abrams smiled but again made no reply to the comment. Instead he said, "If there's nothing else regarding Charlie?"

"Actually, I do have another question about Mr. Bryant," Berlin said. "Do you remember what time he left here on the 12th?"

"No, I'm sorry. I wasn't here that day. I had meetings in Massachusetts. I'm sure my secretary can help you, though. The girls usually see who's coming and going throughout the day."

Girls, thought Berlin. *Liking this guy less and less*. "We'll make sure to ask before we leave." She paused and then thought, *ah, the hell with it*, and asked, "Was there any indication Mr. Bryant was sleeping with someone other than his wife?" She caught Pete's wince out of the corner of her eye. *Who do you think I learned it from, pal*? She didn't apologize to Abrams for her crassness.

Abrams was quiet, but he appeared more thoughtful than anything else. Finally, he said, "Charlie and Kay had some issues early in their marriage. They were both young when they got married, Charlie was still in law school. It's a tough time getting through those classes. Very stressful. He confessed to me, this was many years ago, that he'd stepped out on Kay. It happens quite a bit to law students, even when they're in loving relationships. Anyway. Kay never knew about it and it was a fairly short-lived affair." He paused. "When he told me about it, he seemed very relieved Kay had never found out. Given his reaction, I wouldn't have guessed he'd ever chance a second affair."

"Did he tell you the name of the woman?" Pete asked.

Abrams shook his head. "No, he didn't mention it. I got the impression that she was somewhat, expendable."

Berlin's eyebrows arched. "Could you explain what you mean by that?"

"My apologies," Abrams said, smiling insincerely. "That was a poor way of describing her. She sounded like the type of woman who attached herself to Charlie because of what she could get from him. Financially." He shrugged. "Again, not uncommon around the more prestigious universities."

Berlin smiled tightly. "Got it. Thank you, Mr. Abrams."

"I wasn't trying to be insulting, Detective. It's the reality of the world. And to be frank, she proved that's all she was after when she took money from Charlie to keep quiet about their affair."

"Of course," Berlin said, just as insincere. "And I'm sure the money was completely her idea. You've helped paint a much better picture of Mr. Bryant, Mr. Abrams. We appreciate it." She looked over at Pete.

"Did you have anything else?"

Pete shook his head and stood up. "Nothing else for now. We may have additional questions for your receptionists, if that's not too much trouble?"

"Anything." Abrams stood, offering his hand. "Anything we can do to help."

Berlin and Pete shook hands with him and thanked him again. Berlin fought the impulse to wipe her hand on her slacks as she walked back down the hallway, just in case they had cameras.

Katie was still at the reception desk. Pete was there first, offering his card to her. "If you think of anything else, please call me. Anytime."

Katie smiled at him. "I will, Detective Lewis. Thank you."

Berlin refrained from rolling her eyes and said, "If you could please pass the number along to Ms. Butler as well?" At the younger woman's nod, Berlin added, "Please ask her to give Detective Lewis a call if she can remember what time Mr. Bryant left on the 12th. We'd appreciate it."

"I'll leave a note for Andrea to call when she gets in," Katie said, still looking at Pete.

"Thank you, Miss Albert."

The sun was setting when they stepped back on the street. Berlin headed to the passenger's side of the car. "Would you drive again? I need to think."

The street was busy with typical afternoon traffic. For all of his questionable male behavior, Berlin had to admit Pete was an excellent driver. As he cruised smoothly down the road, she thought about what they'd learned.

"So, we know Bryant cheated on Kay at least

once in their marriage, prior to this latest involvement. We also agree there may have been a proposition to Alex Johnson at some point, probably early in their coaching relationship."

"I'm with you so far," said Pete. "Did you notice the thing with his name?"

"Mean 'Charlie'?"

"Yup. Kay never called him Charlie once. But the lady at the college, and the receptionist here. There's an intimacy with the nickname."

"Abrams used it, too," said Berlin.

"True," agreed Pete. "But they were also childhood friends."

They were both quiet for a few minutes. Then Pete said, "He was in a position to piss people off in court. Big business-type people. Especially if he was as good as Abrams made him out to be."

Berlin thought for a second and then shook her head. "No, if someone with a lot of money wanted someone dead and was the type of person to act on it, they'd hire a professional. They wouldn't use a shelf with a bunch of shit on top of it and hope it would do the job if it eventually fell." She rubbed her eyes, applying slight pressure. "I don't know what to think. I need to make notes or something and see if I can get this information straight."

Pete looked over at her. "Do you want to go somewhere or back to the office?"

"I don't know. Don't you have plans tonight?"

"Yeah, but not until late. I've got some time yet."

"Okay. If you're willing, let's go back to the office for a bit and see if we can make heads or tails of this."

CHAPTER SIX

Letting out a frustrated sigh, Berlin straightened up in her chair, stretching her back and shoulders. They'd been looking over their combined notes on the case for over two hours and were no further along than before they started.

Pete looked at his watch. "I'm done, Redding. I should have been at the bar thirty minutes ago."

Berlin raised her eyebrows. "I'm guessing you wanted to keep whoever she is waiting?"

He grinned. "Yup. This just gave me a good excuse." He grabbed his coat off the back of her chair. "You should head home, too. You're not getting anywhere on this tonight."

"I know. I'll leave soon. Promise."

Pete shook his head as he walked down the aisles. When he was almost to the door he called back, "Go home, Redding."

Berlin leaned back into her chair and closed her eyes. She knew she should go home. Pete was right. She wasn't going to get anywhere tonight. There was too much information that added up to nothing concrete. She needed time to let everything settle and seep into her brain. She needed food and sleep.

She opened her eyes and stared at her dark computer screen before her gaze was drawn to a white card lying by her keyboard. Berlin leaned forward slowly and picked it up, studying the dark blue printing on the front. Before she could talk herself out of it, she picked up her phone and dialed the number on the card.

Butterflies tangoed in her stomach as she listened to the other line ring three times. Slightly relieved there was no answer, Berlin took the receiver away from her ear when a voice on the other end said, "Hello?"

"Hello, Nichole? This is Detective Berlin Redding."

There was a pause on the other end and then, "Good evening, Detective Redding." The warmth in Nichole's voice came through the phone line. "How can I help you?"

Berlin took a deep breath and said, "I was wondering if you were free to meet for a drink this evening?"

There was another pause and then Nichole's laughter filled Berlin's ear. Berlin silently cursed herself for being an idiot. "I'm sorry Nichole-"

"No please. Wait," Nichole said, getting control of her laughter. "I was sitting here, staring at your card. Trying to decide if I should call and pretend I thought of something meaningful about Charles."

Berlin relaxed into her chair. Smiling, she said, "I was trying to think of questions I haven't already asked you. But then I just decided, to hell with it. So how about it? Would you meet me for a drink?"

"I would love to, Berlin. Do you know The Bob House on Whittier Highway?"

"I haven't been there, but I know it. Give me about an hour."

*****

The Bob House and Reel'n Tavern was more restaurant than bar. Berlin had always meant to try their food but never seemed to make it, even when most of the department went on trivia night. She parked her old Outback in the second row of the parking lot and studied the other vehicles parked there.

It was fairly full for a Wednesday night, which could mean it was one of the few places open and still serving at eight o'clock in the evening, or it could mean they had good food. The vehicles were a mix of old but capable and new-used. Nothing looked expensive, and other than one beat up truck, nothing looked like junk. So far it was her kind of place.

Inside, there was a sign directing customers to seat themselves. Berlin quickly scanned the room, taking in the couple dozen customers occupying large wooden tables, black metal chairs and the comfortable-looking wooden bar.

She spotted Nichole sitting toward the back corner of the room at one of the smaller tables. Berlin walked through the room and slid into a chair next to the wall, opposite of Nichole. She angled the chair so she faced the room but could talk to Nichole and still be comfortable. "Thanks for meeting me," Berlin said, smiling.

Nichole smiled back. “Thank you for calling and asking.”

They were both quiet then, the awkwardness building between them. The waitress arrived with two glasses of water and released the tension with a cheery, “Can I get either of you ladies a drink from the bar?”

“Yes please,” both women answered and then laughed.

After placing their orders, Berlin asked, “How are Kay and Cassie doing?”

Nichole raised her eyebrows. “So, we are talking shop tonight.”

Berlin shrugged and took a sip from her water. “It’s common ground, so it feels like a safe topic for now. Plus, I really am interested in how they’re doing. I feel bad for them.”

Nichole sat back in her chair. She was wearing a dark green sweater, the V-neck showing a hint of freckles. “I think the shock is wearing off for Kay and reality is setting in. There’s a lot of legal bullshit she has to deal with that came as a surprise. Stuff Charles should have had together but didn’t.”

Berlin nodded. “My dad always said electrician’s and plumber’s houses were never up to code. I guess lawyers are the same way about their legal paperwork.”

The waitress brought their drinks. “You ladies eating tonight?”

Looking at Nichole, Berlin said, “Pete swears they have the best fries here. Better than anywhere else he’s been.”

“Those must be good French fries. I’m game to

try ‘em.”

“Just a plate of fries for now.” Berlin told the waitress.

“With malt vinegar if you have it,” Nichole added. After the waitress left, Nichole said, “You and your partner are close, huh?”

Berlin nodded. “Yup. I’ve worked with him since coming to Lakes Region five years ago. I’ve known him twice that many years. He’s one of the best people I know.”

“But is he a good cop?” Nichole held out her hand as soon as she said it. “I didn’t mean it like that. It’s just the couple of times I talked to him, he seemed,” she smiled, “distracted by things other than the case.”

Berlin couldn’t argue with Nichole’s assessment. Pete did come across as a bit of a lunk. “Pete has his downfalls, but believe me, there’s always a reason for everything he does.” *Just not one I always agree with.* “Anyway, you were telling me how Kay is doing.”

Nichole looked like she wanted to argue the change of subject but instead took a sip of her drink. After the glass was back on the table, she said, “Kay has been sorting through the mess left when he died. It’s been kind of good for her. She’s more pissed at him right now than sad. It’s at least letting her take care of things.”

“Pissed because of how out-of-order things were?”

“Mmm, some of that.” Nichole hesitated for a second and then said, “She hasn’t said anything specific, but it sounds like she found things out about him she didn’t know before.”

Berlin took a sip from her Jameson and ginger ale and considered her options. She could feel Nichole's gaze on her, studying her. She said, "How much business can we discuss before it'll be a turnoff for you?"

A slow grin started across Nichole's face, and then she laughed. "You are not what I expected, Detective Redding. And that doesn't happen often."

"I'm not sure how I should take that."

Nichole was suddenly thoughtful and then frowned. "I'm not sure how I meant it." She took a healthy swallow of her whiskey and put the nearly empty glass sharply on the table.

Berlin wanted to ask her about her comment but before she could, Nichole said, "You go ahead and ask whatever you need. Then we'll move on from there." Her face was still serious, but at least she was no longer frowning.

Berlin nodded and took another drink. The whiskey did the slow burn she loved, sliding down her neck and into her shoulders, helping ease the tension from the week. "Okay." She considered her options and asked, "Was Charles cheating on Kay?"

Nichole shrugged. "He had in the past. At least a few times. I don't see why he would have stopped."

"Did you see him with anybody? Or is this just speculation?"

"Not speculation, at least not on my part. Kay told me. She said he got drunk one night a few years ago and told her about some woman he'd been seeing when they were younger. Like college days younger." She gave a partial laugh but didn't sound amused. "Selfish bastard, after all those years of keeping quiet and he finally felt the need to tell her about it."

More people had wandered into the tavern and customers occupied a good portion of the main dining room, including the tables closest to them. Lowering her voice and leaning in towards Nichole, Berlin asked, "How did Kay take it?"

Nichole leaned in as well, doing very nice things for her cleavage. "I think she wanted to be mad because she knew it was the proper response. But by the time he told her, things had pretty much gone to hell for them, anyway."

"You said he'd cheated a few times."

Nichole nodded. "Yeah. Well, about a year after his first confession, he felt the need to come clean again. He told her about a more recent transgression. This one only six months prior to his confession. He told Kay he was only with the woman one time. At some conference."

Berlin turned her glass in her hands, wondering why he would start confessing to his wife. The glass stopped moving. "How long ago was this?"

Nichole shrugged and shook her head. "I don't remember. Last year, sometime. Maybe a year and a half ago."

"What did Kay do that time?"

Nichole grinned, showing her dimples. "She slept with me."

Berlin raised her eyebrows and picked up her glass, only to find it empty. She set it back on the table. It hit a little heavier than she intended. "Listen, if I'd known there was something between you and Kay-"

Nichole placed her hand on Berlin's arm. "There isn't. We fooled around once or twice, but it was just a safe way for her to get back at Charles." She squeezed Berlin's arm. "Really."

Berlin met Nichole's eyes and then looked away, unsure of how she felt about the information. She met Nichole's eyes again and said, "Fair enough," and then looked around for the waitress. When it looked like she was headed their way, Berlin turned her attention back to Nichole. "Did he find out?"

Nichole let out a small snort. "Of course not. He'd have to been around and paying attention."

The waitress dropped off their plate of fries and a bottle of vinegar. She picked up their glasses and asked, "The same?" and moved off at Berlin's nod.

"So why do you think he started confessing to her?" Berlin asked, nodding again when Nichole held the bottle of malt vinegar over the fries and watched as she drizzled the dark liquid over the basket. The smell of the salt and vinegar was divine.

"About screwing around?"

Berlin nodded and took some fries.

"Because he was a selfish bastard and wanted to upset her." Nichole recapped the bottle and took some fries for herself.

"You mentioned the selfish bastard part already. You don't think he was trying to fix things?"

"Please. If you want to fix things you sign up for therapy and spend time with your wife. You don't keep having sex with other people." Nichole ate more fries. "No. He was trying to upset her enough she'd walk away from him."

"Why would he want that?"

"They had an agreement that if one of them tried to end the marriage, that person walked away from everything they had. Including children. It was a ridiculous thing they created when they got married. Like a prenup, but worse. But Kay wasn't going to leave Charles, no matter what he did."

"What if one of them died?"

She shook her head. "No, Kay didn't do that to Charles. Cassie adored her father, and Cassie is Kay's everything. No matter how angry she was at Charles, she wouldn't do anything to him because it'd break Cassie. Not that he ever deserved her devotion."

Berlin digested everything Nichole had said, trying to keep it clear through the fog of the whiskey. "Did you dislike him because of him or because of Kay?"

Nichole looked thoughtful. After a few seconds she said, "I like Kay, and I'd get angry with how Charles treated her. I guess disregarded her is more of what it was." She paused again when the waitress arrived with more drinks. After she was gone, Nichole said, "Kay reminds me of me during my marriage. Seeing what she put up with makes me angry that I put up with mine for so long." She grabbed a few fries.

Berlin took a couple, trying to cover her surprise. "How long were you married?"

"Too long," Nicole said and took a sip of her drink. "Ten years."

Letting out a soft whistle, Berlin said, "That is a long time. Is that when you moved to your current house?"

Nichole eyed her. "What makes you think that's not the house we lived in together?"

Berlin munched the fries, enjoying the tanginess from the vinegar. "There's no actual personality put into your house, nothing of you. If I had to guess, I'd say you've been there two years. Four tops. And based on the generic landscaping and exterior features, I'd also say you're renting."

Nichole was quiet. Berlin wondered if she should have kept her mouth shut. Then Nichole leaned forward and whispered, "Can you talk to dead people?"

Berlin grinned and took another drink. "Sorry. Analyzing a scene is a habit. I didn't mean to get all coppy on you."

Shaking her head, Nichole said, "No, no. It's impressive. And sadly, accurate. I couldn't stand staying in our house, so I sold it as fast as I could and moved out. I grew up around here, though. And my parents are still here. Can't move too far from mummy and daddy, you know." She finished in a lousy accent, making Berlin laugh.

"Ahhh. You were one of those kids."

"What those kids?"

"Rich. Snobby. Entitled." Berlin took a drink.

"Of course I was," Nichole said. "Still am. Which is good, because as nice as the academy is, they don't pay me enough to deal with the hoity-toity parents of our students."

"Did you go to school there?" Berlin asked.

Nichole shook her head. "No, not that one. But one similar. Then a private college. It's boring, since that's what every rich kid does." She touched Berlin's hand. "What about you? How did you end up in law enforcement?"

It was only seconds of physical contact, but it sent pleasant chills across Berlin's skin. Trying to stay cool, she said, "Like many lower-class kids, I couldn't afford college. So, I joined the Air Force and ended up in security forces."

"Did you want to be a cop when you were a kid?"

"I don't know that I wanted to be anything. I just knew I didn't want to stay around home and college wasn't an option. My brother joined after he graduated and liked it." She took one of the last fries. It was cold but still good. "I didn't go in with a guaranteed job and when they found out I was good at shooting and could handle the physical requirements, they put me in with the cops. My dad was a cop, so it made sense for me."

Nichole shook her head, laughing. "There's no way I would have made it through something like that. Is it like what they show in the movies? Getting yelled at and having your face in the mud while doing push-ups?"

Berlin shrugged. "Yes, and no. We got yelled at. A lot. And we were always running or marching, doing push-ups or pull-ups if you screwed up. But it was good, too." It was her turn to touch Nichole's hand. "You'd be surprised what you can make yourself do, and what you can get through."

Nichole smiled but didn't respond to Berlin's comment. Instead, she said, "So you liked it."

"Yup. I did. For a long time."

"What happened? Why aren't you still in the military?"

Berlin laughed. "You don't want to hear all of this."

Nichole looked at her, her expression serious. "Yes, I do. This is so different from what I did. I mean, you really did something adventurous."

"This doesn't have a happy ending."

Nichole took Berlin's hand. This time she held it. "What happened?"

Berlin looked at their linked hands, and then she looked at Nichole. Her face was serious, and there appeared to be genuine concern and interest, too. Something there made Berlin say, "I was raped by one of my superiors. A really hot lieutenant. He was used to women saying yes, especially the younger enlisted women." She felt Nichole squeeze her hand. "I wasn't supposed to be out with him, but he was fun, and it felt dangerous after doing everything else I was told to do. And it happened fairly often. Enlisted going out with officers, I mean. Anyway, he didn't take 'no' for an answer very well."

She stopped talking. Nichole stayed silent. Just waiting. Finally, Berlin continued. "I didn't tell anyone at first. He acted like I had agreed to the sex, like it had been a normal evening. But then, a few months later, I found out he'd done the same thing to a few other girls on my flight. We all talked about it and I convinced them to go forward with me to our Commander and file a complaint."

"Did they do anything?"

She looked at Nichole again. "After a very brief investigation they determined there was no proof it wasn't consensual. He was reprimanded for having an unprofessional relationship with an enlisted member and he had to wait an extra three months for his promotion."

Nichole didn't look surprised. "What about the other women who complained?"

There was no humor in Berlin's smile. "My

complaint was the first one they investigated. After they'd closed it, they gave the other women an opportunity to retract their complaints. Which they all did. I was given an administrative reprimand for fraternizing with an officer, transferred out of my unit, and when my reenlistment came up, they denied it. I got an honorable discharge and was told I should be grateful it wasn't a general discharge or worse."

"Jesus." Nichole sat back but kept Berlin's hand. "And they wonder why people don't report sexual assaults."

Berlin nodded and threw back the rest of her drink. "Yup. The real bitch of it is, even though I can look at it and know I did the right thing, I still wonder what would have happened if I'd kept my mouth shut. Nothing changed by me speaking up. I didn't help anyone. If anything, I made it worse by putting those other women through the reporting and all the questions. And he was still free to move on and assault other women."

Nichole tightened her grip on Berlin. "Hey, you did what you were supposed to. He's the asshole who deserves to be beaten down, not you. Him and all the other bastards who let him get away with it." She shook her head. "It's such a broken system."

"The system isn't perfect," Berlin said, "but we get a lot of them and we keep them off the street."

"I don't know. The news makes it seem like there are way more of those fuckers running around hurting people than people out there helping." Nichole looked hard at Berlin. "Be honest. Wouldn't it have felt great to smash the lieutenant's face in with a crowbar?"

Berlin had to grin at the seriousness on

Nichole's face. "I envisioned doing it with my baton, but I suppose a crowbar would be good, too."

Nichole laughed. "Sorry. I just hate that all this awful shit happens, and nothing seems to get fixed."

Berlin sat up and sighed. "Don't apologize. I'm the one who got all heavy tonight. It was supposed to be a flirty evening. Not all gloom and doom."

"I still had a good time with you," Nichole said.

Berlin smiled. "So did I." She hesitantly withdrew her hand from Nichole's. "I suppose I should get going, though. Work starts early."

Nichole nodded. "Yeah, me too. Thank you again for calling."

Berlin walked Nichole to her car. The wind had picked up, leaving the night damp and chilled. She hugged her jacket around her as she waited for Nichole to start her car. "You're okay to drive?" Berlin asked as Nichole got back out of the car and stood by the door.

"Don't worry, Detective. You won't have to pull me over for a DUI."

"Good. It'd look bad in a report if I had to write up where you were and who you were with."

The awkwardness was back. "Well, good night Nichole. Thank you again for meeting me." She stepped forward and leaned down to kiss Nichole on the cheek, but Nichole moved at the last second and their lips met.

Berlin stood still, afraid to make a wrong move but also reluctant to lose contact.

Nichole pressed her lips a little more firmly to Berlin's and then stepped back, still looking up at Berlin. "Would you like me to come over and make you dinner tomorrow night?"

Berlin's voice was quiet. "You don't have to do

that."

"I want to."

This time Berlin aimed for Nichole's mouth and gave her a soft, quick kiss. Still standing close, she said, "I would love to have you come over. I'll send you the address."

"I'll be there by six."

They kissed one more time and then Berlin stepped back and Nichole got in her car. She waved before driving away.

CHAPTER SEVEN

"Please tell me you haven't been here all night."

Berlin looked up from the papers on her desk and found Pete holding out a box of donuts. She peeked inside and chose one with lemon and cream filling. Around a mouthful of donut, she said, "Close enough," and went back to the papers.

Pete set the box on the edge of her desk and stood behind her, reading over her shoulder while eating a Boston Cream. "What is that?"

"Records."

"From what?"

"Alex Johnson. Abrams & Abrams. The firm Bryant worked at prior to Abrams & Abrams. Kay Bryant." Berlin sat back, sighed and took another bite from her donut. "I'm looking for anything that jumps out as unusual."

"And?" Pete asked.

"Nothing concrete." She took one more bite of her donut and put it down on a folder. She shuffled through the papers, pulling one from near the bottom. Berlin handed it to Pete and said, "Alex Johnson's husband filed a petition for divorce fourteen months ago, but it doesn't look like he took it any further."

Pete scanned the information. "Irreconcilable differences. That could mean anything from abuse to irritating in-laws." He looked at Berlin. "The timing would make sense if Johnson and Bryant were fooling around and got caught. They stop for a while and then maybe start up again, and Bryant threatens to tell her husband."

"That seems like a stretch."

Pete grabbed another donut. "The whole thing is a stretch, Redding. I'm humoring you at this point." He shoved a third of the donut into his mouth.

Berlin rolled her eyes and handed him another sheet. "This one has to do with a harassment complaint against Charles Bryant from a co-worker at the first firm he worked at, Campbell and Sons. The woman's name is Diane Long. They found the claim unsubstantiated and nothing more was done."

"But you think otherwise," Pete said.

Nodding, Berlin handed him another sheet. "Three months later Bryant started working for Abrams. I know it could be a coincidence, but I still find it interesting. I left a message for Ms. Long, not that I expect to hear anything back."

"Except maybe a complaint against the department for rubbing salt into old wounds. Come on, Redding. You have to do better than that." Pete made a grab for the pile of papers, knocking over a stack of folders in the process. The folders and papers slid to the floor.

Berlin stared at him, not saying anything.

Pete stared back. "Were the folders important?"

"I don't know. I haven't gone through them yet."

He looked down at the mess on the floor. "Huh. Well, that sucks." Pete glanced up when she didn't say anything else. "Is your eye twitching?"

"I hate you," Berlin said. She crouched down and started picking up the mess. "Help would be awesome, Pete. Since you did it."

"I brought you donuts and you're still mean." Pete crouched beside her and started shuffling papers together in one heap until Berlin smacked him on the arm.

"I had those organized. Could you at least try to be neat?"

He said, "I am being neat!" but began straightening the papers, scanning the contents as he went. After a few minutes, Pete stopped at one, staring at it.

Berlin glanced at him. "What?"

"What was Alex Johnson's husband's name?"

"Hold on." She stood up and grabbed her red notebook off the desk, glancing over her scribbled notes. "Shawn. Why?"

"This is a missing person report for one Shawn Dale Johnson. Dated 26 April 2016."

Berlin felt her heart speed up. "That's only a few months after he filed the petition." She held her hand out for the sheet and Pete gave it to her. She read through the document, noting the last time and location he'd been seen. "His wife was the last person to see him." She looked up at Pete. "Maybe she found a way to get rid of people who were pissing her off?"

"Maybe we should see if Coach Johnson is free for another discussion," Pete said.

"I'll call after we get this cleaned up."

Pete handed over his stack of papers. "Sounds good. I'll go see if I can get hold of anyone in Missing Persons." He was gone before she could argue.

Berlin called the academy's administrative office and after being put on hold several times was informed Coach Johnson was traveling with the volleyball team for several away games. "She should be back at school on Friday if you want to leave a message."

"Please let her know Detective Redding needs to speak with her."

"I will. Have a nice day."

Doubtful the message would get passed on, Berlin hung up and wrote herself a reminder to call Johnson at the end of the week. Then she left their cubicle to find out if Pete's luck was any better.

She found him in the hallway talking to Phillips. The Weasel and the department's PR rep were also there, both talking to Phillips at the same time as Pete. Berlin stopped a few steps back and heard Pete say, "Yes, Sir. We're confident that this evidence could be the missing information we've been looking for. We need some time to substantiate the lead and cross reference the circumstantial evidence so we can corroborate our efforts."

What the hell, Pete? But it was easy to see Phillips wasn't paying any attention to Pete; he nodded occasionally but his head was bent to the other men, his focus on what they were telling him.

Berlin stepped forward and said, “Sir, I think-”

Phillips looked up for the first time, scowling at Berlin. He turned back to Pete. “Fine, Detective Lewis. Keep me updated.” He turned away and walked back toward his office.

“What the hell was that?” Berlin asked, her voice hard. She was used to Pete’s goofy, non-stressed attitude about life, but this was an extra level of ‘don’t give a damn’ for him.

As Pete walked past her, he turned Berlin around and pulled her with him. She stayed right on his heels. “What was what?” he asked.

“That bullshit you were giving Phillips.”

“I was using the same terms you’re always throwing around.” Pete glanced back at her. “You should be proud of me for paying attention.”

“Great. Except what you said didn’t make any fucking sense! Why didn’t you let me say anything?” Her chest was tight, warning her she was about to lose it on Pete.

Pete halted, and Berlin bumped into him. He held up his hand for her to wait and smiled at a co-worker walking past. “Hey, Walt. Great game last night!” They high-fived but once the other man was gone Pete looked at her, his face serious.

Lowering his voice, he said, “Because you would have told him the truth, and right now I need to buy us some time. This case is all over the place and mostly we have dick to go on. Phillips is breathing down my neck about it because we should have closed it two days after the guy was dead.” He paused and then added, “But I agree that something’s off and we at least need to figure out what the hell it is.”

Berlin closed her mouth, cutting off what she had been about to say.

Pete just watched her.

After a few seconds she said, "I can't help it. It just doesn't occur to me to lie."

Pete nodded. "I know. And most of the time I count on you being so damn honest. But there are times I wish you'd reserve that honesty just for me."

*****

Berlin made it home with enough time to do a quick sweep of the house and pick up any stray items she'd left lying around. She was exhausted and cranky with nothing much to show for it.

Pete had contacted missing persons with minimal results. Because all evidence showed that Shawn Johnson had left on his own accord, they didn't consider his disappearance suspicious. Due to higher priority cases, the officer in charge of Johnson's case said they'd made little effort to look for him after the initial investigation. They would contact Pete if they came up with anything new.

Berlin had returned to her desk to sort through the rest of the paperwork mess from earlier but had found nothing helpful. Burned out, she left well past when she'd intended to, and now felt rushed and disorganized.

At ten minutes to six there was a light knock on the door. Berlin tried to still the fluttering in her stomach and opened the door. Nichole stood on her porch with a bag of groceries in her arms. Berlin took it from her and backed into the living room. "Hi. Come on in."

"Thanks." Nichole said, stepping into the small entryway. "This is a cute house."

Berlin forced a smile as she set the bag on the kitchen counter. "Thank you, but you don't have to be nice. There's nothing particularly cute about this place."

"Okay. Your house is as bland as mine."

"That's more accurate. You can throw your coat on that chair," Berlin said, nodding to a royal blue chair in the corner of the kitchen. "So, what are we having?"

Nichole paused while removing items from the bag and studied Berlin. "Are you ok? You look, well…" she grinned. "You sort of look like hell."

Berlin shook her head, brown wisps of hair hanging in her face, and gave Nichole a genuine smile. "Thanks, I appreciate the honesty. I'm just beat from work."

"Are you sure you don't mind me being here? We can do this another night."

The tension from the last few days left Berlin with Nichole's question and she said with complete honesty, "No, I'm sure. I'm glad you're here."

Nichole smiled and nodded. "Good. To answer your question, we're having pan fried steak and salad." She looked skeptically at Berlin. "You're not a vegetarian, are you?"

"Nope, you're safe. Can I help?"

Nichole continued to pull items out of the bag. "Show me where your pans and knives are first and then you can wash the veggies."

Berlin moved to the stove and opened the cabinet to the left of it. She pulled out a frying pan and a strainer and set them to the side of Nichole. Then she opened the drawer above it and pulled out knife options. "Will those do?"

Nichole glanced at them. "Yup, they'll do. Thanks." She pulled the steaks from the bag and then folded it up and handed it to Berlin. "Salt, pepper, and garlic?"

Berlin reached above the stove, opened the cupboard and pulled down the requested items.

"Cool, thanks. I think that's everything I need for now."

Berlin stashed the paper bag in a slim space between the fridge and wall, then pointed to the clear plastic produce bag Nichole had set on the counter. "Does everything get washed and sliced?"

"Yup. I just got the basics for the salad, since I wasn't sure what you liked."

"Works for me," Berlin said. She grabbed the bag and strainer and moved over to the sink.

They worked in comfortable silence for a few minutes before Nichole said, "I mentioned to Kay today that I met you for drinks last night and that you'd asked after her."

Berlin ignored the slight jolt of jealousy and rinsed the romaine lettuce. "How is she today?"

"Okay. It sounds like they figured things out for the service and I think once it's done she'll be able to move forward. Olive oil?"

Berlin looked over her shoulder. "It's where the salt and pepper were."

"Thanks," Nichole said. She opened the cupboard above her head and pulled the bottle down and added oil to the pan. "She did ask me if you'd said anything about the report being finalized. Something about the insurance company asking. Maybe for the payout on the policy?"

She almost cut herself. Could Kay have killed him for the insurance money? Finally got tired of the cheating and figured, screw it? Being more careful with the knife, Berlin began slicing the cucumbers and considered what information she wanted to get back to Kay. Deciding it wouldn't matter one way or the other, she said, "We're planning to sign the certificate tomorrow. I imagine that's what the insurance company is waiting for."

Nichole turned and grinned at her. "Well, I hope you have wine because it sounds like a reason to celebrate. You'll be done with Charles and Kay gets something for putting up with him all these years." She flipped the steaks. "I think these will be done in about five minutes. Will you be ready with the salad?"

Berlin put down the knife and moved the sliced vegetables into a serving bowl. "Yes ma'am. I have two or three options for dressing in the fridge if you want to look. And then the salad is ready to go."

The evening was warm, so they carried their plates out to the small back deck to a little wrought-iron table Berlin had picked up at a flea market. She lit mismatching candles and went back in the house for a bottle of La Belle wine and glasses. She handed the bottle and an opener to Nichole. "Per your request."

Nichole took both from her and studied the label on the bottle. "My, my. Trying to impress me with such high-class wine?"

Berlin sat down. "Yeah, yeah. But it's all us lower-class girls can afford. Besides, fourteen dollars a bottle is expensive around here. You should feel special.

I rarely spring for the good stuff until the third date."

Nichole pulled the cork with an ease only gained with opening a lot of wine and passed the bottle back.

Berlin poured the wine and waited for Nichole to take a sip. "Well?"

"Damn," Nichole said before taking a full drink. "That is good." She raised her glass towards Berlin's. "A toast?"

Berlin brought her glass close to Nichole's. "What should we toast to?"

"How about good stuff on a second date?"

"I'll drink to that," Berlin said and met Nichole's glass with her own.

After dinner Berlin told Nichole to stay seated while she cleared the table. She took the dishes into the house and came back to the deck with a second bottle of wine and an enormous bar of milk chocolate. She placed the chocolate on the table and refilled their glasses. "Sorry I don't have something more exciting for dessert. But it's fantastic chocolate." She sat back down and opened the bar. She broke off a piece and handed the rest across the table.

Nichole took it and laughed.

"What?"

Nichole shook her head but broke off a chunk of the chocolate. "I don't think I've ever been on a date like this."

"Like what?"

Nichole bit into the chocolate and chewed. "I don't know. So relaxed." She took another bite and chewed for a few moments. "Are you always like this when you're out with someone?"

Berlin shrugged. "Honestly, I'm too exhausted

to be anything other than this. I really had planned to have tonight be more romantic." She took another piece of chocolate. "Does it bother you?"

"No. I like it." Nichole was quiet and then added, "It feels real."

They sat in the silence listening to the last crickets of the season, eating chocolate and drinking wine.

Choosing to blame it on the two empty bottles, Berlin asked, "Do you want to see the rest of the house?"

Nichole cocked her head. "What did I miss on the original tour?"

The butterflies were out of control. "The bedroom."

"I can't miss that. That's where the really good stuff is, and we already toasted to the good stuff. It would probably give me rotten luck to not see the rest of the good stuff."

Berlin laughed and shook her head. "And I thought I was crazy." Still smiling, she stood up and offered Nichole her hand. "Come on. I'll show you where the good stuff happens."

Nichole took her hand, and they went back into the house.

*****

There was enough moonlight to keep the lights off but still see everything in hazy detail. Without letting her brain catch up, Berlin stepped close to Nichole and found her mouth, enjoying the shared taste of cranberry from the wine and the sweetness of the chocolate.

They both let their hands roam, removing clothing as it got in the way until there was nothing between them. At last, they were on the bed and Berlin couldn't remember the last time she'd felt anything as wonderful as Nichole's skin brushing against her own. And then Nichole's hands and mouth were working down her body, paying special attention to all the good stuff until Berlin couldn't think at all.

CHAPTER EIGHT

It was still dark when Berlin opened her eyes, unsure of what had woken her. A car starting up outside her door brought her upright and reaching for her gun. It was quickly followed by the realization she was nude. The night with Nichole came back to her, and she relaxed back into her pillow. She looked over at the clock on her nightstand. Quarter to five. Berlin switched on the bedside light and looked at the side of the bed Nichole had ended up on. There was an indent on her pillow and a few strands of curly blond hair showed up against the green sheets. There was also a bright pink sticky note on the pillow. Berlin reached over and picked it up. *Thanks - N.*

*****

She stopped for coffee and was still fifteen minutes early, but amazingly Pete was already working at his desk. He looked rumpled and disheveled and very un-Pete-like.

"What are you doing here so early?"

He looked at her and went back to his computer. "I couldn't sleep last night."

Berlin looked over his shoulder at the computer screen. He had the notes pulled up from their original interview with Kay. "Were you thinking about the case?"

"Nah. Amber snores but insists I stay over. I can't get any sleep when I do. At about three this morning, I couldn't take it anymore."

She couldn't help it, she patted him on the head and grinned. "Poor baby." She placed his coffee on his desk.

Pete scowled up at her but took the coffee. "Why are you so chipper this morning?"

She took her own coffee and moved over to her desk. "I just slept great, that's all." She turned and looked at Pete, still grinning.

Pete was quiet, just studying her.

"Stop staring at me. You're creeping me out." She hung up her coat.

"You got laid, didn't you?" He didn't look so grumpy.

Berlin sat down and started up her computer. "Yeah, like I'm going to tell you something like that."

"Oh, come on, Redding. Give me something good. I'm a mess over here."

"Sorry, I don't kiss and tell."

Pete laid his head against the back of his chair. "Well, at least I know you made it to first base. That's a start." He closed his eyes. "You seeing her again?"

Berlin's silence had him opening his eyes.

"You're not?"

She frowned at her coffee. "I don't know. She left before I got up, so we didn't discuss anything future. She left a note but all it said was 'thanks'. I'm not sure how to take it."

"Huh." Pete took a big drink from his coffee. "I thought only guys pulled shit like that."

"That doesn't make me feel better."

"Don't worry about it, Redding. I'm sure you'll hear from her again." He tapped his fingers on his coffee cup. "I don't suppose she gave you any helpful information about Kay and 'ol Charlie boy?"

"Actually, she did."

Pete sat up in his chair, looking more awake. "Do tell."

Berlin filled him in on what she'd learned the previous night regarding their weird agreement about walking out on the other person. She also told him about Charles confessing his sins to Kay over the last several years. Finally, she told him about Kay asking Nichole about the death certificate, and how it may have had something to do with the insurance company. After she finished, she waited for him to say something.

"That would be awfully convenient for us if she offed him for the money."

"It would," Berlin agreed. "But it's happened before. Probably more times than anyone ever figures out. And we still need to talk to her today, anyway."

Pete nodded. "Should we go play stupid and see what we can get her to admit to?"

"Might as well. We don't have a better plan."

*****

They arrived at Kay Bryant's house two hours later to find everything quiet.

"Maybe she still hasn't come back here," Pete said as they walked toward the front stoop.

Berlin rang the bell and they waited. There was no noise from inside the house. She shook her head, "I got the impression she was. Although, I could be wrong." She rang the bell again and then knocked firmly on the wooden door. In a loud voice, she said, "Mrs. Bryant?"

"Jesus Redding, I'm sure if she was home, she would have heard the bell."

From around the house a voice called, "I'm back here!"

Berlin looked at Pete and raised her eyebrows. He ignored her and led the way off the stoop and followed a granite stone walkway that went along the house to the back.

The rear of the house was even more amazing than the front. A huge brick patio was laid out with different gardening and seating areas and an outdoor grill. Everything looked out on the lake.

Kay was dressed in an old pair of jeans and a flannel shirt. She had her hair pulled back into a short ponytail, and her face was smudged with dirt. She looked younger than when they'd first met her and a good deal happier. Berlin had to admit that Kay looked down-right cute. She slapped down the quick jolt of jealousy, wondering how in the world she could compete with someone like Kay.

Kay pulled off her gardening gloves and offered her hand. "Detectives. I hadn't expected to see you again." She motioned to her outfit. "Please forgive me, I'm trying to get the gardens in order for the winter."

"No apologies necessary, Mrs. Bryant. We're the ones who arrived unannounced," Berlin said, trying for something between friendly and sincere. She looked around the backyard. "This is gorgeous. I can only imagine what it looks like in the spring and summer."

"Thank you." Kay looked around at the yard. "Charles always hired someone to take care of it, but I used to love gardening. So, I thought I would give it a go."

"Have you decided to stay in the house, then?" Berlin asked.

Kay shook her head. "Nothing's definite yet. I have to see how everything goes financially. We had a few debts I wasn't aware of and this is an enormous place for just me and Cassie. Well, just me, most of the time." She looked questioningly at them. "I know this sounds horrible, but the insurance company has been asking for his death certificate. Do you have any idea when I should receive it?"

Pete smiled. "That's one reason we're here. We're finalizing the report and had just a few questions for you regarding that day. Is that all right?"

"Yes. Anything you need."

"Thank you. Could you please go over your day again, prior to coming home? When you left, where you went?"

Kay shook her head, looking confused. "I'm sorry, I thought I gave you all of this information already."

Berlin said, "This is very standard questioning, Mrs. Bryant. Sometimes the people closely involved forget information during the initial discussion, because of shock. We like to follow-up after a little while, to see if they've remembered any other details. It just helps us fill in the time-line."

Kay looked at her and Berlin got the feeling she wasn't buying it.

"Okay," Kay said, crossing her arms over her chest. "Well, I left the house around nine that morning. It takes about forty minutes to get to the volunteer center from our house and we were meeting with one of the charity coordinators at ten. I left early enough so I would have time to review my notes for the meeting."

"About what time did you get to the center?" asked Pete.

"Maybe ten minutes before ten. There was an accident in town so that slowed everything down. I remember thinking I was glad I'd left as early as I did."

"Did you hear anything from Mr. Bryant during the day? A phone call, text, email?"

She shook her head. "No. As I told you before, Charles didn't like to communicate over personal matters during the day. He said it took him away mentally from what he was working on." She frowned slightly.

Berlin said, "Was there a way to get in contact with him if there was an emergency?"

"If I had to get hold of him, I called the reception desk. He kept his phone turned off during the day, so having one of the girls give him a note was the only way to let him know I needed to speak with him."

Her emphasis on the word girls and her tone made it obvious how Kay felt about that.

Pete continued with their questions. "Were you

at the center the rest of day?"

"Mostly, yes. I had lunch with one of my friends who used to volunteer there. We hadn't seen each other for quite some time, and we wanted to catch up. I think I got back to the center around two."

"Could we have your friend's name and a contact number please?" Berlin asked.

Kay did not look pleased by the request but provided the information readily enough.

"Thanks," Berlin said and jotted the information in her notebook. "What time did you leave the center for the day?"

"At five-thirty. I walked out with two of the other volunteers." She paused and looked pointedly at Berlin. "Would you like their information, too?"

Berlin smiled. "That would be very helpful, thank you." She wrote down the names Kay gave her.

Pete smiled his 'I'm a good guy' smile and said, "We really appreciate you going over all of this again, Mrs. Bryant. We know it's tedious. We just have one last question, but please know it's not meant to upset you."

Kay nodded.

"Did you have any indication Charles was seeing someone else?"

Berlin watched her closely as Pete posed his question. Kay froze for just a second before a look of shock came over her face.

"Of course not! My husband was a good man. He would never have done something like that."

"Sometimes even good men can stray, Mrs. Bryant. It's not a reflection of you or your marriage."

"No. Charles was not having an affair." She

sounded sure.

"Unfortunately, we have evidence that proves otherwise," Berlin said. "We suspect the reason he was home so early was because he met whoever he was seeing here."

Kay's look became one of genuine surprise. The look turned thoughtful.

She knows something.

"And this is why you're so interested in my whereabouts?" Kay asked, shaking her head. "Is this how you get your kicks? Or maybe you have a murder quota you're expected to fill?"

Berlin kept any hint of apology from her voice. "Mrs. Bryant, you must know how it looks from our side. Your husband was cheating on you, you have a very expensive property to keep up with, your daughter is in an expensive school. And Charles had a considerable sum for a life insurance policy. Which you get now that he's dead."

Kay stood up straighter, squaring her shoulders. "Call the volunteer center. There are multiple people who will verify when I arrived, who I was with, and when I left for the day. I didn't kill my husband. And I don't understand why you're so intent on turning his death into a murder instead of acknowledging that it was a stupid, senseless accident." She looked at them, calculatingly. "Perhaps that's something I should ask your supervisor?" After a brief pause, she said. "Now, if that's all, I have a lot to do. You can show yourselves out."

They were quiet as they re-traced their steps to the front of the house. At their car, Berlin paused and looked back at the house. "Well, I'd feel a little bad about myself except we know she's lying. Her shock seemed a little rehearsed, which makes me think she was expecting us to bring it up."

"You think your new girlfriend mentioned something about telling you?" Pete asked.

"She's not my girlfriend. And I don't know, but I assume that's why Kay knows."

"You want her to be."

"What? Make sense, Peter."

He looked like a bratty little brother. "You want her to be your girrrlll-friend."

She narrowed her eyes at him. "Why do you always do this? Would you please focus on the fucking issue at hand?"

"Fine, I'll be serious. Blame it on the lack of sleep if that helps." He was still smiling. "So, what's the issue?"

"Kay didn't kill her husband."

"Why do you say that?" Pete opened the driver's side door and got into the car.

Berlin followed his lead. "She wasn't happy about giving us names and contact info, but she did it and she gave us numerous names. Even if one person was willing to lie and give her an alibi, four or five people would be too difficult to coordinate. She was where she said she was when it happened."

Pete nodded and started the car. "We still need to verify."

"I know. If nothing else, we need to prove to Phillips we weren't just stalling for time."

He backed out of the driveway and out on to the road. He shifted into drive and looked at her. "Which is what we're doing at this point."

Berlin sighed and pounded her head against the headrest a few times. "I know. And we're almost out. The report is due by the end of the day."

"And don't forget. Your mother is expecting us at five-thirty."

She glared at him. "What?"

Pete shrugged. "She called and asked. I said we'd be there." He gave her a quick look. "Hey, I can't disappoint your mom."

"I hate you, Pete. I don't have time to deal with my family. I have to figure out this case." Berlin looked out the window.

Pete patted her leg. "Don't worry, kid. You'll figure out something."

CHAPTER NINE

As Berlin suspected, Kay's alibis turned out to be airtight. Pete entered their cubicle as she was hanging up the phone with the volunteer center.

"So? Get anything good?"

"Kay's story checks out. I talked to three people who saw her in the morning and two other people who left with her. Oh, and the friend she had lunch with sent pictures of them from the restaurant. With date and time stamps." She sighed and slumped down in her chair.

Pete sat at his desk and leaned back in the chair. "So, she didn't have time to go home, whack him, and go back to the organization?"

"Stop patronizing me, Pete. It's not helpful." She smacked her hand on her desk. "There has to be something else."

"Redding and Lewis!" Phillips's voice came bellowing from the hallway.

"Great. Just what we need." Berlin said, sitting back up.

Phillips burst into their cubicle looking ready to spit nails. "Do you both have your heads up your asses? Or have you forgotten what your job is here?"

Berlin and Pete both stood up. "Protect and serve?" Berlin said, a little too snarky. She looked at Pete.

He shook his head. "Sorry, I've got nothing. I think my head is still up my ass."

Phillips, humorless as ever, tossed a folder at Pete. It hit his chest and fell to the floor. Pete looked down at it and then at Phillips.

"Kay Bryant wants to file a formal complaint against you both. For harassment."

Berlin stepped forward. "Now wait a minute. We were just doing our -"

"I don't give a damn what you think you were doing, Redding. Whatever you were doing, you must have been doing it with the same half-cocked attitude you seem to do everything with."

She glared at Pete, but he gave a small head shake. She took a step back but lifted her chin. In a calmer voice she said, "Kay knew her husband was cheating, and she was asking about his life insurance policy. We thought it was worth looking into. Sir."

Phillips looked over at Pete. "Is this correct, Lewis?"

"Yes, sir. Mrs. Bryant was understandably unhappy with our questions, but we would have been ignoring something fairly major if we hadn't asked."

Sill ignoring Berlin, Phillips asked, "And now that you've questioned her, is there any reason to think she was responsible for his death?"

Pete glanced at Berlin and then back at Phillips.

"No."

"Is there anyone else who you think may have had something to do with his death?"

Come on, Pete! Give him something so we can keep digging!

"No, sir. Not at this time."

Phillips looked at Pete. "This should have been closed as an accidental death the day after it happened. I don't know why you let her screw around with it for this long." He focused on Berlin. "I want the report on my desk and the certificate filed before you leave for the day, Redding. Got it?"

He moved towards the door without waiting for a response from her. Before exiting, he turned back and looked at Berlin again, shaking his head. "You're like the little boy who cried wolf, Redding. You try to make every minor thing into something big. One day that's going to bite you in the ass. I can squash this thing with Kay Bryant. But you'll piss off someone with your super cop bullshit and the department isn't going to protect you." He shook his head again. "It's time to think about the people around you. It's not just your career you screw with when you pull this shit." With that, he walked out the door.

The office was quiet. Berlin could hear signs of life just past the wall; voices, a phone ringing, someone walking down the hall, but inside it was hard to breathe. Like someone had punched her in the stomach.

"Don't worry about it, Redding." Pete had his serious face on. That was never good.

"Which part do you not want me to worry about?" She hated how quiet her voice was.

Pete stepped forward and guided her to her

chair. He pushed her down until she was sitting. Then he crouched so he was looking into her face. He looked… concerned.

This is definitely not good.

"Any of it," he said. "You're an excellent cop because you care about the people you're trying to protect. I rather have that any day than these self-serving assholes who are only worried about moving up the ladder."

She studied his face, searching for answers. "Is Phillips right, though? Do I bull forward so hard I lose sight of anything else?"

Silence for a beat. Then another. Pete nodded. "Sometimes. Sometimes you become too focused and you grab on to something without considering if you should be hanging on."

Berlin's head dropped forward. *I will not cry. I will not cry. I might punch someone, but I will. Not. Cry.*

"Stop being such a pussy."

Her head snapped up and she glowered at him.

"That's better," Pete said. "I know how you operate, Redding, and I expect that type of focus from you. And it works for us since I'm more of a big picture guy. So, if you're done feeling sorry for yourself, can we get back to work?"

"Doing what? You told Phillips we had nothing else on this. We're supposed to close it and file the death certificate."

"I trust you to handle it and get it filed. The right way." He stood up.

"Where are you going?" Berlin stood up, too.

He still looked serious. It was a weird change.

"I trust you to do what you're good at. You need to trust me to do the same." He looked at her until she gave him a nod. "Good." Pete stepped away and grabbed his jacket. Just before walking out of their cubicle he said, "Don't forget dinner at five-thirty."

He was gone before she had time to throw anything.

*****

Berlin worked for another ninety minutes, looking for anything that might convince Phillips they needed to continue to investigate. She took Kay off their list of suspects, which realistically left Alex Johnson and whoever Bryant had sex with the day he died. Johnson was unavailable for another two days and they had less than nothing on the person he was sleeping with.

"What are you doing, Berlin? There's nothing here." She sighed, stretched her shoulders and back, and then pulled up a report template on her computer. Skipping the 'cause of death' section, she moved directly to 'details' and began filling it with everything they'd found.

Pete called her desk phone an hour later. "Why are you still there?"

"I'm trying to get the report finished. The one you left me with, remember?"

"Well, Christ, we didn't have that much in the file. How can you still be working on it? Finish it up already and get over here. Your brother is in a bitchy mood and we're tired of dealing with him."

Berlin hung up on him without bothering to say

goodbye. She read through the report and decided she felt good about it. She filled out the 'cause of death' details, saved the report, and forwarded it to the county.

"There, Phillips. I did what you told me to. Jerk." She shut down her computer and left to have dinner with her family.

*****

Pete had been right. James was being a bitch. Berlin made the mistake of asking, "Where's Ellen and the kids?" and received a look of death. She ignored him and went to her dad's room. She stopped at the doorway when she saw he was asleep in his chair. Berlin studied him, saw how frail he'd become over the last six months and felt the sting of tears.

An arm crept around her waist and her mom was there, leaning against her but still offering Berlin her strength. Quietly, her mother said, "He had a rough night and morning, so he's been sleeping all evening. The doctor thinks it's this new medication they're trying."

"I'm sorry, mom."

Christine looked at Berlin. "Whatever for?"

Berlin shook her head and looked back at her dad. "That this is how it turned out for you guys. He spent all those years away from us, away from you. Always on the job. And finally, when that's all done, he gets sick. It's like you never got time to just be together."

Her mother laughed quietly. "Berlin, your father was a bear when he wasn't at work. Being a police officer was the only thing he loved."

Berlin gave her mother a sharp look, but Christine waved it off. "I don't mean it like that. You know he loved us. But his job was his love and passion. He would have been devastated if he'd gotten sick while still working." She smiled and shook her head, squeezing Berlin's waist. "If this had to happen, then this is the only way he would have wanted it."

Berlin was quiet for a moment and then whispered, "I don't know if I could look at it the same way. From your side, or his."

Christine turned Berlin towards her and looked up at her face. "Peter mentioned the captain has been giving you a rough time lately. Are you okay?"

Berlin shrugged. "Yeah. Pete is talking me through it."

"You know Berlin, you've already sacrificed so much to be a cop. You did it while you were in the military, and then when," Christine caught herself and changed it to, "and then at college. Just make sure you don't let someone like Phillips make you question what you know in your heart and gut are right. Okay?"

Pretending she wasn't crying, Berlin hugged her mother. "Thanks mom."

Christine hugged her back. Into Berlin's shoulder she said, "So tell me about this woman you've been seeing."

"I really, really hate Pete."

Her mother laughed.

*****

The house was dark and quiet when she got home. Her answering machine was just as dark and quiet. Berlin stamped down thoughts of Nichole, brushed her teeth and went to bed.

CHAPTER TEN

The phone ringing Friday morning broke Berlin's focus on a report of an attempted holdup at South Side Market. She fumbled for the receiver without looking away from the report.

"Detective Redding."

There was silence on the other end and then a click.

Berlin shook her head and hung the phone back up. "Weird."

"What's weird?" Pete breezed into the cubicle.

"That's like the third hang up call I've had in the last twenty-four hours."

Pete sat at his desk and pulled a few folders from the middle drawer. "That's too bad. I was hoping it was your girl. Maybe then you'd stop being in such a crappy mood." Whatever he was doing must have been important. He threw the insult at her without looking at her for a reaction.

Deciding to ignore the whole thing, Berlin

asked, “Are we doing anything on this South Side not-a-hold-up?”

“You can. I have a few other things I have to chase down.” He looked up at her. “Sorry kid. You’re solo again today so try to stay out of trouble, okay?” He collected the folders and his coat and headed back out.

“Yeah, great to see you, too,” Berlin called after him and went back to the report.

Thirty minutes later her phone rang again. Irritated, Berlin snapped, “What?” into the receiver.

“Detective Redding? I’m sorry, this is Alex Johnson. I had a note from the office that you’d asked me to call you.”

Slightly stunned they’d passed on the message, Berlin tried to collect her thoughts on why she’d needed to talk to Johnson. “Yes! Coach Johnson. Thank you so much for calling me back. I was wondering if you would have a minute to meet with me today. I promise I won’t take much of your time.”

Johnson was quiet for a few seconds and then said, “If you can be here at three, I can give you fifteen minutes.”

“Great. Thank you. I appreciate it. I’ll see you this afternoon.”

“Fine.” There was a click and then the dial tone.

“What is with people and hanging up?” She hung up the phone and then pulled out her notebook from the Bryant case. She leafed through it until she came to her notes on Johnson. She had written *missing husband???* at the top of the page with the minimal information they’d gathered from the missing person report.

On the next page she’d written a to-do list,

including to follow up with Johnson on Friday. Directly beneath Johnson's name was Kay Bryant's name and follow up next to it.

Berlin frowned at the two names for a minute. What were the chances?

She picked up the phone and dialed Kay's home number. She got an answer almost immediately.

"Hello?"

"Mrs. Bryant. This is Detective Redding."

The friendliness of the initial greeting disappeared. "I have nothing else to say to you, Detective."

Berlin harnessed her inner-Pete and said, "I just wanted to call and apologize for upsetting you the other day. That wasn't our intent. We can't imagine how difficult all of this is for you, and we know our questions didn't help."

The line was quiet for a moment. There was less frostiness when Kay answered. "Oh. Well, thank you for the apology. I know you were just doing your job."

"You're very welcome. I appreciate you understanding. I also wanted to let you know we filed the report and you should be receiving official notification from the department any day now."

There was relief from Kay this time. "Thank you, Detective. Cassie and I just want to move forward with our lives. This will be a huge help."

"Well, I'm sorry it's taken this long. And if there's anything else we can do for you…" She let the comment hang.

"Of course, Detective. And the same here. Anything I can do."

Bingo

"Thank you, Mrs. Bryant. Actually, since I have you on the line, I did have a quick question. And this is nothing major so if you can't remember it isn't a big deal. When did you say you saw Alex Johnson last?"

"Oh." Kay was quiet.

Come on, come on…

"Well, I talked to her a few days ago. She called to offer her condolences and check up on Cassie and me. But I honestly can't remember the last time I saw her."

"Ok, it's not a problem. Thank you, Mrs. Bryant. Again, we apologize and thank you for your help. And remember, if you need anything, just let us know."

They said goodbye, Kay a little uncertainly, and Berlin hung up the phone.

*****

The academy looked just as pretentious as the first time Berlin visited. She parked in the lot closest to the athletic building and took the stairs to the third floor. She found Johnson's office from memory and knocked on the door. At the response, "It's open," Berlin opened the door and entered the office.

Alex Johnson looked much like she had on the first day they met. She had her hair pulled back in a tight braid and she was wearing a long-sleeved, black top and comfortable looking running pants. Her face was free of makeup, making it easy to see the lines of exhaustion around her mouth and under her eyes. Berlin briefly wondered what was keeping her up at night but let the thought pass.

"Thank you for agreeing to see me," Berlin said, and sat in a chair in front of Johnson's desk. Before Johnson had time to respond, Berlin asked, "How long have you been friends with Kay Bryant?"

Johnson was still for a moment and then leaned back in her chair. "I'm sorry, who?"

Smiling, Berlin said, "I would have gone with something different."

Genuine confusion settled on Johnson's face. "I'm sorry, Detective, what -"

"Even if you had no personal involvement with Charles Bryant, I find it nearly impossible to believe you wouldn't know his wife's name. Especially considering his recent death."

"Ahhh. Well, if you had identified her as his wife -"

"On top of that, I know you called Kay a few days ago to check in with her."

Johnson raised her eyebrows and smiled. It made her face look uncomfortably tight. "I was trying to be kind and offer condolences to my colleague's widow."

Berlin nodded and smiled back. "Right. A colleague you claim to know nothing about, and whose wife's name you didn't recognize sixty seconds ago." She made a show of checking her notes. "But who you still spoke to for twenty-seven minutes." She looked up at Johnson. "Must have been an instant connection, right?"

Johnson drummed her fingers on the arm of her chair and then sat forward. The chair popped with the quickness of the movement. "What do you want, Detective Redding? You obviously already know that

Kay and I know each other. So why are you here?"

"The problem with your lie," Berlin corrected herself when it looked like Johnson would protest her choice of words, "I'm sorry, temporary loss of memory, is it makes me suspicious about other information you may have temporarily forgotten." Berlin paused, considering her next move. She went with, "What I wonder is if your relationship with Charles Bryant was really as hands off as you initially stated."

"I wasn't sleeping with Charles." Johnson met Berlin's eyes without hesitation.

"But he tried." Berlin was just as deadpan in her statement. "We know about his history of sleeping with, or at least harassing the women he worked with. I very much doubt he was any different with you."

Johnson sighed and settled back in her chair. "Fine. Yes, he tried. And kept trying."

Berlin waited and when nothing was added, she asked, "What did you do about it?"

Johnson shrugged. "What makes you think I did anything?"

Berlin studied Johnson. She took in the tidy braid and common-sense athletic wear. Her desk was organized down to the colored paper clips in several little clear plastic holders, and the office was organized with the same efficiency. Johnson was definitely a woman used to controlling her domain. Berlin thought it more likely Johnson was the type to maim an attacker than cry for help. Keeping it simple, she just said, "Because you're the type of person who would. At least something to stop the harassment."

Tilting her head in acknowledgment, Johnson said, "I told Bryant I would tell his wife, tell the school board, and have him removed from his position as an assistant coach. Anything I thought that might have an impact."

"Did any of it work?"

"I don't know." She shrugged. "He just stopped at some point, but I don't know if it was because of my threats or because of someone else."

"Like who? You said 'someone', not 'something'."

"Listen, Detective -"

Switching tactics, Berlin said, "Where's your husband, Coach Johnson?"

The abrupt change in topic seemed to throw Johnson. She looked uncertain for the first time since Berlin had entered her office. "What does Shawn have to do with this?"

Berlin opened her notebook and removed the report. She handed it over to Johnson and watched her as she read it. She didn't appear to be worried or upset. When she'd finished, she offered the report back to Berlin.

"Shawn's sister filed the report. She's never liked me."

"Okay. So, where is he?"

Johnson narrowed her eyes. "Again, what does he have to do with Charles Bryant?"

Fed up with the back and forth, Berlin bit out, "Your husband is missing. You were the last one who saw him. Charles Bryant is dead, and you've admitted he was harassing you. You also have some type of relationship with his wife. And we've caught you in several lies." She leaned forward. "Coach Johnson, you're looking damn suspicious. So how about you answer the question here, in your nice comfortable office. Otherwise, I'll give you a free tour of our police department. Your choice."

After a minute of staring each other down, Johnson said, "*Shana* is in Colorado. At a center for transitioning adults."

Berlin sat back. She had no idea how to respond to that without it seeming like needless prying. She took a minute to process the information and looked back at the report. She cleared her throat and said, "You said the woman who reported him, her missing, this Carol Sweeney, she's the sister?"

Johnson nodded, looking slightly amused at Berlin's embarrassment.

"Let me guess. She doesn't like that Shaw-Shana, is transitioning?"

"No, Carol does not approve. And she doesn't approve that I fully support Shana's decision."

Berlin shook her head. "Why didn't you share this with the person investigating the disappearance?"

"I was never told why I was being asked. And it was none of their business where she was. She wasn't in trouble."

Berlin was fairly certain Johnson was telling the truth. She wrote the number to missing persons on the corner of a page in her notebook, tore it off, and handed it to Johnson. "Please call them and close out the report. There are too many people actually missing they should focus on."

Johnson took the paper and nodded. "Anything else? Or are we done here?" She started to rise from her chair.

Berlin stayed seated. "Did you kill Charles

Bryant?"

Johnson sat back down. Slowly. "Is that a serious question?"

"Absolutely. And one that needs an answer."

"Charles Bryant was a womanizing, condescending bastard. But we would run out of men fairly quick if we killed them for that." She paused. "To answer your question, though, no. I didn't kill him." She raised her eyebrows. "Anything else?"

Berlin looked down at her notes. Nothing jumped out at her. She shook her head and smiled. She offered her hand to Johnson. "Thank you for taking the time, Coach Johnson. I appreciate it."

Johnson took Berlin's hand. She had a nice, firm handshake. "Take care, Detective Redding."

Berlin walked down the hallway, back the way she'd come, thinking of Johnson's words. Why had they sounded more like a warning than just the standard departing phrase?

She made it to the stairs, still lost in thought, and started down. There was an older man on the first landing, standing with another person. They turned at Berlin's footsteps and Berlin saw the other person was a fairly young girl. Something in the man's stature made the hair on Berlin's neck stand on end. He was also standing way too close to the girl.

"Good afternoon," Berlin said, keeping her voice light and cheery. She kept her eyes focused on the girl.

The man nodded, but the girl didn't react.

Berlin stopped beside them and pulled her notebook back out. She spoke to the girl, saying the first thing that popped into her head. "I don't suppose you or your dad knows where Nichole Kellner's office is? She teaches Spanish."

The man laughed, unamused. "Professor Kellner isn't in this building. Why don't you try the front office?"

Berlin smiled at the girl who was tucked tight against the wall, a thick book held tightly across her middle. "Parents think they know everything, don't they?"

Now the guy just looked pissed. "Listen lady, knock it off with the parent crap. I don't know who you think you are, but I recommend -"

Berlin had her badge out and the smile off her face as soon as he told her to cut the parent crap. She waited for him to finish his statement, but his mouth snapped shut at the sight of her badge.

"If you aren't her father, and you're not related to her, I'm really interested to know what your relationship is with this young lady? Mister?"

He looked around the stairway, saw nothing helpful and straightened up, away from the girl. "Harold Houston."

"Thank you, Mr. Houston. And what is your relationship with Miss?" Berlin looked at the girl and waited.

The girl looked up at Berlin and then side-eyed Houston, then back at Berlin. "Brittney Thompson." She looked at her shoes.

"Hi Brittney. I'm Detective Berlin Redding." Berlin pulled a card from her pocket and handed it to the girl. Brittney checked Houston again. When no movement from him was forthcoming, she grabbed the card and clutched it in her hand against her book.

Berlin focused on Houston. “Now, Mr. Houston. You were just about to explain your relationship to Miss Thompson.”

“She’s in one of my classes.”

Berlin nodded. “Interesting.” She turned back to Brittney. “Brittney, are you hard of hearing?”

The girl shook her head.

“How about your eyesight? Is that okay?”

She looked a little confused by the question, but Brittney shook her head again. “No. I can see and hear fine.”

“Great. Thanks.” Berlin squared her shoulders and took a step forward, putting herself in Houston’s personal space. He immediately backed up but hit the wall. “Tell me, Harold. Why were you crowding Miss Thompson when she obviously can hear and see you just fine? Or do you enjoy having someone this close to you?”

He raised his hands just enough.

“Go ahead, asshole,” Berlin said, her voice low and hard. “Put your hands on me and see what happens.”

His hands went back down, and he looked to his left, up the stairs.

Ignoring whatever he was looking at, Berlin said, “Ah ah, Mr. Houston. Focus on me, please. We haven’t finished our conversation.”

He met her eyes again.

“If I hear even a whisper of you getting into someone’s personal space again, and I don’t care if that person is eight or eighty, I will come find you and I will make sure you aren’t happy to see me. Do I make myself clear?”

He nodded, and Berlin backed away one step. She smiled back at Brittney. “Miss Thompson, I want you to use the number on that card any time, day or night. And I want you to share it with anyone who might need my help. Okay?”

The girl looked at Berlin, then at Houston, and then at Berlin again. She nodded once and gave Berlin the briefest of smiles. And then she scooted around them both and dashed up the stairs.

Berlin looked after her and found Alex Johnson watching with no expression on her face. She spoke briefly to Brittney, who nodded and then left. Johnson turned her attention back to Berlin and Houston. She looked at Houston until he looked away, and then she nodded at Berlin. She said, “Detective,” and then walked off after Brittney.

Alone with Houston, Berlin said, “I will follow up on this, Mr. Houston. I promise.” She continued down the stairs and out of the building.

*****

Berlin had just gone to bed when there was a knock on her front door. She stayed still and when the knock came again, she pulled open the drawer on her nightstand and removed her 9 mm shield. She got out of bed and made her way to the front entryway. Staying to the side of the door, Berlin flipped the porch light on and peeked out the curtain of the side window. A small woman with blond, curly hair was standing on her porch.

She unlocked the deadbolt and opened the door.

Nichole looked up at her, a shy smile on her

face. "Hi."

Berlin shook her head. "What are you doing here? It's past ten."

Nichole's smile dropped from her face, and she looked around. "Can I please come in?"

"What do you want Nichole? It's late. I haven't heard from you since Wednesday, and I'm just not up for a big discussion."

"Oh, come on Berlin, I was teaching, and I knew you were working! It's only been a couple of days. And it's not like you called me." She shoved her way past Berlin into the entryway. Once inside, she turned and looked at Berlin.

Berlin could tell from the set of Nichole's face she was getting ready to argue another point, and then her expression changed. She looked Berlin up and down and grinned. "Were you already in bed?"

"It's late. And I had a long day," Berlin said, trying to keep the defensiveness from her voice.

"I like your sleepwear choice."

Considering she was wearing an oversized t-shirt that boasted, 'My Penis is Bigger Than Yours,' Berlin didn't take her compliment seriously.

"Was there something you wanted, Nichole? Or can I go back to bed?" Berlin crossed her arms across her chest, acutely aware that she wasn't wearing a bra.

Nichole's grin got bigger. "I have another question. Are you wearing anything under that shirt? 'Cause it certainly doesn't look like it."

Berlin felt the flush wash over her body. She uncrossed her arms and tugged at the hem of the shirt. "Go home, Nichole."

"I missed you this week," Nichole said, moving

closer. She took Berlin's hand from the hem of the shirt and replaced it with her own. She ran it up under the shirt and across Berlin's hip.

Berlin's body was instantly on fire.

Nichole slid her hand further back, over Berlin's ass. "I can make you breakfast in the morning."

Pretending it was the offer of breakfast and not the unspoken promise of sex that changed her mind, Berlin said, "Fine," and moved forward into Nichole's arms.

CHAPTER ELEVEN

The smell of coffee and sausage brought Berlin out of a sound sleep. She lay still for a minute, trying to figure out why her house smelled good. A crash from the kitchen followed by colorful swearing, and the realization she was once again in bed, naked, reminded her who was making so much racket in the other room.

Berlin rolled onto her back and stretched, feeling pleasantly tired. Another muffled curse from the kitchen had her out of bed and slipping on a worn sweatshirt and ratty jeans. She stumbled out of the bedroom but paused before entering the kitchen.

Nichole was at the stove, dressed in the penis t-shirt, which covered her much better. She'd completed her outfit with a pair of bright pink socks with zebras marching all over them. She'd attempted to put her hair up, but the curls had other plans and a good majority had escaped and sprung out all over her head. Her face was clean of makeup, her skin pink and flushed from the heat of the stove. She looked young and innocent and beautiful, and the sudden urge to protect her was almost overwhelming. Nichole moved away from the stove and stretched up to reach into the cupboard for plates. The t-shirt rode up as she reached, revealing she'd copied Berlin's fashion choice from last night. The protective instinct was shattered and replaced with something definitely more primal.

Berlin waited until the plates were safely on the counter. "Good morning," she said and entered the small, sunlit room. She walked up behind Nichole, now focused on eggs in the frying pan, and hugged her from behind. "I wasn't sure if you'd be here when I woke up." She placed a soft kiss on the back of Nichole's neck.

Nichole leaned back for a moment before turning her attention back to the eggs. "Good morning. I thought you'd sleep forever."

Berlin released her. "Sorry. I was a little more tired than usual."

Grinning, Nichole split up the eggs and sausage. "Would you grab the coffee? Do you think it's too cold to eat outside?"

Berlin took a moment to study Nichole's t-shirt and socks. "Nah. I'm sure the socks will keep you warm enough."

Nichole stuck out her tongue but put the plates down and went back to the bedroom. She was back in a few minutes wearing jeans and a thin sweater. "Better?"

"Don't worry, you're still cute as a button," Berlin said as she picked up the coffee mugs and creamer. She made her way to the porch, deposited her items and went back for the coffeepot.

Nichole followed her with the plates, napkins

and forks. They got settled at the table and Berlin poured the coffee. "How did you sleep?"

Nichole surprised her by pulling her over for a kiss. They parted, grinning at each other. "I slept great. Thanks for letting me stay."

Berlin snorted and ate a bite of the eggs with some sausage. "Like you gave me a choice, tempting me with breakfast. It's great, by the way."

"Thanks. Breakfast is one of the few things I've mastered in the kitchen," Nichole said, pouring a healthy dose of creamer in her coffee. She held it up for Berlin and added some to her cup when Berlin nodded.

"Thanks."

They ate for a few minutes in silence, and then Nichole asked, "So, do you have to work today?"

Berlin shook her head. "No, they'll call for any serious emergencies, but I'm not on call this weekend. Something catastrophic would have to happen to get called in." She took a sip of her coffee. Perfection. "I planned to go up north today and spend the night."

"Oh," Nichole said.

When she didn't say anything else, Berlin looked at her. "What about you? Do you have plans?"

Nichole shrugged and played with the food on her plate. "I have some lesson plans I need to work on, and some grading to do. Plenty to keep me busy." She looked less than pleased about the prospect.

Berlin took a bite of eggs, enjoying the strong flavors of Swiss cheese and sausage. She wasn't used to considering someone else when making plans. She wasn't even sure they were at a point where she should consider Nichole when making plans. Finally, she thought, *ah, the hell with it* and asked, "Do you need internet access?"

"For the papers?"

Berlin nodded and sipped her coffee.

Nichole shrugged. "No. It's all hard-copy. Why?"

Berlin couldn't tell if Nichole was being coy or if she was feeling as uncertain about the situation as Berlin was. "Do you want to go with me?"

Another shrug, more food-pushing around the plate. "You said up north, but where?"

"I have a place a little north of Lancaster. I go once a month just to check on it and get out of here for a couple of days."

Nichole looked a little uncertain. "What would I need? Clothes-wise? I keep a small overnight bag in the car but there isn't much in there."

"Not much." Berlin peaked under the table and the zebras. She lifted her head back up, grinning. "Maybe something a little heavier for socks, but I have those up at the cabin. Extra sweatshirts and flannels, too. So really, as long as you have clean undies… unless you want to go commando all weekend?" She raised her eyebrows.

Nichole remained quiet and for a moment, Berlin wondered if she'd misread Nichole's interest in going with her. But then her face broke out in a big smile. "You really don't mind if I go with you?"

"Of course not. It'll be nice to have the company."

*****

"This is so beautiful," Nichole told Berlin a little

over an hour into the drive. She had her head craned back so she could look up at the tops of the granite cliffs.

Berlin grinned. It was like being in the car with a little kid. But she had to admit, it was a beautiful drive. She'd always loved the starkness of the cliffs compared to the green of the trees. "Haven't you been up here before?"

"A long time ago. But I never paid attention." Nichole looked over at Berlin. "So why have a place up here?"

Berlin passed an old station wagon crawling down the road. "I grew up in the north country. I couldn't wait to leave it when I was younger, but we moved south for dad's job when I was a teenager and I found I missed the north. And the longer I was away from it, the more I missed it. So, when I got the chance, I bought a little place."

"Would you live up here permanently?"

Berlin shrugged. "Maybe someday. It's just a camp, so I'd have to do a lot of work to it. But maybe when I'm older and ready to get away from the city."

Nichole looked thoughtful. Turning back to the window, she said, "It would be nice to have a place to get away."

A little while later Berlin pulled onto a gravel road lined on both sides with evergreens. Nichole was still looking around like she'd never seen the mountains or a forest before. Berlin entered the clearing of her cabin and parked the car.

They got out, and she watched Nichole's face for any hint of what she might be thinking. The nicest word for the cabin was rustic, but James called it ratty.

It was old but as well-kept as something over a hundred years old could be, but it wasn't a place a true city girl would necessarily feel comfortable. "Are you still sure you want to stay up here?" Berlin asked.

Nichole came around the front of the car toward Berlin. She was scanning the cabin, taking in the hewn logs and thick chinking, small windows, and the ample porch. Finally, she turned to Berlin, an enormous smile on her face. "This place is brilliant, Berlin." She took Berlin's hand and squeezed it. "Seriously. This is amazing."

Pleased, Berlin waved Nichole forward. "Come on in and I'll show you around."

The tour took about three minutes. The cabin had originally been only one room made up of a postage-sized kitchen, a small sitting area, and a sleeping area. A previous owner had added to it, creating two tiny but dedicated bedrooms and a bathroom.

"This place looks like you," Nichole said.

Looking at the small, slightly shabby rooms, Berlin raised her eyebrows and said, "Thanks?"

Nichole laughed; her whole tone warm. "I meant it as a compliment." She moved closer to Berlin and put her arm around her waist. She looked around the little sitting room, taking in the worn corduroy couch and scarred wooden table. "Everything here is warm and comfortable. It feels like a home. Like you."

Berlin smiled and kissed Nichole's temple. "I'm glad you like it. And I'm glad you're here with me."

They stood together for a few moments, both enjoying the feel of the other. Finally, Nichole asked, "So now what do we do?"

"Now we work, and later we'll play."

*****

They set to work unpacking the car. Berlin brought in a bag of groceries, and Nichole grabbed her overnight bag. They met back outside, and Berlin opened the back of the Outback. "Can you help me pull this out?" She had her hand on the end of a piece of wooden lattice.

"What's that for?" Nichole looked skeptical.

"I need to replace some sections on the back deck. This will hopefully keep anything big from making a home under there." She started pulling the section out, and Nichole joined her.

"What would live under a deck?"

Berlin walked backwards around the corner of the cabin, moving towards the backyard. "Mostly things like raccoons or woodchucks will hide out. But the occasional skunk or even a young black bear will find their way in if they're desperate enough."

Nichole stopped moving. "Bears?"

Berlin laughed, walking and pulling Nichole with her. "Come on, Nichole. Don't worry. I'll keep you safe."

They propped the wood against the deck and returned to the front of the house. There wasn't a garage, but Berlin had a small shed tucked away on the side of the cabin. She unlocked it and swung the doors open and switched on the light.

"This is awfully snazzy for an outdoor shed," Nichole said, looking around inside the shed.

"Why have good tools if you don't take care of them? And it gets dark up here early, so I splurged and had the electricity added. Which also gives me a dry place to work if I need it." She handed Nichole two red tool cases and held out an extension cord. "Can you take this, too?"

Nichole put down one case and took the coiled cord. She put her arm through the coil and fit the cord on her shoulder and picked the case back up. "Yup, I'm good."

Berlin looked up from putting hand tools in a case and smiled. "Yes, you are."

Nichole grinned back.

Grabbing another tool case and two sawhorses, Berlin led the way back around the house. She nodded toward the steps, and Nichole placed the cases on the ground. "There's a plug just to the right of the steps. Hold on to the end with the plug and toss the coil toward the bottom of the yard."

Nichole did as Berlin said, and the cord uncoiled in an almost perfect line.

"Nice job," Berlin told her. "We'll make a professional carpenter out of you yet."

Nichole flushed pink; her eyes bright. "Now what?"

"You can unpack the two tool cases you carried over. The bigger one is a circular saw, and the second is the skill saw. We'll use the circular saw to cut the new pieces, and we may need the skill saw to remove the old sections."

She watched Nichole kneel and flip the latches on the first case and then open it. She grabbed the saw easily, removing it from the case. There was no hesitation with getting her hands dirty. No complaining about the roughness of the work; all things Berlin would have expected from someone raised as Nichole had been. It was possible she was trying to impress Berlin, but Berlin had the feeling Nichole wasn't as helpless as she made herself out to be. After a few more moments of watching, Berlin continued setting up the sawhorses.

The job went fast. Berlin did the work on the first section of lattice. She explained what she was doing as she went. She removed the broken and rotted pieces of lattice first, careful to remove any nails still stuck into the bottom frame of the porch. Then she measured what they needed to replace it. After measuring the new section twice, she cut the new section and installed it.

She helped Nichole with the second section, making corrections as Nichole worked, and explaining why she made them. She had Nichole repair the third section on her own, only helping when asked.

The women stood back and admired their work when it was done. "What do you think?" Berlin asked, glancing over at Nichole. Nichole's hair was a curly cloud all around her head and she had wood dust and shavings all over her.

"I think it looks amazing." Nichole's voice held a distinct note of pride. "Now what?"

Berlin started gathering the scrap wood and put it into a neat pile. "I'll clean up the wood scraps if you'll put the saws away. Once we've cleaned up, we'll have some lunch and I'll take you swimming."

"There's a pool around here?"

"Nope, no pool." Berlin finished creating her stack and picked it up. She stood up and found Nichole looking at her.

"Swimming where?"

Shaking her head, Berlin said, "Trust me, you'll like it."

*****

They took a picnic lunch with them instead of eating at the cabin. Nichole made them turkey and cheddar sandwiches and Berlin packed bottles of water, chips, and chocolate into a small cooler. She added the sandwiches on top. Adjusting the strap over her shoulder, she looked at Nichole and nodded towards a worn quilt folded on a chair. "Will you carry that?"

Nichole picked up the quilt and grabbed the car keys. "Yup. Let's go."

"We don't need the keys. We're walking."

Nichole's hold on the keys tightened. "Walking? Where?" She looked out the window at the trees. "In the woods?"

Berlin approached her and pried the keys out of Nichole's hand. She placed them back on the counter. "We'll be fine. I do this all the time. Plus, I'm always armed when I go in the woods." She gave Nichole a quick kiss. "Come on."

It was a beautiful day. The cooler morning had given way to an unseasonably hot afternoon. Berlin was fairly certain it would be one of the last warm weekends they'd have. The small patches of yellow and orange leaves on the trees, and the leaves already on the ground, were strong indicators that fall was on its way.

She loved being in the woods. The quietness and smell of evergreens soothed her in a way nothing else could. Every time she was away from her cabin, she seemed to miss it more. Thinking of Nichole's question, she wondered if she'd be ready to move up north permanently sooner than later. She glanced over at Nichole, who had finally stopped jumping at every sound, and wondered if she'd be more willing if she had someone to move with.

Berlin had taken them on one of her favorite walks. The worn path was wide enough to easily accommodate them walking side by side. The lane had been cut years before and now mature raspberry canes, goldenrod, and late summer wildflowers boarded the path, giving it a natural feel instead of man-made.

"Sorry for being weird about the walk. I was picturing us darting through trees and bushes. Not… this." Nichole waved her hand at the short grass under her feet. "This is so cool."

"I can't take all the credit." Berlin shifted the cooler to her other shoulder. "All I do is maintain it. The people I bought it from did the major work. They were big cross-country skiers and cut trails throughout the woods." She glanced at Nichole. "And don't apologize. I know this has to be a new experience for you."

Grinning, Nichole agreed. "Lots of new experiences. I never thought I'd be the type of woman who'd like using power tools."

Berlin laughed and bumped Nichole's hip with her own. "You did great. You looked like a pro."

"I had an excellent teacher," Nichole said, bumping back. "So, how much further until we hit this mysterious swimming paradise?"

Berlin stopped and placed her hand on Nichole's arm. "Stop for a second."

Nichole stopped. In a quieter voice, she asked,

"What? Is it a bear?"

"No. Just listen."

They listened to the birds overhead and the chipmunks and squirrels scolding from the trees and underbrush. And something else…

"Do you hear it?" Berlin asked.

Nichole said, "I hear a rushing sound."

"Yup, just ahead." Berlin picked up her pace and Nichole followed.

The path veered off to the right, following the tree line, but Berlin took them through the trees for a few yards. "It slopes down here, so be careful."

They finally broke through the tree line to the bank of the river. Huge boulders and granite slabs created perfect spots for sitting or laying out. Another slab gently sloped into the clear water.

Nichole gazed around and then looked at Berlin. "This is where you want to swim?"

"This *is* where I swim. It was one of the reasons I bought the property." Berlin stepped onto the flat rocks and put the cooler down. She removed her sneakers and socks and held her hand out to Nichole. "Come on, city girl."

Nichole placed her hand in Berlin's and stepped onto the rock. "I mean, it's beautiful. It really is. But it doesn't look deep enough to swim in."

"See that section there?" Berlin asked, pointing out toward the far side of the river. At Nichole's nod she said, "That darker section is a channel. It's deep enough that I can't touch the bottom without being completely under water. The whole thing is deeper than it looks." She pointed to another section. "There's an incredible current that flows through there, and it's like swimming in an infinity pool. You have to fight to stay in one place."

Nichole still looked skeptical.

"Let's eat first, because I'm starving." Berlin sat down and started unpacking the cooler. She handed Nichole a sandwich and a bottle of water and took one of each for herself. Nichole finally sat down with her.

They ate in comfortable silence for a few minutes.

"What are we wearing to swim?" Nichole asked, looking innocent.

Berlin shrugged. "I'm swimming in what I'm wearing."

"Seriously? You're wearing shorts and a t-shirt?"

She looked down at her worn out police trainee t-shirt and Under Armour shorts. "What's wrong with that?"

Nichole pulled the cooler over and took out a bag of chips. She opened it and offered it to Berlin. "Is that what you usually wear when you swim?"

Berlin flushed. "No. Not usually." The other side of the river suddenly became quite interesting.

"What do you usually wear, Berlin?" Nichole's face was still innocent, but there was a wicked glint in her eyes.

"You can stop now. I am not swimming naked with you."

"Oh, come on!" Nichole's face broke out in a gleeful grin. "You got naked with me last night!"

"That was different."

"Why? Naked is naked."

"No," Berlin corrected her, "last night was dark.

Now it's daytime. You'll see…" She stopped, her face burning.

Nichole nudged her. "See what?"

Sighing, Berlin looked at Nichole. "Everything. Me."

Tilting her head to the side, Nichole studied Berlin. Shaking her head, she asked, "So. What's wrong with that?"

Berlin sighed again. "I'm not pretty like you are, Nichole. I'm not feminine. I don't have a pretty, womanly body."

Nichole was quiet again, and then she reached for Berlin's hand. "Berlin, you have a wonderfully strong, powerful body. There aren't many women who can do what you do for a living. And not many who could do what you're doing up here. I think you're amazing, and your body reflects that. Stop beating yourself up for not looking like other women."

She threw her garbage into the cooler and stood up. In one smooth motion Nichole had her shirt off, quickly followed by her bra. She toed off her sneakers and slid out of her shorts and underwear and peeled off her socks. "Come on, slowpoke. You promised to take me swimming."

Without another word, she stepped down along the granite slab that dipped below the surface of the river. And slipped off the rock, crashing into the water. She came up sputtering, shrieking loud enough to silence the birds. "Jesus fucking Christ! You didn't tell me how cold it was!"

Berlin laughed so hard her stomach hurt.

Still sputtering, Nichole swam toward the deeper channel and Berlin relaxed on the rocks to watch. The paleness of Nichole's skin was easy to see through the clearness of the river, the distortion of the water only magnifying the curves of her body. Berlin watched her bob up and down and saw Nichole take a deep breath before she disappeared under the water. She reemerged only moments later, shrieking and laughing as she shoved wet, blond curls out of her face.

"It's so cold! And so deep! I couldn't touch the bottom, even when I shoved myself down against the rocks!"

Berlin smiled at the excitement in Nichole's voice. "Told you."

Nichole treaded water and looked up at her. "Are you coming in?"

"In a minute." Berlin admired her a little longer before lying back on the rocks and closing her eyes.

The sun felt wonderful. She listened to Nichole splashing in the water, smiling now and again at a curse or a giddy shriek. Finally, it grew quiet. She opened her eyes and lifted her head. Nichole was standing by her feet, water droplets clinging to her skin. Berlin gazed at her body, taking in Nichole's breasts, the curve of her waist, and the fullness of her hips before she closed her eyes and leaned her head back on the rock. "Hi."

Cold drops of water landed on her body, letting her know Nichole was now above her. She felt Nichole sit down beside her on the rock and then felt hands tugging at the hem of her shirt.

"Lift please," Nichole said.

Without letting herself think about it too much, Berlin lifted her torso off the rock and let Nichole pull her shirt over her head.

"Compliant. I like that."

Her sports bra followed after some pulling and cursing, making Berlin grin. Her grin turned to shivers when Nichole's fingers started exploring her skin, first gently and then rougher. She arched again when Nichole's attention turned to her breasts. After a few minutes, she felt tugging on the waistband of her shorts.

"Lift please," Nichole said, her voice husky.

Berlin lay still, trying to decide what to do. A sharp pinch low on her ass stole the decision from her. She arched her hips off the rock and before she knew what had happened, her shorts and underwear were down and gone. She opened her eyes and glared at Nichole, who only grinned at her.

"Next time move faster," Nichole said. Her hands started moving up Berlin's legs and then back down. Each pass a little higher and more insistent.

"Nichole, you can't! I'm sweaty and filthy. And I'm -"

"Thinking too much. Close your eyes and shut up, Berlin."

There was no room for argument in Nichole's voice, but Berlin still wanted to. She was unsure and embarrassed, but Nichole's hot mouth was suddenly on the inside of her thigh, and then between her thighs. Suddenly thinking was impossible and then she just didn't care anymore.

They stayed at the river until the evening became cool and bugs were out in full force.

"You were right. This is an amazing place to go swimming." Nichole finished packing up the cooler while Berlin shook out the quilt and folded it.

"I thought I would die laughing when you fell in," Berlin said, grinning again.

Nichole stuck her tongue out. “I thought you promised to protect me.”

They walked up the incline from the river’s edge into the trees. Once back on the path, Berlin said, “From the bears. There’s not much I can do to protect you if you want to go running around all crazy.”

“The story of my life, my friend. The story of my life.”

CHAPTER TWELVE

The next morning Berlin woke up before Nichole. She slid out of bed, careful not to jostle the mattress. She slipped into a pair of jeans and a flannel shirt and left the bedroom. Morning light spilled into the kitchen, warming the entire room. Berlin pulled coffee out of the freezer, poured some into the filter, and added cinnamon on top. She hit the on switch and moved into the bathroom.

She pulled the quilt and their river clothes from the washing machine and carried them outside to the small clothesline. She draped the quilt on two lines and hung the rest of their clothes on the remaining line. When she reentered the kitchen, Nichole was up and staring at the coffeemaker.

"Good morning, sleepyhead. I put that on a few minutes ago so it shouldn't be much longer."

Nichole smiled, still looking half asleep.

Berlin took two coffee mugs from the hanging rack under the cabinet and held one out to Nichole. "I hoped you'd sleep long enough for me to make you breakfast."

"Mmm… breakfast. What are we having?" Nichole walked over and took her mug. She then gave Berlin a hug but ended it as soon as the coffee pot beeped. "Oh, thank God!"

"I see how it is. Dumped for caffeine."

Nichole filled both mugs and added creamer to her coffee. She offered the carton to Berlin.

Berlin took it and added a generous amount to her mug and said, "Pancakes or French toast. Your choice. And bacon with whichever."

"French toast please." Nichole took a drink of coffee and closed her eyes. A look of pure bliss on her face. "I love coffee." She opened her eyes and found Berlin looking at her. "What?" She put her mug on the table and put her hands to her head, feeling around. "Is my hair all crazy?"

"Yes. But you look cute." Berlin smiled and started pulling bowls and a frying pan from the cabinet. "I was just thinking this has been great. Having you here this weekend."

Nichole relaxed and picked her mug back up. "It's been great being here with you." She stood up and moved over by Berlin. "If you get me another pan, I'll fry up the bacon."

After breakfast Berlin tidied up the cabin while Nichole took a shower. She swept and ran a vacuum through the living room and was filing up the sink for dishes when Nichole came out looking pink and scrubbed.

"I'll dry," Nichole said and grabbed a dishtowel.

"Thanks." Berlin rinsed a pan and handed it to

Nichole. "I'll shower and then we can pack up and head back south."

"Do we have to go back?" Nichole pointed to a spot on the pan. "You want me to just wipe that out with the towel?"

Berlin grabbed the pan back and gave it another quick scrub. "Funny girl. And yes, we have to go back. Or at least I do." She smiled smugly at Nichole. "You can stay here and keep the bears away if you want to."

Nichole shook her head and looked sad. "Such a shame the honeymoon is over already."

Berlin laughed and handed over the second pan.

She took a quick shower and then dressed in the same jeans and flannel she started the morning in. She wiped everything down in the bathroom and gathered the wet towels and floor mat, carrying everything into her bedroom to get packed up. Nichole's bag was on the bed, but the room was empty. Berlin did a quick job of braiding her hair and left the room.

"Nichole? You ready to go?"

The kitchen and living room were empty. Berlin looked out the back window and saw the quilt and clothes were gone from the line. She found Nichole in the second bedroom, the quilt and clothes in a pile on the bed.

Nichole was staring at a small, framed picture on the dresser in the bedroom. It was of two young women; the taller of the two had her face pressed into the cheek of the other and they both were laughing. The taller, darker girl was Berlin. The other girl was slight and had strawberry blond hair. "Who is she?" Nichole's voice was icy, and she looked accusingly at Berlin. "She must be someone special if you're hiding her away up here. Or is she hiding because you don't want your family to know about her?"

Berlin took the picture carefully from Nichole, smoothing her thumb across the face of the smaller woman. She placed it back on the dresser. "That's Laurel."

Nichole had her hands on her hips. "And she was? A wife? A girlfriend? What?"

Berlin tried to kill the irritation bubbling up. "Laurel was my sister. She's dead." She turned away from Nichole and walked out of the room.

Nichole followed a few minutes later, the anger gone from her face. She knelt at the chair where Berlin sat and touched Berlin's knee. "Jesus. I'm sorry, Berlin. I'm such a jealous bitch. There's such evident love on both your faces, and I just," she shook her head, "I just lost it. I had no right to question you. I'm sorry." She squeezed Berlin's knee.

Berlin shook her head. "It's okay. I know you didn't mean anything."

"Can I ask what happened?"

Taking a deep breath, Berlin said, "We were living in Manchester. Laurel was working, and I was going to school. She had been dating the same guy for a while, and he started getting heavy into drugs. I told her she should stop seeing him, that he would pull her into that scene or hurt her. So, she tried to break it off with him and he became abusive. We filed a report. The police picked him up, held him for a few days but eventually released him. I told her to get a restraining order against him. She did." Berlin smiled humorlessly. "He grabbed her from the parking lot of the building she worked at and shot her. Then he shot himself."

Berlin closed her eyes against the memories, missing her sister so much it made her stomach hurt. She opened them again and wished it was Laurel sitting there with her. But the pain and concern on Nichole's face looked real, and Berlin felt her irritation at Nichole fade. "Because he was dead, they did nothing. They put it down as a tragic murder-suicide of a young couple, working through some issues. The police didn't care. They had too many live dealers and abusers that were still active on the streets. They also figured since Laurel was involved with him, she must have been using, too." Berlin sighed. "It eventually only hardened my determination to be a cop, and one who took every investigation, every complaint, seriously."

Nichole sat quietly, still touching Berlin's knee, but she looked far away in her thoughts. Finally, she focused on Berlin again, as if she'd decided something.

"When I was in college, I had a friend." Nichole paused. "She was my first girlfriend. Her name was Becky. She was everything I wasn't. Tall. Beautiful. Thin. And so smart. She was studying to be a doctor. I had never met anyone as caring as she was. She was just so determined to find the good in people, and to help everyone." Nichole smiled, "She was really something." She stopped again and Berlin just waited, knowing there probably wasn't a happy ending to the story.

"For one of our spring vacations, her family went to Formentera. Have you been there?"

Berlin shook her head, but remained silent, not wanting to interrupt the narrative.

"It's one of the islands off of Spain. It's gorgeous. Anyway, Becky went with her parents, her two brothers, and her sister. Her father had business associates who lived there. Super wealthy clients. They paired Becky with the youngest son. I guess everyone was hoping they'd hit it off and fall in love, or some bullshit like that." She shook her head. "She told me he was a creep, and he kept trying to have sex with her. The last message I got from her, she told me he was getting a little scary and she planned on letting her parents know she wasn't comfortable with him." Nichole stopped again.

Berlin covered Nichole's hand, still on her knee. "What happened?"

"They found her body towards the bottom of La Mola. The police said she was there visiting the lighthouse and was drunk. That she must have stumbled and fallen off the edge of the cliff. A terrible accident."

Berlin studied Nichole's face. "And what do you think?"

"I think someone who was terrified of heights, and of falling, would never go anywhere near that place. I think the business associate's son took her there and got angry enough when she wouldn't have sex with him, he shoved her over."

"There wasn't an investigation? They didn't check to see if she'd been assaulted?"

Nichole shook her head. "There was no need. It was an *accident*."

Berlin slid off the chair to sit on the floor and put her arm around Nichole's shoulders. She drew Nichole's head down to her shoulder. "I'm sorry," she said into the blond curls. "I'm so sorry."

Nichole stayed there for a few minutes. Eventually she said, "You remind me of Becky in a lot of ways, and part of that makes me angry. Both so determined to fix the world, to save it. Your sister was murdered, and you took that and decided you needed to help people. Even the people who are like her killer."

"It took me a long time to get there, though," Berlin told her. "I went through some serious depression, first. A lot of drinking. A lot of anger. But Laurel pushed me to be a cop. She knew I wanted to help people, and it's in my blood. And being a cop was the best way I knew how to help the people who were being hurt."

Nichole drew away, shaking her head and wiping the tears from her face. "Is it really? You've seen how screwed up the justice system is. And not just ours. Look at how often these assholes get away with whatever they've done."

"It really doesn't happen that often, Nichole. They show it in movies, but if we've done our job, and the evidence is there, we put those people in jail."

"But what about the ones who don't get caught?" demanded Nichole. "Or the ones who can buy their way out of trouble? Like the guy who killed Becky?"

Berlin said, "That's the exception. Not the rule."

"Really? Your sister? Becky?" She pushed away from Berlin. "Some fucking exception."

"That's why we need more people in law enforcement. Honorable people. More people helping others. It will never be an easy fix. We get these assholes off the streets, but someone else comes in to take their place."

Nichole shook her head. "That's a thoroughly depressing answer."

Berlin shrugged. "Do you want me to lie? To tell

you it's all going to work out?"

"It would be nice. Nice to know that the good guys win."

"Sometimes they do," Berlin said, standing up. "Just not every time."

*****

They were both quiet as they packed up the car and did a last check of the cabin and immediate property. Berlin left Nichole to her thoughts and tried to turn her own away from Laurel and Nichole's revelation, but their conversation kept replaying in her head. She wondered what she would do if Laurel had been murdered now, instead of when she was younger. Would she have reacted different and fought harder for justice?

She looked over at Nichole loading their bags in the car. How would she have acted if it had been her lover who was murdered? Would she still be adamant that the law was the right answer? Unsettled by her line of thinking, Berlin locked the cabin and joined Nichole at the car. "You okay?"

Nichole shrugged. "I'll be fine." She looked around at the shabby little building, a sad smile resting on her face. Then she looked at Berlin again. "I'll be fine."

They weren't quite an hour into their drive when Berlin pulled off the road and parked in the lot of a small bar and grill.

Nichole had been quiet during the drive, her head turned to look out the window. When the car was off, she turned to look at Berlin.

"I'm hungry," Berlin said. "And I need caffeine. I've stopped at this place before and they have decent food." She couldn't read Nichole's face. "Will you come in with me?"

Nichole stayed silent but opened her door and got out.

The inside of the building was poorly lit and outdated. Vinyl covered stools at the bar were mismatched and mostly torn, showing what was left of the roached filling. The bar itself was scarred and stained, rough enough looking that Berlin was sure stripping it and refinishing it wouldn't help it much.

There were only four customers inside. An elderly couple sat at a table, completely focused on shoveling food into their mouths. Two men sat at the bar, staring at the grainy television, half-finished beers in front of them.

Berlin picked a table away from the bar but with a view of the rest of the room, sat down and picked up the sticky menu. Nichole sat down across from her.

"I'm sorry."

She looked at Nichole. "For what?"

"For bringing down the feeling this weekend. We had such a wonderful time yesterday and then I had to get all stupid and emotional." Nichole looked down at the orange plastic tabletop.

Berlin put the menu down and covered Nichole's hands with her own. "I'm glad you told me about Becky. And I'm glad you know about Laurel." She shook their hands, and Nichole looked up at her. Berlin smiled. "Look at how long it usually takes couples to get to the first emotional break through. We're doing this on fast forward."

Nichole finally smiled. "Couples, huh?"

Berlin felt her face flush. "I didn't mean it that way. Poor choice of words."

"Nope, now you said it," Nichole said. She leaned forward over the table, pulling Berlin at the same time.

Berlin took the hint and met Nichole in the middle for a kiss. Nichole drew back slightly and said, "You can't take it back."

The waitress interrupted, dropping two glasses of water on the table. She was as worn out as the bar was, nicotine and disappointment completing the job that genetics and poor eating had started. And she did nothing to disguise her disapproval over two women kissing. "You ladies know what you're having?"

Back in her chair, Berlin said, "A bacon cheeseburger and a coke, please."

Nichole gave the menu a quick glance. "I'll have the chicken sandwich and a coke."

The waitress swiped the menus off the table and went away. When she reached the two men sitting at the bar, she stopped and said something to them. They both turned to look at Berlin and Nichole after she entered the kitchen. Berlin met their gazes, and they quickly looked away.

Nichole tugged on her hand, drawing her attention again. "Why are you so interested in the guys at the bar? I thought we were talking about being a couple?"

Berlin smiled. "I think it's safe to say there's some definite potential."

Heavy steps and old cigarette smoke signaled the waitress's return. "Cook said we're out of the chicken breast and bacon. You want to try something else?"

Berlin watched the two men move down the bar and settle into stools closer to their table while Nichole was asking if they still had burgers.

"Cook didn't say we didn't," the waitress answered, sounding put-upon. "Guess I can check." She left again, shaking her head as she passed the men.

"Maybe we should go somewhere else," Berlin said. The two men now had their heads bent toward each other, and one of them laughed out loud, slapping the other on the back.

"Why?" Nichole took a sip of her water and winced. "You said the food was decent here, although, if I have to go by their water, I'm not expecting much."

"I think maybe they changed management since I was here last."

"What makes you say that?"

"Well," Berlin said, "the last time I was here, there was a different atmosphere to the place." The men were still laughing, stealing glances at them. "*Friendly*, I would say. And I'm getting the feeling now that they don't like women like us."

Nichole turned her head to see what Berlin was looking at. The men were talking louder, every other word audible. They were looking at Berlin and one of them said something, the words *butch* and *dyke* coming through loud enough for the women to hear.

Berlin flushed but kept her temper in check. Steps approaching the table drew her attention from the men. It was the waitress.

"No burgers - hey!" She cursed as Nichole shoved past her and approached the men.

"Nichole, leave it!" Berlin said, but Nichole had already sashayed her way to the bar.

She spoke loud enough for the entire bar to hear. "Hello gentlemen." She stopped at the side of the larger of the two men. His beard did little to hide the damage of too much beer and fried food over his lifespan, but Nichole was looking at him like he was a young Paul Newman. "My friend and I couldn't help but overhear some of your conversation. You have a problem with two ladies being real close friends?" Her voice was sugar-sweet, and she wore a big fuck-me smile.

The beard said, "Nah honey, we don't have a problem with girls being friends. We was just confused, that's all." He leaned toward Nichole just a little.

Nichole's expression changed to sweetly bewildered. "Well, what's the confusion about, sweetheart? I'm sure I can help straighten things out for you."

"You're a real pretty girl," Beard said.

His friend licked his lips and echoed, "Real pretty."

Nichole's smile deepened, showing her dimples. "Well thank you, boys! That's sweet of you to say that."

"Why we're confused is, what's a real pretty little girl like you doing with her?" He nodded in Berlin's direction but kept his eyes on Nichole.

Berlin's heart sped up and she flushed hotter. Though the blood pounding in her ears she heard Nichole say, "I don't see anything wrong with her."

"If a pretty girl like you is gonna be with another girl, that girl should at least be pretty as you!" Beard grinned, looking pleased with his logic. "If you're gonna be with someone like that, just find yourself a nice big man to give you what you need."

Nichole nodded her head slowly, a look of serious contemplation on her face. "Ahhh, I think I get it now." She fluttered her eyelashes and played with a strand of her hair. "You happen to know where there's a nice, big man who's looking for a pretty little girl like me?"

He stood up so fast his stool toppled over and held his arms wide. "You're looking at him, baby!"

Nichole stepped forward, still smiling up into his eyes. Then, quicker than Berlin thought she could move, Nichole's knee came up and struck him in the crotch.

He made a dry, sucking sound, his mouth opening and closing like a fish, before he hit the ground.

The waitress came around the bar and the Beard's friend said, "Hey, you can't do that!" while reaching inside his jacket.

Berlin was up and stepping forward before his hand had completely disappeared. Her voice calm, she said, "Hands where I can see them, asshole," and showed him her badge.

"That stupid bitch can't do that!" he said again but put his hands back by his sides.

Nichole was crouched down by the Beard, and Berlin moved closer, not trusting Nichole to keep her hands off him. But all she heard was Nichole say, "I'd become a nun before fucking you. I can't wait for the day for men to become obsolete." She stood up, looking down at the large man, now in a fetal position, her face fixed in an ugly sneer. "Fucking pathetic."

Berlin flexed her shoulders, forcing herself to relax. She put her badge away and threw a twenty-dollar bill on the bar. "Are you done?"

Nichole turned to Berlin; her eyes still hot. Without a word she turned on her heel and stalked towards the door.

*****

They were both silent as Berlin drove south. She couldn't decide what she was angrier about. Her inability to act on what the Beard and his friend had said, or the way Nichole reacted to it. She'd learned from her time in the military and being a cop that there would always be prejudiced people who didn't like the choices she'd made in her life. As much as she would have loved to respond to the stupid, ignorant, and thoughtless comments people made, or better yet, hit a few of the people who made them, she also knew that wasn't how you changed someone's mind. And realistically, most people didn't want their minds changed.

But a tiny, petty part of her was flattered that Nichole had reacted. It was the first time Berlin could remember someone standing up for her. So why was she so… disturbed?

She turned the events over in her mind, looking for the point where things had felt off. She had seen Nichole flirty before, although not to that extent. But that didn't bother her. Berlin decided it had been the level of manipulation Nichole used on the Beard, and how quickly she turned violent. It was like watching a snake strike; cold, calm, and calculated.

It was another twenty minutes before Nichole spoke. "Are you mad at me?"

"I don't know," Berlin said truthfully. "I'm still trying to process what happened."

Nichole nodded. "Okay, that's fair." She didn't make it another minute before blurting out, "I just couldn't let them get away with talking about you like that."

Berlin glanced over. "Why not?"

Nichole turned in her seat to face Berlin. "Because it was wrong! It was disrespectful." After a moment, she added, "And you obviously weren't going to do anything about it."

"I was going to leave," Berlin said.

Nichole flopped back in her seat, facing forward again. "Yeah, that really would have showed them."

"So, are you upset because of what they said, or because I didn't react?"

Berlin jumped when Nichole slapped the center console. The plastic creaked in protest. "What the fuck, Berlin! How could you just sit there and let them talk shit about you?"

Berlin looked over at Nichole. "Nichole, I'm a police officer. It's my job to not get upset by some moron whose brain is smaller than his dick. I don't care what they said about me." *Mostly.*

Nichole shifted so she was again facing Berlin. "What if they'd been talking about me? Would you have stood up for me?"

"Honestly?"

Nichole nodded.

"If the situation had been exactly the same, but they had directed the comments at you, no. I wouldn't have reacted. At least not the way you did. We would have left, but I'm still a cop and idiots talking shit isn't a crime."

Nichole leaned forward, her face dark. "What if they'd gotten physical? Would you have stepped in then? Or just sat there, spouting your ethical cop bullshit?"

"Enough!" The white-hot anger was back, this time directed at Nichole. Berlin pulled off the road, receiving irritated honking from the car behind her. She braked hard and glared at Nichole. Her voice husky from holding back, Berlin said, "I'm sorry I didn't react the way you thought I should. I'm sorry I didn't freak out because some mountain redneck hicks were talking shit. And at the moment I'm sorry I asked you to go up north with me. This is who I am, Nichole. I don't know how to be different, and even if I did, I wouldn't." She took a deep breath, counting to ten. "Sorry you don't approve." The tires spun gravel as she got back on the highway.

They didn't speak the rest of the drive.

*****

Berlin pulled into her driveway and put the car in park. Nichole was out the door before she even turned the engine off. Berlin took her time getting out and watched as Nichole unlocked her car and threw her bag across the driver's seat and got in the vehicle. She was already pulling out by the time Berlin closed her door.

She walked up to the porch and stood there, looking at the front door. There were no decorations, no personal pieces that made it welcoming or approachable. When had her front door, always a welcome sight before, become such a depressing reminder of her life? *Since Nichole came through it and showed me what I was missing.*

Berlin sighed and trudged up the three steps. She unlocked the door and swung it open. The house was quiet, but instead of comforting, it was suffocating. Everything was too dark, the walls, the wooden floor, the brown furniture. She threw her bag on the floor and her keys on the hall table.

The old gold-framed mirror over the table was as mocking as the men had been. Her face was too broad, her skin too dark, rough, and freckled from the sun and wind, her hair too frizzy. Looking at her reflection, Berlin couldn't see any reason Nichole would have defended her. The cold manipulation she'd used crept back into Berlin's head. She had to at least consider that Nichole had been manipulating her the entire time, too.

Angered and hurt by the thought, Berlin met her reflection's eyes and said, "Fuck you, Nichole."

And fuck me, too.

CHAPTER THIRTEEN

Berlin stalked into the department thirty minutes late Monday morning. Pete took one look at her and turned back to his computer. She was hanging up her coat when Phillips walked in, the ever-present look of irritation on his face.

The Weasel was right on his heels, whispering loudly, “Sir, we really don’t have time for this!”

“Detective Redding. What type of shit are you trying to pull?” Phillips held a file in one hand and slapped it against the other.

“What?” she asked, glancing at him briefly over her shoulder.

The irritation turned to disgust. “What is that?” He took a step forward, pointing at her.

“What are you talking about?” She turned fully to face him.

“That mark on your neck. Your hair doesn’t look styled so I’m assuming it isn’t a burn from a curling iron.”

Even Pete was looking now.

"Is there a problem, Captain?" She was careful to use the same level of sarcasm present in Phillips's voice.

He took another step forward, leaving the Weasel simpering about "no time," by the door. "Yes, Detective. There is. You represent this department and when you come in looking like you pulled an all-nighter with a vampire, you make the department, and me, look bad. Do I make myself clear?"

Berlin looked down at her hands, determined to keep her cool. Phillips apparently had other plans.

"Redding! Do I make myself clear?"

The anger from the previous day was back. "Yes, Sir. You've made yourself perfectly clear. In five years, I've come in with one mark on my neck and it makes me a slut which reflects badly on the department. Never mind the multiple male officers who have come in with similar marks on them, and nothing gets said. So, what you've made perfectly clear, once again, Captain Phillips, is you're sexist and you don't like having a female detective working in your department. Or did I miss something?" She turned to the Weasel. "I bet the voting public would love that."

Phillips was red and shaking. "I will open a disciplinary file on you, Redding. And I'll have you out of this department so fast it'll make your military discharge seem like a spa trip."

Berlin looked him straight in the eye, refusing to back down.

"Captain, we have to leave now." The Weasel's voice split the tension. He backed into the doorway when Phillips turned his gaze on him. "Really, Sir. Your meeting is in fifteen minutes. Downtown." His voice was pleading.

Phillips looked at Berlin one more time and then walked out of the office. The Weasel was right behind him.

Pete looked at Berlin, shaking his head. "I thought I taught you better."

"Don't piss off the boss? Whatever. Screw Phillips and his temper tantrums."

"No, you moron. If you're going to neck, remember to hide the evidence. How am I going to teach you anything if you refuse to listen?" He waggled his eyebrows. "Good weekend, huh?"

"If you consider her kneeing some guy in a bar and driving away from my house as fast as she could good, then sure." She narrowed her eyes at him when he opened his mouth to ask another question. "What did Phillips want, Pete?"

Pete shrugged. "I don't know. That was the first time I've seen him since I've been in. Whatever it was, it sounded like it was something you did."

Berlin frowned, trying to remember what Phillips said when he'd come in. Something about what was she trying to pull. She looked toward the door and saw the file sitting on the corner of the desk. She hadn't noticed him put it down. Berlin walked over, picked it up and opened it, not even considering if she should.

"Oh, shit." No wonder he was pissed.

"What?" Pete stood up and walked over to read over her shoulder. He started laughing. "You marked the cause of death as pending?" He shook his head. "I guess you have been listening to me."

"I don't know why he's being so bitchy. I did

technically file the completed report."

"Yup. And put it into the County's hands. Bet Phillips is just thrilled with you for that." Pete took the file from her and sat back down at his desk, reading.

"Wait a minute," Berlin said. "What?"

Pete was still focused on his reading. "This is a good report, Redding. Very detailed."

Berlin kicked his shoe. "What do you mean I put the report in County's hands?"

Pete looked up at her. "Standard procedure, Redding. Anything that gets stamped pending has to be approved by County once it gets finalized."

"Since when?" What the hell did I do?

He shrugged. "I don't know. Don't you remember that big-to-do about cases being mishandled and misidentified? They changed the procedure to fix the issue after that whole mess."

"Well. Shit." Berlin dropped into her chair, her shoulders slumped.

Pete sat up, his brow furrowed. "I thought this is what you wanted. You get more time to prove Bryant's death wasn't an accident."

"I don't have anything, Pete. Zip. Zilch. Nada. The County will ask for additional information and I'll look like a moron for not closing it when I should have."

"What about Johnson?" He started paging through the report again.

Berlin shook her head. "She's clean. Her husband is going through gender reassignment. His sister made the report because she doesn't like Johnson." Her head was starting to pound.

He flipped a page. "What about Johnson and

Bryant being in some relationship?"

"She admitted that he tried multiple times and was insistent about it. She finally threatened to tell whoever she had to, including his wife, to get him to back off. Eventually he did, but she says she doesn't know why." Berlin pinched the bridge of her nose between her thumb and forefinger. "Forget it, Pete. There's nothing there."

Crickets from Pete. Berlin looked up and found him still buried in the report. "What the hell, Pete? Are you even listening to me?"

"Yeah. I'm trying to decide what type of cheese I should get you for your wine." He shut the file and stood up. "If there's nothing there, close the case for real and tell Phillips he was right." He pulled his coat down and headed for the door.

"Where are you going?" Berlin asked.

Ignoring her question, he said, "Otherwise I'd make myself scarce," and walked out.

She thumped back into her chair, pissed at everyone. "Awesome."

*****

Berlin's afternoon was no better than the morning. With no idea what step to take next, and having no wish to deal with Phillips, she took Pete's advice and left the office. She drove around with no destination and got nothing accomplished during the three hours she was gone.

On top of that, she received two more hang-ups. Each time the phone rang her heart picked up its pace with the thought it might be Nichole, but the caller came up as private with no number. After the second call she shut her phone off.

Pete was back in the office when she returned. She ignored him and sat at her computer, determined to do something useful. Her desk phone rang as she was booting up her computer. She snatched up the handset. "Redding."

She could hear someone breathing and then a click.

Berlin slammed the phone back into its cradle. "What is wrong with people?" Her voice sounded shrill even to her.

Pete turned from his computer and stared at her; one eyebrow cocked. "I think I was wrong. Sex seems to be very bad for you."

"That's like a dozen hang ups I've had in the last several days. What the hell?"

He looked at the phone and back at her. "Seriously? That many?"

Berlin nodded. "My desk phone and my cell. But everything comes up as a private number."

"Did you star sixty-nine it?" He looked serious. *He can't be serious. This has to be some sexual joke.*

"You aren't serious," she said.

"It still works. It should dial the last caller -"

Her phone rang. Berlin wanted to throw the phone across the room. "Mother. Fucker!"

"Answer it, Redding."

She glared at him but picked up the phone. "This is Detective Redding."

"Hey Redding. This is Dawson down in records. Would you tell Lewis we have the files he requested?"

Berlin closed her eyes and decided she should

throw the phone at Pete. "Why don't you call him?"

"Uh-uh. This is the number he listed." Dawson hung up.

Berlin hung the phone up carefully and turned to Pete. "Whatever files you asked for are down in records. And next time, give them your number." She ran her hands over her head, at a loss. And then remembered her cell phone. "Will it still work even if I turned my phone off?"

Pete shrugged. "I don't know. You can try it."

Berlin pulled her phone out of her jacket pocket and powered it back up. And saw she had missed calls from Nichole. Her stomach started doing its roller coaster routine.

"Well?" Pete asked.

She shook her head. "I've had calls since the last hang up." She went to her voicemail and picked the first one.

"Hey Berlin. Listen. I'm sorry about this weekend. I think I really messed up. I'd like to talk to you tonight and see if we can figure out what happened. Please call me."

There were three more messages from Nichole. With each one, her voice got sharper and her messages shorter. The last one was just the dial tone after she hung up.

"She didn't sound real happy," Pete said.

"You couldn't hear her; how do you know?"

"Believe me, Redding. I know the sound of an unhappy woman, even if I can't hear the exact words."

Still staring at the phone, Berlin said, "It doesn't matter. It's her problem." She tossed the phone on her desk and started logging in. "I'm working."

"I don't know if I would call it working…."

"Go to hell, Pete."

He turned back around and didn't say another word.

*****

The urge to scrub the weekend with Nichole from her mind was overwhelming. Unable to rid herself of her memories, Berlin did the next best thing and worked to scrub any trace of Nichole from her house. She started in the bedroom, ripping the light grey flannel sheets off her mattress. She stuffed everything, including her blanket, into the washing machine and changed the setting to hot. She vacuumed the wooden floor, even using the crevice attachment where the walls and floor met.

Then she started in on the bathroom. She scrubbed the bathtub until her arms hurt and she could have prepared a meal in it. Berlin gave the tile floor the same treatment, resenting the blandness of the tan tiles the entire time.

She was working in the kitchen when there was a knock at the front door. "What the fuck now?" She threw her gloves on the floor and stomped to the door and flung it open.

Nichole stood on the stoop, a paper bag in her arms. Her blond hair was pulled tightly back off her face, letting Berlin see the dark circles under her eyes. She wasn't wearing makeup and her skin was ghost pale, but instead of making her look exhausted or sick, she looked fragile and lost.

Berlin stared at her, saying nothing.

Finally, Nichole said, “You didn’t call me back. I started to worry.”

“About?” Berlin kept her voice flat.

“You!” Nichole shoved the bag at Berlin. Reflexively she grabbed it and missed blocking Nichole from entering the house.

“God damn it, Berlin. I tried to apologize, but I can’t if you won’t answer your phone.” She paced around the tiny living room.

The pain and uncertainty that had built up in the last twenty-four hours bust to the surface, and Berlin briefly wondered how someone she’d known for such a short amount of time could bring forth so many emotions. “I didn’t want to see you, Nichole. I didn’t answer because I wasn’t ready to talk to you. I’m allowed to have time to figure things out.”

Her chin up, Nichole said, “You could have told me that. At least I would have known you’re alive.”

“Great. Now you know. I’m sure you have things to do.” She started toward the door.

“Those need to go into the freezer. Unless you want to drink it.”

Thrown off course by the change in topic, Berlin stopped and looked down at the bag, realizing her arm was getting numb where the bag rested again it. Ice cream. Hershey’s Cookies and Cream, Mint Moose Tracks, and Chocolate Marshmallow.

Berlin looked up from the bag. “Three kinds? You don’t think that’s over-kill?”

Nichole shrugged. “I didn’t know how angry you were.”

“Ice cream doesn’t fix this.”

“I know,” Nichole said, nodding.

"And you can't stay the night."

The corners of her mouth turned up. "Okay."

Sighing from deep in her toes, Berlin nodded toward the kitchen. "Come on. I even have clean bowls."

Hours later, Berlin was almost asleep when an elbow nudged her. "What?" she mumbled.

"Thanks for letting me stay."

CHAPTER FOURTEEN

It was early in the afternoon when Berlin's desk phone rang. She picked it up, but before she could even identify herself, she heard the all-too familiar click. *Okay, Pete. Let's see if your little trick works.* She hit *69 on the keypad and listened to the phone redial the caller. By the seventh ring, Berlin was sure it either hadn't worked or the person wasn't going to pick up. On the eighth ring, the other end picked up, but she only heard silence.

"Hello?" Berlin said.

Nothing.

"Do you realize you've been pranking a police department, and that's a felony? I have your number now, and I can get your information within five minutes. So -"

"I wasn't pranking you." It was a young woman. She didn't sound like a punk or a brat. She sounded professional and no-nonsense in her short but direct answer.

"Then what would you call calling me and hanging up immediately?"

The woman sighed. "Indecisiveness caused by guilt trips from my mother."

Berlin had no idea where to go with that. She started over. "This is Berlin Redding. I'm a detective with the Lakes Region Police Department. Could you please identify yourself?"

There was a pause on the other end, long enough Berlin wondered if the woman had hung up again.

Finally, the voice said, "My name is Heather Christiansen."

"And the reason you've been calling me, Ms. Christiansen?" Berlin wrote the name down on her notepad.

"I think you need to look at deaths related to the school."

It was Berlin's turn to pause. "What school, Ms. Christiansen?"

"Listen, Detective. I know you've been investigating the death of a man tied to the academy. The private school on the lake."

Berlin's mind raced. She'd handed out her business card to several people during the investigation, but very few who sounded quite this young… "Ms. Christiansen, I can't comment on that without knowing who you are or why you're contacting me."

Another pause, this one much longer. Finally, "Do you know where the Mello Moose coffee house is?"

"Yes," Berlin said.

"I'll be there tomorrow morning when they open. And Detective Redding, you need to look at deaths tied to the school." She hung up.

Berlin hung up the phone and sat still for a few seconds, processing what Heather had said. Deaths related to the school on the lake. She had to be referring to Lake Kanasatka. But what deaths? There couldn't be that many, it was a school. And deaths at a school tended to get talked about.

She flipped through her notebook to the first day they'd started investigating Charles Bryant's death. Most of the people she'd given her information to had already talked to them. She went through all the names she'd written down, but at the end, she only had four possibles. Diane Long, Katie Albert, Andrea Butler, and Brittney Thompson. After re-reading her notes on all four, she moved Long and Butler to probable, based on the fact she hadn't personally spoken to either.

She knew very little about either one, so she woke her computer up and pulled up her saved searches. The academy was the first one. Curious, she typed in 'death' and 'Lake Kanasatka Academy'. A few articles down the page there was a brief mention of a memorial ceremony held for a faculty member. Berlin clicked on the article.

There were very few details about the death, just the name Ben Rivera and that he'd been a psychologist at the school. She changed the search to just his name and found the obituary. Aged thirty-nine when he died at his home from a heart attack. He'd been with the academy for ten years. No children. He was survived by his parents, and his wife, Nichole Rivera, also employed by the academy.

Berlin started at the name on her screen, her stomach weighted with stone. It wasn't conclusive, but something in her gut told her Nichole Rivera was her Nichole. She went to the academy's home page and found the faculty listing. There was no Rivera listed. She tried Kellner and a picture of Nichole with longer hair popped up. The name Rivera was included in parentheses in her bio.

She couldn't make her brain work. All she could do was think about Nichole's husband being dead. From a heart attack. And why Nichole said nothing about it.

*****

That evening there was a knock on the door. Berlin opened it. Like the night before, Nichole stood on the stoop, but this time she was carrying flowers. She smiled and held out the bouquet of orange, red, yellow, and dark purple Shasta daisies. "For you." Her smile was huge.

Berlin opened the door wider and backed into the room, saying nothing.

Nichole lost her smile. "What's wrong?"

Berlin shut the door and walked into the kitchen. She picked up a printed sheet and handed it wordlessly to Nichole.

Nichole put the flowers on the counter and took the sheet. Her face washed white as soon as she saw the name at the top. "Fuck."

"Yeah, that was pretty much my reaction when I found it this afternoon." Berlin opened a cupboard door and removed a glass and her emergency bottle of Jameson. She filled the glass to the top and picked it up, leaving the bottle out. She took a long swallow. "I thought you were divorced."

Nichole placed the paper on the counter and stuffed her hands in her pockets. She shrugged. "I never said I was divorced."

Berlin slammed the glass down on the counter, splashing whiskey against the ugly laminate. "You said he left. That indicates separation or divorce. Not death. You fucking lied to me!"

Nichole straightened her shoulders. "Why does this matter, anyway? So, he's dead."

"What am I supposed to think when I read your husband died? In your house. *Accidentally.* And you never said a word about it."

Nichole was still, but Berlin could see her mind working. There was no anger on her face, but no surprise, either. She almost looked amused when she cocked her head and said, "You think I killed Charles."

Berlin just looked at her, and Nichole started to laugh.

She grabbed Berlin's glass of whiskey and drained it. "Why would I kill him? Because he was an adulterous schmuck?" She picked up the bottle and refilled the glass. "The world will be damn short on men if we kill them for that." Nichole raised the glass in Berlin's direction and took another long drink.

Her words sparked something in Berlin's memory, but she pushed it aside. She crossed her arms over her stomach. "So, tell me I'm wrong, Nichole. Tell me this is all one big coincidence, that Charles really died in an accident. That your husband really died of a heart attack." *Please, please tell me I'm wrong - that I'm not that much of an idiot.*

Nichole shook her head and handed back Berlin's glass. "You might need this." She sighed. "I'd love to tell you that, Berlin. But I can't. Because you're right. I killed my husband."

Berlin watched Nichole's face, hoping for some sign she was lying again, just trying to shock her. There was nothing. Needing to do something, Berlin turned away and walked into the little living room, taking the glass with her. She sat on the dark wooden rocker and waited for Nichole to join her. After a few minutes, Nichole walked in and sat on the love seat.

"Tell me," Berlin said.

Nichole stared at her clasped hands. "I already told you we'd been married for ten years. We dated off and on through high school and college. I was with him because my parents liked him, and they left me alone as long as I was dating him. We got engaged during college, while I was with Becky. He didn't know about her. My parents didn't know, either." She shook her head. "After Becky died, it was like I was dead, too." She paused, and Berlin handed her the glass. Nichole drained it. "My parents had no idea what was going on with me and wanted me to go into therapy. I loathed the idea, so married Ben instead." She smiled grimly. "I thought it would be the lesser of two evils. Anyway, it gave my mother something new to obsess about."

"What happened?" Berlin asked.

Nichole shrugged and placed the glass by her feet. "He was abusive. Just verbally and emotionally for the first five or six years. He was a psychologist, and he liked to play with my head. I was stupid. I was ugly. I was getting fat. The typical bullshit. When I started working, I gained back some self-confidence, and I started ignoring him. That's when he started getting physical."

Berlin wanted to comfort Nichole, but she held back. Instead, she asked, "Did you tell anyone?"

"Just my brother, Paul. We were really close growing up, but Ben was jealous and didn't like him. We hadn't talked much in a few years. But I called Paul one night, crying, and told him what was going on." She finally smiled. "He didn't miss a beat, just asked if I wanted help leaving. Said he'd be here on the first flight he could catch. I told him no, not yet." Nichole picked up the glass, found it empty and put it back down.

Berlin got up and retrieved the bottle from the kitchen. She offered it to Nichole.

Nichole took it and drank straight from the bottle. "Paul sent me a stun gun, police grade. About six months later, Ben went after me. He hit me the hardest he'd ever hit me before, and it knocked me out for a few seconds, maybe a minute. I really don't know. We were in my bedroom and when I came to, he was still there, leaning over me. I grabbed the gun, and I hit him in the chest with it. I just kept pulling the trigger."

"Nichole, that shouldn't have killed him."

Nichole smiled. "He had a heart condition. I knew he did, he'd had it since he was young. But I was so scared he'd kill me I didn't care. I just kept shocking him until he fell over." She wiped tears from her face. "I called the police. Ben had a medical history; he'd had open-heart surgeries. When they saw his medical alert bracelet and learned about his history, they didn't even ask questions."

Nichole's face was bloodless, and her eyes were huge. Berlin left her place on the rocker and sat beside her, taking her hand.

"I kept waiting for them to come and get me,"

Nichole said, her voice a whisper. "At the house, at work. I imagined it happening everywhere I went. Like one of the police shows, where they come in, guns and fingers pointed, shouting they knew I killed Ben." She finally looked at Berlin. "He had these ugly scars from surgery. I don't know if they hid any damage I did. Or if I didn't get him as many times as I thought. I just don't know."

Berlin closed her eyes, relieved. She opened them and squeezed Nichole's hands. "If you were afraid for your life, and you were protecting yourself, then it was self-defense."

Nichole shook her head, "But I was glad he was dead!"

"Nichole, it doesn't matter if you're glad. The motivation is what's important here, and you were motivated to save yourself."

There was disbelief in Nichole's voice, but also hope. "Are you sure? It's just… done? I don't have to worry about it anymore?"

Making sure she kept eye contact with Nichole, Berlin said, "You still need to report it."

Nichole shook her head. "But you just said -"

"I know. But it still has to be reported and most likely there will be an investigation. It just may include you being questioned, or they may want to talk to other people. Like Paul. But you won't be in trouble, Nichole." She squeezed Nichole's hands again in emphasis.

Nichole took a deep breath. "Do I have to do it now? Tonight?"

Berlin shook her head. "No. But tomorrow you need to go in. I'll go with you, okay?"

Nichole nodded quickly and gave Berlin a shaky smile.

*****

The bedroom was black, not even moonlight to show off the shapes of the room. Berlin lay on her side, almost asleep, not quite touching Nichole's body with her own. She traced lazy shapes on Nichole's hip. Nichole captured her hand and pulled it down, so Berlin's arm was across her stomach.

"Do you ever think of running away?" Nichole's voice was small and quiet in the darkness.

Berlin closed the last half inch between them and pulled Nichole tighter against her. "What do you mean?"

"Do you ever think of just leaving here? Leaving your job? Going some place where no one knows you."

"Sometimes. It would be hard because my family is here. But sometimes. Mostly up to the cabin." She turned her head so she could kiss Nichole behind her ear. "Do you?"

Nichole nodded. Even quieter, she said, "We could go together."

Berlin smiled into the darkness. "Where would we go?"

"Anywhere," Nichole said. "Anywhere away from here."

CHAPTER FIFTEEN

Berlin woke up, confused for a moment by the sound of a chainsaw running softly in her room. Relaxing back into her pillow, she grinned slightly. She hadn't figured Nichole for a snorer. She turned her head and squinted over at the digital clock on her nightstand. Five-twenty. She could let Nichole sleep another hour and then head in -

"Shit!"

Nichole jerked awake next to her. "What? What is it?"

"Sorry, go back to sleep." Berlin tugged on Nichole's arm and pulled her back down on the bed. "I didn't mean to say it out loud."

Nichole laid back down. "What is it, though?" She still sounded sleepy.

"I have a meeting this morning. If I'm going to be on time, I have to get moving."

Nichole started moving around again. "Sssok, have to be at school couple hours…"

Berlin stopped her, pressing her hand on Nichole's shoulder. "No, stay in bed and sleep. Just lock up when you leave, and text me when you head over to the department. Okay?"

Nichole nodded, her eyes closed again. "Okay."

Berlin brushed blond curls off Nichole's forehead and gave her a soft kiss. Then she slid out of the bed and went to get ready for her day.

*****

Berlin arrived at the Mello Moose at quarter after six but found they were already open. She walked up the stairs and entered the warm, well-lit restaurant and was assaulted by smells of brewing coffee, frying sausage, and freshly made pastries. Her stomach rumbled.

There was a man in his forties sitting at one table, typing furiously on his phone. The only other person in the room was a young woman behind the counter. She looked at Berlin, nodded and went back to shifting pastries behind the glass display case.

Berlin walked up to the counter and eyed the menu. When the woman finished with the pastries, she wiped her hand on a towel and walked over to the cash register. "What can I get you?"

The voice was right... "I'll take a cafe mocha with an extra shot of espresso, and an egg, sausage, and cheese on a croissant. Heather."

She didn't even blink. She just rang up the order. "That will be eleven dollars and thirty-three cents."

Berlin handed over a twenty.

Heather counted out Berlin's change, handed it to her, and then nodded at a table away from the texter. "I'll be over in a little while."

With little choice, Berlin sat at the table and waited. A few people wandered in. Two were customers and Heather took their orders. One was another young woman who apologized multiple times for being late and disappeared through a door behind the counter. A few minutes later Heather brought Berlin's coffee over. She placed it on the table without a word and went back behind the counter. She made the coffee orders for the other two customers and then someone yelled something from inside the kitchen. She went in and came back out with two plates. The late girl was behind her. Heather brought the plates to Berlin's table and the other girl manned the register and counter.

Heather set the plates down, went back to the counter, grabbed a bottle of water and returned to the table and sat in the chair across from Berlin.

She took a bite of her breakfast sandwich and then said around the egg and ham, "I only have ten minutes, so ask whatever you need to ask," and went back to chewing.

"Why did you call me?" Berlin took a bite of her own sandwich. It was excellent.

"You called my mom a couple of weeks ago and asked her to get in touch." Heather took a big drink of her water and then another bite of her sandwich. She was a tall girl and thin, almost to the point of looking unwell. But from the way she was wolfing down her sandwich, it may have been genetic more than a lack of eating. She had unexciting features but pretty, green eyes, and, as her voice had indicated, she was no nonsense.

“Your mom is Diane Long?”

Heather nodded and popped the last bite of sandwich in her mouth. “Did you look up deaths at the school?”

“I did. But nothing jumped out at me.” *Well, nothing tied to the case, anyway.*

Heather’s eyes narrowed. “You didn’t look very hard, then.”

Irritated by the conversation, Berlin pushed her plate away and tapped her fingers on the coffee cup. “I’m still confused by your involvement in all of this. And why am I talking to you, and not your mother?”

Heather looked at her watch, then the counter, and then back at Berlin. “Mom got your call and then heard about Charles Bryant’s death. She freaked out because she was sure she was a suspect.”

Berlin shook her head. “Why would she think that? I mean, she had a complaint against him from years ago, but that’s not exactly a major connection.”

“I know.” Heather sighed. “That’s what I told her. I’m a criminology major so I should know, but she was nervous about talking to you. I kept telling her I was going to call you and then she’d give me this major guilt trip about not loving her and wanting her to go to prison.” Heather shook her head and shrugged.

“I’m assuming she didn’t hear from him again after he left Campbell and Sons.”

“No.” Heather was tearing her napkin into little bits.

Interesting. She’s nervous about something. “Okay. You could have told me that on the phone.” Berlin sat back in her chair and took a drink of coffee.

"You're sure she didn't see him again? Was there something going on between Charles and your mom? Beyond the harassment? Maybe it wasn't really harassment, and she got mad he ended things between them?"

The napkin pieces got smaller and smaller. Heather told the table, "As I said yesterday, you need to look at the deaths tied to the school."

"We'll get back that in a minute," Berlin said. "Tell me about the affair between your mom and Charles. That's why she didn't want you to call me, right? I'd find out about the affair, which definitely makes her a suspect. Bad enough if he was just harassing her, but the fact they had sex-"

"It was me, all right?" Heather's voice was too loud in the nearly empty cafe and they received looks.

Berlin smiled at the girl at the counter and ignored the other customers. She turned her attention back to Heather, who had swept her napkin into a neat little pile. "What do you mean it was you?"

Heather sat back; her arms folded tightly over her chest. "Charles Bryant wasn't harassing my mother. He was harassing me. I helped my mom at the office when I wasn't in school, and he asked her if I could help him, too. She thought he was nice, so said yes. It didn't take long to figure out what he was after and I told mom right away. Mom didn't want to drag me into it, so she filed the complaint and said he was harassing her."

"Let me guess," Berlin said, her hands clenched around her coffee cup, "no one took her claim seriously?"

Heather shook her head. "They offered her some

bullshit settlement if she agreed to drop the complaint, but it wasn't about the money, it was about stopping him. Mom figured they must be scared if they were offering to pay her off, but they just dragged everything out." She smiled tightly. "Then he ended up leaving the firm anyway, and she was told there was no evidence. It was her word against his and they weren't going to do anything to him."

Berlin's thoughts rolled. The complaint from Diane Long was from before Bryant started with Abrams. So at least eight years prior. She looked at Heather, her stomach in an angry knot. "You can't be more than, what? Nineteen?" She got a patient smile in return.

"I'm twenty-two. I was fourteen when mom filed the complaint." Heather stood and threw her water bottle into the trash and came back for her napkin pile. That also went into the trash. She stood by the table, hands in her pockets. "Mom saved me and protected me. I'm fine. And just in case you're wondering, we have alibis for the day Charles Bryant died." The hands came out of the pockets with a folded piece of paper. She put it on the table in front of Berlin and then her arms went back across her chest. "But he wasn't the only one who liked little girls, Detective. You need to look at the deaths tied to that school."

"Heather, your break was over like ten minutes ago." The girl behind the counter looked uncertain. Heather nodded at her and then looked back at Berlin, her face serious and wiser than her twenty-two years. "Will you look into it?"

Berlin's thoughts turned to Brittney and Harold Houston. "Yeah," she told Heather, and nodded. "I'll look into it."

Heather was a few steps from the table when Berlin said, "Hey, let me know if you need help with the academy."

"Academy?"

"You said you were a criminal justice major." Heather shook her head. "Thanks, but I'm not going to school to be a cop. I'm going to be an advocate. To help people."

*****

When Berlin left the Mello Moose, she found the morning had turned bright and sunny. A complete contradiction of her mood. She checked her phone but had no missed calls or text messages. Frowning at it, she stuck it back in her pocket and got in her car. She closed her eyes and thought a minute. She definitely did not want to go back to the department and chance dealing with Phillips, but that was where her computer was. She tapped on the steering wheel, thinking. The next best thing would be to go directly to the source.

She put her sunglasses on, started her car and headed to the academy.

*****

Berlin parked and headed straight to the athletic building. She went up the steps and down the hallway and found Johnson's door closed. She knocked, but there was no sound of movement or voices from behind it. She knocked again and listened. Still nothing.

She looked down the hall in both directions, saw

no one and briefly flirted with the idea of picking the lock, but discarded it just as quickly. Berlin stared at the door again and for the first time it registered there was a large cork board attached to the wall next to the door frame.

There were game and practice schedules posted along with announcements for upcoming events in the school. There were also quite a few notes left for Johnson. Most were from students letting her know they'd be late or needed to meet with her. A few appeared to be from other teachers regarding staff meetings and other personal issues.

"Might as well join the crowd." Berlin tore a piece of paper out of her notebook, wrote a quick note requesting that Johnson contact her, and then looked for a place to put it. Most of the notes were sticky notes just stuck to other papers on the board. There was a little cluster of them that stuck up slightly, and Berlin pulled it off, revealing a thumb tack. She added her note under the thumb tack and tried to stick the clump back on the board, but it fell on the floor. She picked it back up and separated the notes, hoping they would stay up individually, at least long enough for her to walk away. As she stuck them back up, a message written on a florescent pink note caught her eye. *Call me ASAP! N.* The hair on the back of Berlin's neck stood up as she looked at it. She knew that handwriting.

Steps in the hallway drew Berlin's attention away from the board. Without thinking, she crumpled the pink note and shoved it into her pocket and looked toward the footsteps.

An older man was headed her way, his shoulders slightly stooped. He looked exactly as a professor should, down to the white beard, dark blue cardigan sweater, and stack of books in his arms.

"Can I help you, young lady?" He stopped beside her.

"Thank you, but no." She smiled and held out her hand, only then realizing she still held several notes off the board. Berlin quickly put them back up and offered her hand again. "Detective Berlin Redding. I was just leaving a note for Coach Johnson."

He shook her hand, but not before she saw the slightest tremors. "Ahh, yes. Our Coach Johnson is quite the popular person. Well, if you left a note, I'm sure she'll get it." He looked around them. "I imagine she'll turn up eventually."

Berlin smiled again. "Well, it was nice to meet you, Mr?"

"Albert Griffin. I'm one of the psychology professors here. Well, at least until they decide my ideas are too old-fashioned and ask me to leave."

Unsure if he was joking or not, Berlin asked, "Does that happen often?"

Albert Griffin laughed. "No, not often. Do you mind if we walk, Detective? It gets tiresome to stand still carrying a stack of books."

"Of course not. Can I take them for you?" They started walking.

"Wouldn't they just love that? Letting a lovely girl like you carry books for me." He laughed again, but it quickly turned into a coughing fit. He bent over as he coughed, and Berlin took the books from him before they slid to the floor. He caught his breath after another minute, but it was several more before he could talk. "My apologies. I've been fighting a chest cold for quite some time and I just can't seem to shake it."

"Are you all right?" Berlin asked, the concern in her voice genuine.

"Yes, yes. Perhaps I will let you carry the books, at least for a bit." They started walking again. Berlin noticed he kept his right hand tucked into the pocket of his sweater.

"Now, you were asking about how the school gets rid of old teachers like me?"

Berlin grinned at him. "Something tells me you'd be fairly difficult to get rid of, Professor. But does it happen? Teachers forced to leave after a certain amount of time?"

The old man sighed as they made their way down the stairs. "Fortunately, no. Although it would probably do the school some good. And the teachers. But most who come here and are still here after the first year, stay."

"How many new teachers have joined the school over the last few years?"

He thought a moment, his brow furrowed. "Well, Alex Johnson is fairly new to us. She came a few years ago. We have a young lady who joined our English department just out of college, although I'm not sure she'll stay. And we had a very nice young lady join us in the Psychology Department about three years ago when one of our members passed away." They exited the door and stepped into the sunlight.

Berlin's heart picked up its pace. "You're talking about Ben Rivera."

Albert Griffin looked at her. "That's right. Ben. Did you know him?" There was curiosity on his face, and something else she couldn't place.

Berlin shook her head. "No. I just recently read about his passing."

He nodded. "Ah, yes. It did make the news. People always seem interested in other people's misfortune." They walked along the path, saying nothing. Albert nodded to a group of students who passed them.

Berlin let another minute pass before she asked, "Did you know him well?"

He shrugged. "Well enough, I suppose. He was quite popular with the heads of our department because he brought a lot of money in. And from what people say, he was fairly well liked around the campus."

But you didn't say you liked him.

Berlin noticed he was slowing down and when they passed one of the stone benches shaded by a tree, she motioned to it. "Do you mind if we sit?"

Albert eyed the bench, smiled knowingly at her, and sat. "Not at all." His right hand came out of his pocket to adjust his sweater. It was noticeably shaking.

Berlin set the books on her other side and sat quietly, watching the people moving around the campus. Finally, she asked, "How long have you had Parkinson's?"

He eyed her, possibly for the first time really seeing her, and said, "Quite a few years now. I usually do better to hide it, but the coughing fits seem to stir things up."

She nodded. "My dad has Parkinson's, so I may be a little more observant than others."

"I'm very sorry to hear that. I hope your father is one of the lucky ones and hasn't had too much difficulty with it?"

Without really know why, Berlin said, "He was okay for a little while, but then the depression set in, and he stopped fighting back. He had a stroke two years ago, and I haven't been able to have a conversation with him since."

"That has to be difficult for both of you."

Berlin nodded and then bit the inside of her lip, ignoring the sting of tears.

Albert looked out at lawn and the people hurrying along. "It's hard on young men, I think. An old man like me, I figured something would get me, eventually. And I've lived an enjoyable life." He turned to look at her. "What did your father do for a living?"

She cleared her throat. "He was a cop."

"Ahhh. And you become a police officer because of your father?"

Berlin looked down at her hands clasped in her lap. She had answered 'yes' so many times when asked that question. But she looked up at Albert, sure the uncertainty was clear on her face, and said, "I don't really know. I joined because I'm a fixer, I think. I guess I thought this was the best way to help people."

"People who needed fixing, you mean?"

She nodded.

"And now?" He asked.

"And now I don't know if this is the best way." She wanted to slap her hand over her mouth as soon as the words were out.

The horror over her words must have been clear because Albert started laughing when he looked at her. Then he patted her hands. "There's nothing wrong with second guessing yourself, Detective. In fact, it's an important thing to do. Always check in with yourself to make sure you're on the right path. You seem like a level-headed young lady, I'm sure you won't steer yourself wrong." He patted her hands again and then looked up. "I've always enjoyed this spot on the campus."

Berlin drew in a deep breath, doing her best to shake off the emotions their discussion brought forth. She looked up and admired the tree branches stretching out above them. "That's an impressive oak tree."

Albert smiled his agreement. "I've been told it's over one hundred years old."

At her look, he smiled. "I don't know if it's true, but regardless, this tree has been here for a long time."

She studied the trunk, standing tall in the middle of the benches and courtyard. There was a teddy bear, several loose flowers, and what looked like a picture frame at the base of the tree. It also looked like a picture was tacked to the trunk. When she asked him about it, Albert's face lost some of its joviality. "The tree is a bit of a remembrance. For students or teachers, really anyone tied to the school, who has died."

"Why this tree? It's not exactly central to the campus."

Albert pointed to a group of building on the far side of the courtyard. "Those are the student dorms. The tree was started years ago by the students for fellow students who had died. I believe they felt they were closer to their friends with the tree so close."

Berlin didn't know what to say and was grateful when Albert asked, "Are you ready to continue our walk?"

She shook her head and gave him a brief smile. "I would love to, but I should be going."

"Indulge me just a little longer, Detective Redding. It's been awhile since I've had such pleasant company. Just until we reach my office."

They continued down the pathway with Albert telling her stories of teaching psychology to a bunch of over-privileged kids who didn't care. They entered another building and Berlin followed him down the first-floor hallway. "Which building is this?" she asked.

"This is the psychology building." Halfway down the hallway, they stopped. Albert turned to a large display case, and Berlin turned to look, too.

The case was filled with group pictures at sporting events, a graduation, several formal events, and medals. There was also a solo picture of a young, blond girl. A plaque at the top of the case read, 'In Memory of Ashley Williams - 1999 to 2015'.

"Who was she?" Berlin asked, turning back to Albert.

His face drawn, he said, "A very nice girl who looked in the wrong direction for help."

Confused, Berlin set the books on a table below the case and looked closer at the contents. This time focusing on the group pictures. Basketball, softball, soccer. The formal pictures could have been from anything; a debate, an assembly, a ceremony. The pictures were mostly of groups of students, and looking closer, Berlin started picking Ashley Williams out in each one. Ashley in shorts and jersey, taking a long-distance shot during a basketball game. Ashely in a dark blue dress at a podium, her hair in a French twist and her face serious. And then, in a group shot of the softball team in what seemed to be a moment of celebration, Ashley stood slightly apart from her team.

A man stood just behind her, his hand on her shoulder. It looked… possessive.

Threads of disgust wormed their way into her stomach, making her feel slightly nauseous. Berlin looked at Albert, and he was staring at her. Waiting. She turned to the pictures again. The man was dark-haired and had a full beard. Something looked familiar about him, but she couldn't put her finger on it. She found him in another picture, again standing just a little too close to Ashley. And then another. Finally, it clicked.

Her voice was flat when she said the man's name. "Ben Rivera." There was another familiar face in a few of the pictures. He looked slightly younger than his picture at the law firm. "And Charles Bryant."

"We get a lot of young people through this school, Detective, who come from very wealthy homes. But wealth does not equate," he bit off the word, "to stability. Or love. Many of these young people turn to the other adults in their lives for that stability and affection. Adults who know better than to exploit those feelings."

"Why are you telling me this?" Berlin asked, looking at the old professor.

"Alex Johnson mentioned she witnessed your fixing tendencies first-hand, and she asked me to introduce you to Ashley." He picked up the stack of books. "She thought it might settle your mind about a case you're trying to solve."

Berlin's brow furrowed as she tried to make sense of what he'd just said. When would Johnson have seen her trying… Harold Houston. She straightened up, suddenly angry. "You can tell Johnson that I know something is going on here and somehow it's tied to the death of Charles Bryant. And as much as I like you, Mr. Griffin, and as much as I can respect Johnson for protecting these kids, I have a job to do. Part of that job is making sure that justice is served. Regardless of my personal feelings. And I will make sure that happens."

Albert Griffin patted her shoulder and started to walk away. "Have you considered that it already was?"

*****

Berlin left the psychology building, her head buzzing with everything she'd learned from Albert Griffin. It was possible that it was all lies. Something he'd made up to mess with her. She dismissed the thought almost immediately since they'd just met that morning, and she could see no immediate motivation for Griffin to make it up. On top of that, it matched with what Heather had told her earlier. She already knew Bryant had a history of preying on young girls, and Heather had warned her he wasn't the only one.

She was also fairly certain that Alex Johnson had sent Albert Griffin to find her, but the only reason Berlin could think for Johnson to do that was Johnson had something to do with Bryant's death. If Johnson had found out Bryant was targeting students, she may have confronted him. There could have been some argument, even a physical altercation, and she could have… "Dropped a shelf on his head?" Berlin stopped once the words were out of her mouth. It sounded even stupider when she said it out loud.

So maybe not that exact scenario, but given Johnson's message through Albert Griffin, Johnson knew more about Bryant's death than she had led them to believe. Berlin sighed and started walking again, trying to sort through everything she'd learned and seen.

One of the most disturbing things was the possession in Ben Rivera's body language. That possessiveness had spoken volumes, as had the separation between Ashley and the rest of her team. If Berlin had to guess, he had created an isolation that forced Ashley to him, making her vulnerable to his attentions.

It made Berlin furious and sick. How had Rivera and Bryant gotten away with it? Hadn't anyone noticed? Other teachers or coaches? Hadn't Kay and… Nichole! Had Nichole known that her husband had been in a relationship with his student? Berlin turned it over in her head, finally deciding Nichole couldn't have known. She would never have stood by and let him get away with it. And given her reaction to abusive men, if she had known she definitely would have confronted him about it… Berlin stopped walking again. Nichole never said what their fight had been about the night Ben died.

"Son of a…" She pulled her phone from her pocket. Nothing. Nichole had mumbled something about work and the school.

The exit back to the parking lot was just ahead of her, and the administrative building was just beyond that. Berlin picked up her pace and skipped the parking lot and instead headed to the administrative office.

There was a young man behind the desk. He was tall and skinny with bad skin but beautiful, curly hair. He smiled uncommittedly when she approached the desk. "Good Afternoon. What can I do for you?"

Berlin showed her badge. “I was wondering if you could tell me what building Nichole Redding’s office is in?”

He looked at his computer screen and made the keyboard click a few times. “It looks like her office is in Washington. On the main floor.” He pulled out a copy of the map they were given on their first visit and he circled one of the buildings. He gave her the map.

“I appreciate it,” Berlin said.

She was almost to the door when he called out, “She isn’t here, though. Emailing her or leaving a voice message might be the best way to get in touch.”

Berlin turned back toward him and took a few steps forward. “I’m sorry, did she call out sick?”

He shook his head. “Nah, it says on her schedule that she isn’t here on Wednesdays.”

Berlin’s stomach dropped, but she just nodded. “Thanks.” She exited the office.

CHAPTER SIXTEEN

The drive back to the department was endless. Berlin's phone remained quiet, and she wished her head would do the same. Too many outlandish possibilities were bouncing around inside her skull and she needed to do some research to remove the scariest ones.

The office was quiet when she walked in. Pete wasn't at his desk, but his coat and sunglasses were, so he was somewhere in the building. She threw her notebook on her desk and started her computer. She needed to look up information on Ashley Williams, first. And Ben Rivera. Her brain stalled, wanting nothing to do with what she might find.

She was still sitting there, staring blankly at her computer screen when Pete walked in, a folder in one hand and a cup of coffee in the other. He took one look at her and handed over his coffee. "Where the hell have you been? And why do you look like someone ate your favorite puppy?"

Grateful for the distraction, Berlin took a long

pull off the coffee and wished it was something stronger. “I had coffee with the daughter of the woman who filed a sexual harassment claim against Charles Bryant. She told me to look at deaths tied to the school, so I went out there.” She handed the coffee back. “We have a problem, Pete.”

Pete sat down on her desk. “Wait a minute. Who did you talk to?”

“Heather Christiansen. Her mother is Diane Long, the woman who filed a harassment complaint against Charles Bryant. She’s been the one calling and hanging up during the day.”

“How’d you figure it out?” He looked smug.

Berlin glared at him and moved on to the next bit of information. “Apparently Bryant made inappropriate suggestions to Heather when she was 14.”

“Inappropriate like…” Pete asked, his eyebrows raised.

“Yeah. That type of inappropriate.”

Pete removed himself from her desk and sat slowly in his own chair. “That’s why the mother made a complaint.” It wasn’t a question. He looked at Berlin. “Alibi?”

She nodded, pulled her notebook to her and took out the piece of paper Heather had given her. She waved it at Pete. “I haven’t called them yet, but I don’t think she lied.”

He leaned forward in his chair, his elbows resting on his knees and his chin in his hands. “Do you think there were other minors?”

The flush of anger washed over her again and Berlin nodded quickly. “Yeah. I know there were. And Pete, I think it gets worse -”

"Lewis! Redding!" Phillips's voice carried from down the hall. "Get out here. Now!"

Pete was out of his chair and through the door faster than Berlin, but she was right on his heels.

Phillips was just outside their cubicle. His face was red and the sheet of paper in his hand was shaking slightly. "You have another *accidental* death." He shoved the paper at Pete, holding on to it even after Pete grabbed it. Phillips looked at Berlin. "Get this shit figured out. Now. You're making the department look like assholes."

"Yes, sir." Pete pulled the paper out of Phillips's hand and passed it back to Berlin.

She scanned the details quickly as they walked. "This is in Tuftonboro. The deceased is David Mitchell."

Pete grabbed his jacket and sunglasses from their cubicle on their way out. "Let's go."

*****

The seventh time Berlin checked her phone, Pete broke the silence. "What are you so damn twitchy about?"

Berlin threw her phone into the coffee cup holder in the console and stared out the front window. "Nichole was supposed to call or text me when she left this morning. I haven't heard from her." *Not good, not good, not good...*

When there was no comment from Pete, she looked over and found him shaking his head, his face caught in a sad expression.

"What?"

Pete shrugged. "I just never figured you as being the clingy type."

She couldn't tell if he was serious or teasing her. "I'm not clingy."

His eyebrows almost met his hairline. "And what would you call it?" He took the exit for 113.

"Concern." *Fear... What have you been up to, Nichole?*

"Over what? And how much time have you been spending with her, anyway?"

Ignoring the second question, Berlin said, "She's had a lot of terrible shit happen to her. She's lost someone she loved; she was in an abusive relationship." She studied the trees flashing by the window. "She has these quick mood swings… I don't know, Pete. I'm a little afraid she'll come unhinged." *If she hasn't already.* After another minute, she chanced a look at his face. He looked serious again. Unable to take the silence, she said, "What?"

"It sounds like you're talking about you."

She threw her hands up and looked back at the window. "I don't know why I tell you anything. You always throw this weird, random shit back at me."

"I'm serious, Berlin."

She bit off a snarky comment at his use of her first name and turned back towards him.

When she stayed quiet, he went on. "Think back about eight or ten years. How screwed up and angry you were. Hell, think back five years, when you got to the department." He glanced at her. "There's a reason no one wanted to work with you, and it wasn't because you were a woman or a newbie."

Berlin shook her head. "You never said

anything."

"I wasn't worried. I knew you'd pull your shit together." He pulled off the main road and started up a long driveway. A large, grey farmhouse and a red barn stood off in the distance, blue and red lights flashing against both. "My point is, you were coming apart at the seams, and you didn't go off the deep end. So, give this woman a break, okay?" He parked the car and looked at her. "Don't assume she's lost it until you have proof."

Berlin nodded, feeling like she'd just received a lecture from her father. "Okay."

Shoving her inner thoughts aside, Berlin exited the car and looked toward the building. Judging from the size and shape of the house and barn, it was an old property. It probably would have followed the same fate as many other rundown farms, but instead, someone had poured a substantial amount of money into it. The property was tastefully renovated and looked expense but still period correct. There were even six horses out in the field, their heads raised towards the lights and activity.

Susan Mitchell was at the edge of the commotion, arms wrapped tight around her thick middle. Her round cheeks were flushed red and wet with tears. Where Kay Bryant had looked lovely in her grief, Susan Mitchell looked raw and broken.

A tall, red-haired officer nodded as Berlin and Pete approached the small group and made the introductions. "Mrs. Mitchell, this is Detective Peter Lewis and Detective Berlin Redding. They're going to look into the death of your husband. If you don't mind, please tell them everything you've gone over with me. Okay?"

Berlin said, “Thanks, Casey.” She turned toward Susan and forced a smile. “Is it okay if I call you Susan?” At the older woman’s nod, Berlin went on. “We’re very sorry to put you through this, Susan. I know this is a terrible time for you and your family. If you need a break at any time, just let me know.” She glanced at Pete, and at his nod, she continued. “Can you walk us through what happened today?”

Susan took a deep, shuddering breath. “I’d been asking David for weeks to do something with the hay out in the barn. The farmer who delivered it put it in the arena, but that’s not where it goes. David was supposed to have him come back to move it, but the farmer insisted that’s where he was instructed to put it. He said I called and told him to put it there, and he wanted more money to move it.” She blew her nose.

“Did you talk to the farmer at any point?” Berlin asked.

Susan shook her head. “David was the one who handled things like that. I told him we should just pay the money, but David refused and said he’d move it himself. That was two weeks ago. I don’t know why he decided to do something about it today. I didn’t even know he was home. I came back from town and I could hear the Bobcat running in the barn, and when I went to look… there was David, and -” She covered her mouth with her fisted hands, a sob caught in her throat.

Berlin moved closer and put her hand on Susan’s arm. “I’m so sorry,” she said quietly. “Is there someone we can call to come and stay with you?”

Casey said, “Mrs. Mitchell’s brother-in-law is on his way over.”

“Thanks.” Berlin looked back at Susan. “Let’s

find somewhere for you to sit down for a few minutes. Detective Lewis and I will get more details and then we'll come back and check in with you. Okay?"

Susan was given more tissues and used them to wipe her face. She nodded and was led away by a female officer.

After she was out of earshot, Pete looked at Casey. "Do you have the details from the barn?"

Casey nodded. "I do. And it was bad." He rubbed a large hand over his face, like he was trying to scrub away the scene. "As far as we can figure it, he was moving bales with the Bobcat and somehow lost control of it. The front tire hit a concrete block and he was flung out of the machine. He went forward and his foot caught the controls. The bucket dropped onto his head. He was probably killed instantly."

"Jesus Christ," said Berlin. "And she found him like that?"

"Yeah. The stuff nightmares are made of."

They were all silent for a moment, lost in their own thoughts. Finally, Berlin said, "She was the only one home?"

"Unfortunately. She said they have one kid away at college and another one in a private school."

Berlin's skin prickled. "Did she say which private school?"

"No. But the son is sixteen, so high school."

Someone from down in the yard waved and Casey excused himself, leaving Berlin and Pete alone.

"You think he's at Lake Kanasatka?" Pete asked.

"He has to be. There aren't that many private schools in this area."

"No one said he was at a school close to home."

"True," Berlin said. "But my gut says he's at the academy."

Pete nodded. "Yeah, mine too."

Berlin shook her head. "This is all tied to the school, Pete." She felt sick. "It's too much of a coincidence not to be."

"Do you want to find out for sure if that's where the kid is?"

Berlin looked over to where Susan was sitting. A grey-haired man dressed in khaki pants and a blue sweater was looming over her like a vulture, one hand on the back of her chair. He was saying something to her, his face tense. Susan was hunched in her chair, watching her fingers shred a tissue.

Thoughts of Heather nervously doing the same thing earlier flashed through her mind and Berlin's jaw clenched. "No." But she started walking toward them. She felt Pete close behind her.

The grey-haired man straightened at their approach. His face lost its tightness as he smiled and held out his hand.

"Detectives, thank you so much for helping us with this matter." His hand wavered and finally fell when no one took it. "Such a horrible accident, and I'm sure you understand that Susie and our family would like to -"

Berlin focused on Susan and cut him off. "Mrs. Mitchell, does your son attend the academy on Lake Kanasatka?"

Susan stared at Berlin, her eyes wide, the ravaged tissue forgotten. She finally nodded. "Yes. Scotty is a sophomore this year."

"Do you teach there? Or volunteer?"

She shook her head. "No. But David did. He offered sports -"

"Susie, I really don't think that's relevant." The older man stepped closer to Berlin, blocking her view of Susan.

Berlin stepped forward. "You must be David's brother."

The man nodded. "That's right. I'm Keith Mitchell. And with Dave gone, it's my responsibility to look after Susie. I really don't see -"

Tired of people fucking with their investigation, Berlin snapped. "I appreciate your concerns, Mr. Mitchell. But interfere with an ongoing investigation again, and I'll have you handcuffed and placed in the back of a police car." When he opened his mouth to argue, Berlin took another step forward and said, "Try me."

"Enough." Pete's voice cut in. "Mr. Mitchell, please let us do our jobs so we can leave you and your family in peace." He glared at Berlin, the warning clear on his face, and then he turned to Susan. "Mrs. Mitchell, please finish with what you were telling Detective Redding."

Susan looked flustered and unsure. She looked at her brother-in-law and then at Pete. At Pete's encouraging smile, she said, "Well, David went to school at the academy. And he said he wanted to give back to the school. So, he spoke to the board and offered to provide physicals to the kids who played sports at the school."

"Your husband was a doctor in this area?" Berlin asked.

"For over twenty years," Susan said, the pride clear in her voice.

"That's wonderful he could give back to the school," Berlin said, the sick feeling back. She glanced over at Keith Mitchell and then handed a card to Susan. "There may be some additional questions today, Susan, but Officer Casey will let you know for sure. And if you need anything," another glance at Keith, "you can reach me at the number on the card. Any time."

A shout from the barn caught Berlin's attention. She looked over and saw Casey waving his arm.

Pete tapped her shoulder. "Let's go."

The inside of the barn was as beautifully renovated as the outside. The ceiling was at least twelve feet high, made in the post-and-beam style. Wooden planks worn with age and at least eighteen inches wide covered the floor. A sliding door on the far end showed another section beyond it, and through the open doors Berlin could see a sandy surface and a pile of hay toward the center of the room. The arena. The tracks from the Bobcat were easy to see, going between the section of the main barn and the arena. A neat pile of bales was stacked on the far side of the main barn, and it was near that stack that the Bobcat rested. Now silent.

The scoop had been lifted, and someone had placed a sheet over the remains of David Mitchell. Casey and three other people stood near the Bobcat. A fifth person crouched near the side of the machine, inspecting something near the controls.

"What's up," Pete asked.

Casey nodded at the machine. "Someone sabotaged the Bobcat."

The fifth man got up from the ground and

approached their group. He was younger than the rest of them and looked like he would be more at home behind a computer than on a crime scene. He handed Pete a metal cylinder a few inches long. Pete studied it for a moment and then handed it to Berlin.

One end was rough and slightly fragmented. She shook her head. “I don’t know what this is.”

The technician took it back carefully. “See the fragments here?” He pointed to the obvious end.

Berlin and Pete bent their heads over the chunk of metal. “Okay,” said Pete.

The man gave Pete a second cylinder, this one smooth on both ends and about an inch and half longer. “See the difference?” He rubbed his finger on the jagged edge of the shorter piece. He looked a little too happy with his show-and-tell session.

“But what does it mean?” Berlin asked, doing little to hide her irritation and got a deep frown in return. *Probably ruining his fun.*

“These are the pins that control the safety mechanism for the bucket. They make sure the bucket won’t come down unless it’s supposed to.” He pointed to the jagged edge again. “Someone sheared this one off so the safety mechanism would eventually fail and wouldn’t engage.”

“But how could they know when the pin would fail?” Pete asked.

The technician shrugged. “You couldn’t. It could take weeks or years, depending on how often the machine was used, and what they used it for.” He palmed the cylinder. “And the safety didn’t fail, anyway.”

Berlin straightened up. “So, it was an accident?”

Casey stepped forward. “Nope. Have to wait for an autopsy to confirm, but he was probably already dead when the bucket came down on his head.” He motioned for them to follow him.

They came to the corner of the barn where an enormous rough post acted as a support beam. Directly in line with the idle Bobcat, there was a splintered section in the beam. There was a small hole in the center with a piece of lead sticking out, barely imbedded in the wood.

Berlin peered at the distorted blob. From the size, she guessed it had been fired from a 9mm handgun. “He was shot?”

“Yes, ma’am. Looks close range, so probably someone who knew him.” Casey looked at the covered form of David Mitchell and then back to the buried lead. “I think someone got tired of waiting for the Bobcat to fail and decided to expedite the good doctor’s end.”

CHAPTER SEVENTEEN

It was almost five when they left the Mitchell's property. Pete got in the driver's side and Berlin didn't even argue with him. She was exhausted and in no mood to drive, anyway. She closed her eyes and leaned her head against the back of the seat.

It stayed quiet for a few minutes, and then Pete asked, "So what else am I missing from this picture?"

Berlin opened her eyes and side-eyed her partner. He had both hands on the wheel and was staring straight ahead, his face expressionless. She'd seen him in his serious cop-mode more times this week than she had in all their years working together. She sighed and sat up straighter in her seat. "Nichole's late husband, Ben Rivera, died several years ago from a massive heart attack. No one looked twice at it because he was known to have heart trouble, including two heart surgeries."

"Okay?" Pete said, drawing the word out. He made a right to stay on 113.

"Rivera was physically abusive the last few years of their marriage. She said he really went after her the night he died. Nichole zapped him with a stun gun in self-defense, which likely triggered the heart attack."

Pete looked at her, his eyes off the road for longer than Berlin was comfortable with. "How long have you known?"

"Eyes on the road, Pete. You're scaring me a little." When he was looking forward again, she said, "Just since last night. I was about to tell you this morning, but we got hijacked by Mitchell's murder." She ran her hands over her face. "So, there's that, and then what I found when I went to the school." She stopped. If she said it out loud, it would make it real.

"What did you find out?" Pete gripped the steering wheel, his knuckles white.

Berlin took a deep breath. "I think Ben Rivera and Charles Bryant were sexually involved with students at the school. I think David Mitchell was involved in some way. I think the night Nichole's husband died, Nichole confronted him about what he was doing at the school, and that's what they fought about. I think Alex Johnson may have killed Bryant and Mitchell and I think Nichole may have tipped Johnson off that I was getting closer to understanding what happened."

Pete slowed down. Berlin thought he was pulling over and then she realized they were back at the department. He parked the car but made no move to get out. "What do you have to support your theory?"

"I know Johnson and Nichole know each other. Nichole left her a note, telling her to contact her right away. I know Bryant and Rivera knew each other and

Johnson knew Bryant. And she knows Kay but lied about it. Johnson was missing this morning when I went to the school, but she had someone show me the pictures of Rivera and Bryant with their students. Pictures that, at least to me, looked like there was something going on. The psychology professor who showed them to me confirmed my suspicions. And it follows what Heather Christiansen warned me about this morning."

"What about Mitchell?"

Berlin shook her head. "I don't know yet, but it's too much of a coincidence he volunteered at the school. Especially giving free health physicals to the kids who Bryant was coaching and abusing? The entire thing says twisted cover up to me."

"Jesus Christ." Pete's face was grim and drawn. He was quiet but eventually said, "It doesn't prove Johnson is the one responsible, but she looks like she's physically capable." He hesitated, and then asked, "Are you sure Nichole…?"

Berlin shook her head. "I don't know."

"Okay." Pete nodded. "Okay. We'll focus on Johnson for now."

"What do we do?"

He turned and looked at her. "You're going home." When she opened her mouth to argue, Pete said, "You've been on almost twelve hours and you need a break. I'll see if I can find anything in Johnson's past that lends itself to violence against anybody. And wait for the reports to come back from the Mitchell crime scene. Be in first thing tomorrow morning and we'll see where we are. Got it?"

Berlin still wanted to argue, but the tightness in

her neck and the headache forming behind her eyes warned her it was pointless. Instead, she said, "Yes, sir."

Pete gave her a tired smile. "See you tomorrow, Redding."

*****

Berlin was almost home when her phone buzzed on the passenger seat. *Nichole!* Her stomach jumped into her throat at the thought, but a quick glance at it showed a picture of her mother on the screen. Not feeling up to Christine berating her for skipping a family dinner, Berlin let it go to her voicemail. She was pulling into her driveway when the phone buzzed again, and her mother popped back up on the screen. She sighed, picked up the phone and answered.

"I'm sorry mom, I'm -"

"Your dad had another stroke. We're at Lakes Region General, but they're getting ready to airlift him to Dartmouth. Can you meet us there?" Christine's voice was high and wobbly.

"I'll be there as fast as I can." Berlin hung up, screeched out of the driveway and sped down the road.

Praying to anyone listening that any patrolmen would look the other way, Berlin put the gas pedal to the floor and drove as fast as she dared. She made it in just over an hour and found her family huddled together in the emergency waiting room.

Christine stood up when Berlin approached, her face ashen and drawn. She'd aged several years since Berlin had seen her a week ago. "What happened?" Berlin asked.

Her mother shook her head. "He's had so many rough days since they put him on that new medication. He barely slept and seemed so agitated. They don't know if it was that, or if it would have happened, anyway." Her face crumbled and Berlin took her into her arms.

"It'll be okay, mom. Dad's tough, he'll pull through this," she said, knowing that she was probably lying to Christine. She hugged the smaller woman tighter. "Let's go sit down."

She led her mom over to where James and Ellen were sitting pressed together on a couch. Ellen had her hands entwined in her husband's and her dark head on his shoulder. She'd been crying but smiled as Berlin and Christine sat down across from them.

"Hey Lin. Fancy meeting you here."

"Hey Len, where are the monsters?" Berlin smiled back and held out her hand to her sister-in-law.

Ellen sat up and took it, squeezing tight. "With my folks. If dad's feeling up to it tomorrow, I'll bring them by to say hi to him."

Berlin's eyes stung, but she nodded at Ellen's words and nonchalant attitude. All they could do at this point was pretend Tom would be fine.

They made small talk and poor jokes, trying to distract themselves from why they were there. As soon as a doctor headed their way, their conversation stopped, and they waited anxiously to see if they would be next to receive whatever news there was on their loved one.

After two hours Ellen finally stood up and stretched, arching her back. Her stomach poked out so far Berlin was sure she'd topple over. "I need to go for a walk and find something to eat. Does anyone want to keep me company?"

Berlin looked over at her mother. Christine was pale, the skin under her eyes bruised. "Why don't you go with Ellen, mom? You look like you could use a little break."

"What if the doctor comes out? What if they come and tell us that…?" She didn't finish the sentence.

"I'll call you if anyone heads our way and looks like they'll actually talk to us. I promise."

"Come on, Christine. You need to get something to eat and keep your energy up," Ellen said, holding her hand out to her mother-in-law.

Christine was quiet for a moment but nodded and stood up. She drew a deep breath, squared her shoulders and looked at her children. "Do either of you want anything?"

James shook his head but didn't say anything.

"Thanks, but I'll go in a little while and get something," Berlin said.

Ellen took Christine's arm, and they wandered out of the waiting room. Ellen using her special talent of pretending things were okay, already rattling off something about the kids.

Berlin looked at her brother and said, "Your wife is amazing, you know."

James looked at her. "Yeah, I know. And I know I screwed up, so spare me the lecture, okay?"

She got up and moved to the seat next to him. "I wasn't going to lecture. I've been meaning to apologize for opening my mouth that night. You were right. People who take my advice rarely end up okay." She looked down at her hands.

James took a deep breath and exhaled through his nose. “Thanks. I appreciate that. But you were right, too. I really screwed up.” He nudged her shoulder with his own, harder than he needed to. “And I shouldn’t have said what I did. You care about helping people, and I know your bossiness comes from a good place. And I’m sure not everyone who takes your advice ends up fucked.” He nudged again.

“Keep pounding me with that shoulder and I’ll put you on the ground, Jamie.” She appreciated his forced laugh. “Are you and Len going to make it through whatever this is?”

He rested his head on the back of his chair and closed his eyes. “Yeah. We’re working on it. And she won’t give up on me. She loves torturing me too much.”

“Nice, Jamie.”

He raised his head and gave her a genuine smile. “Hey, I’m not complaining. It’s one of the many things I love about her.” He nodded his head toward her phone. “Who isn’t calling you?”

“What?”

“You’ve been staring at your phone or flipping it in your hands almost the entire time you’ve been here.”

Berlin looked down and frowned at the phone. “Someone was supposed to call me. I haven’t heard from her since this morning, and I’m getting worried.”

“Why? Is she one of your addict informants or something?”

She smacked him in the leg. “No Jamie. She’s a friend.”

He looked at her knowingly. “This is the friend mom mentioned you were seeing?”

Berlin groaned. “Can nothing stay secret in this

family?" Then she smiled. "Yeah, the woman I've been seeing."

James wiggled his eyebrows. "So, is she an addict?"

"No, James, she isn't an addict. She's actually a teacher at Lake Kanasatka. Spanish."

"No shit. The academy?" James sat up. At Berlin's nod, he said, "That's funny. Ellen and I were there, talking to their admissions office a few weeks ago."

"Why?"

"For Lynn. We're looking at options beyond public schools. Lake Kanasatka Academy has some of the highest ratings in New England."

"But she's only five."

"Yeah, so we're like six years behind with her." He shook his head. "I don't think we're snooty enough to put our kids in a private school, though. But maybe a charter school. I think that would fit Ellen's hippy tendencies a little better."

Ignoring the hippy comment, Berlin asked, "What did you think of Kanasatka?"

He shrugged. "It's a beautiful campus. And everyone seemed nice, though a little too nice." He paused for a minute, looking thoughtful. Then he looked at Berlin and said, "Remember when dad was thinking of joining the Masons?"

Unsure about the change in topic but willing to humor her brother, Berlin nodded. "Yeah. He went to meetings for a few months, but it didn't last too long. Why?"

"Do you remember some of the guys who were members? They were, I don't know." He frowned down at his hands.

Remembering the men Jamie was talking about and then thinking about the academy, Berlin thought of Keith Mitchell. He'd been pretty determined to keep Susan from speaking to them. Berlin said, "Secretive?"

Jamie nodded. "Yeah. That's how the school felt to me. Like we weren't part of them, didn't know the secret handshake, so they only showed us the rainbow and unicorn bullshit."

"What are you two talking about so intently?" Ellen plopped down into the chair across from her husband, startling them both. Christine sat down next to her, looking a little better after their walk.

Jamie sat up and smiled at his wife. "The girl," at Berlin's look he changed it to, "woman, Berlin is seeing is a teacher at Lake Kanasatka. I was telling her about our visit there."

Ellen frowned. "Lynn isn't going there." She reached into the white bag and pulled out a croissant. She tore off a third of it and stuffed it into her mouth.

"I thought you liked it," James said, reaching forward and wiping crumbs from her belly.

She shook her head. "That was before I talked to Sue Parker. Her sister-in-law was a teacher there for a few years but left about two years ago. She said after working there, she wouldn't send her kids. Especially a daughter."

"Did she say why?" Christine asked, sitting forward and looking alert for the first time that evening.

Another chunk of croissant went into Ellen's mouth. After it was gone, she said, "Sue didn't have specifics, but said a girl committed suicide there. She didn't know if it was stress from the classes, or if there was something else going on, but I guess one of the girl's professors took it a little *too* hard." The last piece of pastry disappeared.

"It was an actual suicide, or she was just speculating?" Berlin asked.

Ellen said, "She specifically said suicide. The girl's roommate found her in their dorm room."

Berlin sat back. "Jesus Christ." When she saw the memorial for Ashley Williams, she assumed Ashley had had some type of accident. She hadn't considered suicide, even after learning there was possibly something going on between Ashley and an adult. She knew it was possible they weren't talking about Ashley, but the timing was right, and she couldn't get the image of Ben Rivera's possessiveness out of her mind.

Christine was studying her daughter. "What's wrong, Berlin?"

Berlin looked at her mother's pale and worried face and slipped her phone into her coat pocket. "Nothing that can't wait, mom."

It was another two hours before a doctor came to talk to them. He was tall and thin, looked exhausted and too young to know anything about caring for another person. His voice was deep and kind when he asked, "Are you Tom Redding's family?"

Christine stood up; her hand clenched in Berlin's. "Yes. I'm Christine, Tom's wife. How is he?"

"Your husband is resting right now with the help of some heavy-duty medication. He's stable enough to move to the ICU, but unfortunately that's the best news I can give you for now."

Berlin stood and put her arm around her mother. "Can we at least see him?"

"I'm sorry, no." The doctor shifted, putting his hands in the pockets of his medical coat. "The best thing you can do is go home and get some rest. It will be at least another hour before we get him moved and settled. When you come back in the morning, we should have a better idea of what we're dealing with. But for now, please know he's resting and we're doing absolutely everything we can for him."

Berlin nodded. "Thank you."

He nodded back and walked away.

She looked at Christine. "What do you want to do?"

Christine looked lost; her eyes glassy with tears. She wrapped her arms around her middle and sat back down. "I don't know. I don't know what to do. I can't imagine sleeping, not with Tom here. I don't want to go home without him." Her voice broke.

Ellen looked at James and then her mother-in-law. "Well, I know I could use some help with Lynn and Tommy, if you're up for it, Chris. My back has been killing me and they're running me ragged." She stood up, her hands on the small of her back. "Why don't you come home with us tonight and we'll come back first thing in the morning."

Berlin held her breath and prayed her mother would take the bait. When James looked like he'd protest, she kicked his foot and shook her head at him.

Christine sniffed back her tears and wiped her eyes with both hands. "Are you sure I'd be a help, and not a bother?" She asked Ellen.

"Absolutely. You'd be doing me a huge favor by staying with us."

Christine nodded. "Okay. Thank you."

*****

It wasn't even midnight when Berlin pulled into her driveway, although it felt like it was hours past it. Her head was heavy, and she was slightly dizzy with the lack of sleep and emotional stress. She jerked the car to a stop and just stared at her porch steps in the headlights. There was a figure huddled there. Nichole. Berlin's heart gave a couple of hard beats, but it was too heavy from the day's wear and tear to respond any further.

Berlin shut the car off, pitching the figure back into darkness. She opened her door and pulled herself out. She slammed the door shut and then walked toward her house. She didn't even pause at Nichole, she just said, "I'm too tired to do this. Go home."

Nichole stood up. "I'm sorry I didn't call you today. Or come to the station."

Berlin paused with her hand on the key in the door. "Nichole, that is so far beyond what I'm worried about right now. I have to be back at the department in six hours and I really need to sleep. So seriously, do me a favor and go home."

Nichole moved to the second step, her hand out. "Would you just -"

Berlin swung around, the worry and horror from the day spilling out of her. "No! I'm sick and tired of your shit! This has been such a horrendous day on so many levels I can't even begin to process everything. At the top of that has been worrying myself sick over you. And I'm done. Okay? Just done with it. I don't know what you and Alex Johnson have been doing but I will find out and with the way my luck is running lately, I'll be the one to arrest you. So go the fuck away!"

Nichole's face was ghost white. She backed away from Berlin and down the stairs. "I'm sorry, Berlin. Really, I am."

Berlin looked at her for a few seconds, memorizing her face. "I don't care," she said, and turned back to unlock the door. It swung open, and she walked into the darkness of the house. She looked back to where Nichole had been standing just seconds before. There was no one there. Berlin shut the door without looking back again.

CHAPTER EIGHTEEN

There was no one at the department when Berlin walked in the next morning. Her head was full of jackhammers, and she severely doubted there was enough coffee and Motrin in the office to make them stop. She'd slept a chopped up three hours, sure she would get a call from her mother or that Nichole would come back. By the time four rolled around, she finally gave in and got up. Now that she was at her desk, all she wanted to do was crawl under it and sleep.

Berlin sighed, pulled the small bottle of ibuprofen from the top drawer, palmed four of the little orange pills, and chased them down with hot, black coffee. Then she logged in to her computer and started searching.

She entered David Mitchell's name and tied it with Lake Kanasatka Academy. There was very little information. Two or three articles on his support to the academy over his twenty-plus years as a physician and mention of his alumni status. It was all information they had from Susan.

Further down the page Berlin found an article written by Dr. David Mitchell that discussed the signs of depression. She clicked on the link.

The piece was titled *Preventing Suicide: Knowing the Signs of Depression* and written three years prior. It included a serious picture of David and another of a group of teenagers and adults dressed in somber colors. The picture reminded Berlin of the other group photos on display at the academy. She zoomed in closer to get a better look at the faces of the adults. Two she didn't know and two she did: Charles Bryant and Ben Rivera. Rivera's eyes were black, vacant hollows. His skin was stretched tightly over his cheekbones, his mouth a thin, straight line. The caption under the picture read *Team members and staff mourn the loss of a friend and teammate.*

Berlin scanned the article quickly. It was fairly basic; he listed the signs of depression, mentioned asking questions about intentions of self-harm, and highlighted the most common reasons for depression and suicide in young adults. About three-quarters through it, she finally got the answer to her question from the night before. *Dedicated to the memory of Ashley Williams*. She printed the article and an enlarged version of the group photo.

She opened another search page and typed in Ashley's name. A Facebook page came up, but when Berlin clicked on it, she got a warning the content could no longer be found. She went back to the search page and after two more misses she found an article written just after Ashley's death. There was very little information due to Ashley's age. There was a headshot of Ashley at the top of the piece and the information underneath stated she was found in her dorm room late in the evening on 28 September 2016. EMS reported her as unresponsive and determined she'd died at the scene. Berlin sent it to the printer and continued to search.

On the third page an article titled *Lake Kanasatka Academy Hit By Second Tragedy* caught her attention. Berlin clicked on the link and found an image of a handsome and viral Ben Rivera. The article read: *Lake Kanasatka Academy suffered a second tragedy on Wednesday evening when Psychologist Benedict Rivera was pronounced dead at his home. Officials reported that Dr. Rivera had a history of heart issues and died from a heart attack. Some students and faculty say they believe the loss of Ashley Williams, one of his students, three weeks earlier may have contributed to his heart attack. One of Ashley's athletic coaches, Charles Bryant, commented, "It just broke his heart when we lost Ashley. Dr. Rivera was working closely with her Ashley. And her family. He was like a second father to Ashley and he was devastated by her death." Counseling has been available to students and teachers since Ashley's death and will continue after this tragic loss of Dr. Rivera.*

It still wasn't conclusive. Berlin knew how Rivera died, and it was from too much voltage to the chest, not a broken heart. She pulled up healthy Ben and shattered Ben and studied them. There was definitely a difference between them, though. Ashley's death had affected Ben Rivera to an extreme level, beyond what an educator should have felt for his student. The image of the possessiveness in Rivera's face, his hand on Ashley's shoulder in the picture at the academy flashed through Berlin's mind, bringing back the horror she'd felt at seeing it. She reread Bryant's comment, *working closely with Ashley... like a second father... devastated...*

"How many girls, you predatory bastard?" Berlin asked shattered Ben. "How many lives did you ruin, you and your sick, predatory asshole friends?" It still wasn't conclusive. But in her gut, she knew she was right.

Berlin got up from her computer and headed out of the cubicle to the main hallway and toward the printer. The pictures of Ashley, Rivera and the articles were waiting. She pulled the sheets off the tray and turned to head back to her computer when she heard her name.

"Redding!"

She turned and found Phillips coming towards her. Pete, the Weasel, and several other officers were behind him. Berlin turned fully and faced the group, waiting.

Phillips stopped in front of her and shook his head, a slight sneer on his face.

"Did you want something, Captain, or were you just taking your pet for a walk?" Berlin nodded at the Weasel. She caught the twitch of Pete's mouth from the corner of her eye but kept her focus on Phillips.

His eyes narrowed. "You're dismissed from the Bryant and Mitchell cases. I want your notes and any information you may have discovered during the investigations. From this point forward you are to have nothing to do with either case. Is that clear?"

It was like someone hit her low in the gut. "What?" She looked at Pete. The slightly pained expression on his face was the only confirmation she needed to know Phillips was serious. She squared her shoulders. “Why?”

Phillips was smirking. She wanted to punch him. “It’s been brought to my attention you are involved with an individual who is now a suspect in this investigation. It was also suggested you may be emotionally compromised because of your past.”

Berlin looked at Pete. “What did you find?”

Phillips took a step forward, invading her personal space. “Redding, what part of ‘off the case’ do you not understand.”

White-hot anger poured through her, making her shake harder than a junkie three days removed from the last fix. Any restraint she’d ever shown for Phillips slipped away. She moved forward, purposely stepping on his toes, forcing him to back away. “I understand completely, you spineless piece of shit. I understand you’re so goddamned afraid to have a woman…”

“Redding.”

“… in the department you’ll create any shitty excuse…”

“Redding!”

“… to remove her from a case because she has a chance…”

“Detective Redding. That is enough!” Pete’s voice finally broke through to her. He stepped forward. “Captain Phillips removed you from both cases on my recommendation.”

Berlin’s mouth snapped shut. Of all the people in her world, Pete was the last one she would have expected to do this to her. She kept her eyes locked on him, searching his face for answers. He shook his head.

What the hell is that supposed to mean? She looked back at Phillips. The smirk was firmly in place.

"You're such a prick," she said. She turned on her heel and headed back to her office.

She was throwing files in a pile when Pete came in several minutes later. Berlin ignored him. He sat on the edge of her desk. "Are you going to talk to me?"

Berlin held a folder in her hands and stared at the pile on her desk. Partially under Pete's ass. She glared at him. "No."

He shrugged and settled more firmly on the folders.

She wanted to be livid with him. She knew she should be livid with him. But all Berlin felt like doing was curling up into a ball and crying. She asked the folder in her hands, "Why? Why wouldn't you say something to me if you were concerned?"

Pete's voice was calm when he said, "What's basic protocol in these situations?"

Berlin closed her eyes. Taking a deep breath, she said, "An officer or detective will be removed from a case if they have any personal involvement or interest in the investigation's outcome."

"What would you have done in the situation?"

She opened her eyes and glared at him. "I wouldn't have run to Phillips without warning you, that's for damn sure!"

Pete's expression didn't change. Quieter, he said, "I needed Phillips to have his moment, and I needed him to know you were off the case."

"Why?"

He shook his head. Louder, he said, "Please place anything relevant to this investigation on my desk.

Only take your personal property from the office." A pointed look at her notebook, and then a little quieter he said, "And don't go looking through any of the files in my drawer. Doing so could lead to administrative leave or termination."

Berlin straightened up. Pete looked serious. *Pay attention, Berlin!*

"Do you understand what I'm saying?" he asked.

A dozen thoughts raced through her head as Berlin searched his face, looking for some clue as to what was going on. Finally, she nodded.

Pete nodded back and got up off the files. "Good. See you around." He paused just before exiting and looked back at Berlin. "I'm sorry about your dad. No matter what happens with this bullshit, you know if you need anything, you find me. Got it?"

She blinked back tears and nodded. "Thanks."

He nodded one more time and left.

Berlin tossed the folder onto the pile with the others and dropped into her chair. She'd said it to Nichole; Pete had a reason for everything he did. She just had to figure out what it was. She also needed to do it fast before Phillips had her escorted from the building.

She slid her chair towards Pete's desk and the metal two-drawer filing cabinet sitting beside it. The top drawer was open slightly, inviting her to look inside. She reached for the handle but stopped just shy of it, Pete's words resonating in her head. Administrative leave or termination. She knew it was a warning. Not necessarily for looking at the files in the drawer, because who but Pete would know that she had. The warning had to do with her reaction to whatever was in the drawer.

It was never the action part of a choice that bothered Berlin. It was everything that came before the action. It was the not knowing and indecision that killed her. Once she had the information, she could consider plans of action and determine probable outcomes. And then she could act. In this case, Pete had given her the outcomes: administrative leave or termination. Which meant whatever was in the drawer was not good. If it wasn't good, and had severe consequences, that meant it was something that someone needed to act on.

Enough screwing around.

Berlin opened the drawer.

The drawer held only two folders. She pulled both out and set them on Pete's desk. The first folder contained three sheets; all were photocopies of a police report dated 18 September 2016. Thoughts of the records department calling her about files for Pete came back to her. *So, this is what you've been up to. You sneaky bastard.* Berlin started reading.

An anonymous report had been made to the police department regarding several sexual assaults at Lake Kanasatka Academy. The report alleged that several male faculty members and volunteers had entered into sexual relationships with various students over a number of years. The call requested the department investigate and suggested the police talk to Ben Rivera, Charles Bryant, and Ashley Williams.

The two officers assigned to the complaint were James Edwards and Don Kolenski. Berlin recognized both the names, though she didn't know either personally. She did know both had been reassigned to other departments within the last twenty-four months.

Their notes about the actual complaint were underwhelming. There was a detailed account of their interviews with both Rivera and Bryant. Both men claimed their interactions with the students were strictly professional and academic. When asked if either had ever had any inappropriate interaction with a student, Rivera reported that occasionally students he counseled would project feelings on him, since he was a 'safe' figure in their lives. He assured the investigators he corrected the behavior immediately once he recognized it and had even assigned students to a different counselor when needed. When asked specifically about Ashley Williams he offered that she was a 'good girl' from a family who had very little interest in her, thus she often looked for attention from other places.

Edwards and Kolenski also recorded interviews from other members of the administrative staff. Everyone they talked to seemed to corroborate what both Bryant and Rivera reported about their own behavior and Ashley's. Several of the people interviewed thought it may have been Ashley who orchestrated the complaint to get attention.

Finally, they had reached out to Sylvie and Kirk Williams, who were staying at their home on O'ahu. Both parents were reported as unconcerned and unsurprised about their daughter's behavior or the complaint. Sylvie Williams allegedly told them Ashley had been making up lies for years about abuse from members of Ashley's own family. Which, according to Sylvie, were one-hundred percent false. She finished her interview by telling the investigators that she and Don saw no reason to continue the investigation, as it was obviously another attempt by Ashley to get attention.

The investigation was closed based on the lack of evidence of sexual assault or questionable behavior against Ashley Williams, or at Lake Kanasatka Academy. Everything was signed off by Captain Luke Phillips. There was no mention in the report of talking to Ashley Williams.

In all her years of police work, Berlin had never seen such a poor job of witness questioning or investigation. How anyone could read the report and not see it as a cover-up was beyond her. Her hands shaking, Berlin closed the folder and opened the second one.

There were two sheets. One was a photocopy of a letter dated February 2017, thanking Lake Kanasatka Academy for their generous donation of fifty-thousand dollars to the Lakes Region Police Department. The head of the department's headquarters had signed the letter. The second was another photocopied letter, this one to the Broken Wings Foundation, announcing an anonymous donation in the amount of two hundred and fifty-thousand dollars. The letter was dated 3 December 2016.

Berlin wrote the foundation's name and donation amount in her notebook and then carefully closed the second folder and placed both back in the drawer. Then she shut the drawer, leaving the slight gap that was there before she'd opened it. She sat back in the chair to think. She'd never heard of the Broken Wings Foundation, but Pete thought it was important enough to put with the other paperwork. Which also meant it was somehow tied to Ashley's death.

She had no idea what to do now. This was

bigger than she could have imagined. If the department had failed to investigate the assault claims adequately, and if Phillips had signed off on it knowing the investigation wasn't handled properly, and if the department had taken a payout from the school… They were all huge ifs with no real way of proving any of it.

Footsteps outside the office reminded Berlin she was running out of time. She moved away from the filing cabinet and back to her own desk. She picked up the pile of folders and moved it over to Pete's desk.

See, Phillips? Just a good little detective, doing what she was told.

The papers from the printer were still out. She looked them over and the date of Ashley Williams's death caught her attention. 28 September. Only ten days after Phillips signed off on the investigation of the assaults.

Memories of her own assault and the bullshit investigation came back to her. How many times had she considered killings herself after being told she was a liar and she was trying to ruin the career of a decorated officer? She remembered lying in her bed, trying to curl around the pain and shame of it all, just wanting the entire thing to end. Was that what Ashley Williams had felt when no one believed her? The school refused to back her up. Her parents had been telling everyone for years she was a liar. Had she seen suicide as her only alternative?

This had to stop. She had to find out what happened to Ashley and who was responsible. And she needed to make sure they were held accountable. If the police department was somehow involved, especially Phillips, she would make damn sure it was held accountable, too.

Her decision made, Berlin folded the papers from the printer and placed them in her red notebook. She untucked her shirt and slipped the notebook into the waistband of her slacks against her stomach. She tucked her shirt back in and straightened her coat. If anyone looked too closely they might notice something, but she didn't intend to let anyone look that close.

Berlin exited the cubicle area and marched down the hallway, looking straight ahead. She was outside in the parking lot in under a minute. She didn't see a single person on her way out. Once she was sitting in her car, Berlin took a deep breath before bringing her brain back online. With Pete off limits for now, there was no one safe to talk to from inside the department. Most of the officers thought Phillips walked on water and would take any opportunity to feed him information if they thought it would put them in his favor. There was one person Berlin could think of who might talk to her, but first she needed some place quiet where she had internet access and she could think.

*****

The noise outside her father's hospital room was constant, creating white noise that wasn't unpleasant and helped kill the chaos going on inside Berlin's head. It was still early when she arrived, and for the first hour she sat with her dad and held his hand. She searched his face for any changes since the last time she'd seen him awake. It had been almost a week ago. He was paler now, and she thought thinner, but otherwise looked like the same man he'd been since the first stroke.

A nurse came in about thirty minutes after she'd arrived and let Berlin know that he still hadn't woken up since he'd arrived at the critical care unit, but he was resting comfortably. Berlin saw nothing in her dad that made her think he wasn't, so she thanked the woman and went back to watching him.

At some point the exhaustion from the last forty-eight hours caught up with her and she fell asleep in her chair. She woke up when her mother entered the room.

"How long have you been here?"

Berlin sat up, her neck sore, her head achy, and her mouth tasting like something had crawled inside it and died. "I'm not sure. A couple hours, I think." She stood up and stretched. "Where's Jamie and Ellen?"

Christine smiled. "They'll be here in a little while. It takes longer to get going with kids and I didn't want to wait." The smudges under her eyes looked darker, and Berlin could tell she'd been crying.

She walked over to her mom and gave her a long hug. "Did they have anything new to tell you when you came in?" Berlin asked.

"No. They said he's resting comfortably." Christine smoothed the blanked over Tom's legs. "I know I should be grateful for that, because it means he's hopefully comfortable. But I want him to wake up." She brushed at her eyes, much the way an angry child would, and then looked at her daughter. "Now, what brings you here at this time of day?"

Deciding it wasn't a complete lie, Berlin said, "I had a break in my caseload, so thought I would come see dad for a while. But I need to make a couple of calls, if you want some time alone with daddy."

Christine settled into the chair Berlin had

vacated, leaned forward and took Tom's hand. "I'll be here, sweetie. Go make your calls."

Berlin watched her parents from the doorway, her heart breaking for them and for herself. After another minute, she turned and walked into the hallway.

She called the number she had written down for Alex Johnson. It rang five times before the voicemail picked up. Berlin hung up without leaving a message. Then she dialed it again. She did it eight more times before it was finally answered. "I need to talk to you."

"You are persistent, aren't you?" Johnson's voice held irritation and something else. She sounded almost… buzzed. "You could have left a message. I would have returned your call."

"I didn't want to take the chance you'd ignore me."

"Well, for future reference, I only answered now because my students were getting annoyed by the phone ringing."

Tired of the banter, Berlin said, "I need to speak to you about Charles Bryant."

It was quiet on Johnson's end, long enough that Berlin wondered if she'd lost the connection. Then, "That's interesting, Detective. I received a call an hour ago from an Officer Martinez asking to speak to me. He also told me I wasn't to discuss Charles's death with you. I am assuming this was what you wanted to talk about?"

"Did Martinez specifically say Bryant's death was off-limits? Because I'm more interested in some of his activities prior to finding him in his basement."

Johnson paused again, but this time Berlin could hear pages flipping. She could picture Johnson thumbing through her planner. "I have students until seven tonight. But you can come to my office after that."

"I need to talk to you sooner than tonight," Berlin said.

"Be glad I'm willing to talk to you at all, Detective." Johnson hung up.

"Shit." Berlin stared at her phone. She knew she was on borrowed time and each minute she wasted was another that Phillips could come up with a way of stopping her.

She looked at the time on her phone. She had over five hours to kill before she could meet with Johnson.

Berlin pulled out her notebook and opened it up. The pictures and article she'd printed at the department fell out and uncovered the words 'broken wings'. She picked the folded papers up from the floor and then brought up the search engine on her phone. She typed in the foundation's name and started scrolling.

She had her answer in less than three minutes. Sylvie and Don Williams had started the foundation a month after Ashley died. According to the website, the foundation helped emotionally and mentally unstable children.

"That's right, blame all that shit on your kid being overly emotional," Berlin said as she jotted down the information. She paused when she saw 250k?? written next to the name.

"So, who would have donated anonymously?" she asked herself. Someone who didn't want to be thanked, but that wouldn't have been interesting to Pete. So, someone who didn't want to be tied to the foundation or the founders, which was more likely since it had been in the do-not-touch file. Berlin tapped her fingers on her leg, thinking. The school could have donated and meant it as a kind gesture because of Ashley. But the school wouldn't have had to donate in secret, since they could have done it in Ashley's name. The folded papers next to her reminded her of what and who was on them. Rivera was dead by the time the donation went through. But what about Bryant? How close had he and Rivera been? Going by what he said in the article after Rivera's death, they were close. Would Bryant have donated the money because Rivera would have wanted him to? Or did Bryant donate the money to keep everything about Rivera's relationship with Ashly from leaking out? And to keep everything quiet about his own role in Ashley's death?

Jack Abrams's comment about Charles paying his girlfriend off to shut her up came back to her.

Berlin flipped through her notebook until she found Heather's contact info. She dialed the number and got through almost immediately.

"Hello?" Heather's voice came through as strong as the first time Berlin had heard it.

"Heather, this is Berlin Redding. Do you remember who offered your mom money to drop the charge against Charles Bryant?"

There was a pause. "No, I don't remember the name. I'm sorry, Detective. That was quite a few years ago."

Trying to prod Heather's memory, Berlin asked, "Was it the firm she was working for? The one Bryant left?"

"No… I think it was the place he went to after

he left." Another pause. "Some guy's name. Something and Something."

I knew it. "Abrams & Abrams?"

"Yeah, that sounds right. Why?"

"The next time I come into the Moose and you're working, I'll buy you a cup of coffee and tell you. Thanks Heather, I appreciate it." Berlin clicked off the call.

Well, it looked like she'd found a way to kill some time.

CHAPTER NINETEEN

Katie Albert looked up when Berlin walked into the lobby. She smiled when she saw who it was, but as soon as it was clear Berlin was alone, the smile lost most of its luster.

"Good afternoon, Detective. Is it just you today?"

"Just me, I'm afraid. Detective Lewis is home with his twin daughters." Berlin's smile sweetened as Katie lost hers. "His wife has the flu. Is Mr. Abrams available to speak with me for a few minutes?" She'd have to remember to tell Pete she'd finally managed the art of lying.

Katie could have been sucking on lemons, her smile was so sour. "No, I'm sorry. He's in a partner meeting at the moment. Is there something I could help you with?"

"It's a sensitive question. I should probably ask Mr. Abrams directly…"

Katie stood up straighter. "I can assure you Mr.

Abrams trusts his staff completely, and we know everything that happens in this firm."

We'll see about that. "Okay, great. I was just wondering how many pay-outs he's made over the last ten years to cover up sexual harassment and statutory rape incidents?"

The smile completely slipped from Katie's face, and her brow furrowed. "I'm sorry, I'm not sure I -"

"I know of at least two. I'm just assuming there's more. I thought I'd ask him directly before I go digging around in other places."

Katie stared at Berlin; her mouth slightly open.

Berlin nodded at the door they'd gone through the first time they'd visited the firm. "You know what, I'll just pop in real quick and ask him myself." Katie's half-hearted protest followed Berlin through the door and into the hallway. Berlin gave it sixty seconds tops before Katie was telling whoever else might be around about the accusations.

The door to Abrams's office was closed. Berlin put her ear close to it and could faintly hear murmurs from inside. She thought back to their first visit. If she remembered correctly, the table was at the front of the room, so there was little to no chance of her looking in without being seen. Berlin stepped back from the door to think. When nothing came to her, she said, "Screw it," and just opened the door.

Jack Abrams was sitting at the head of the glass conference table, six other men sitting with him. All seven men turned to look when she strode through the door.

Abrams looked less than excited to see her. "Detective, this is not a good time." He gestured to the suits at the table. "I'm in a meeting at the moment. As I'm sure my receptionist explained to you."

"She did mention something about a circle jerk." Berlin looked pointedly at each man in the room. "Guess I found the right room. My apologies for interrupting, boys." She looked back at Abrams. "But since I'm already here, what can you tell me about the two hundred and fifty-thousand dollars you donated to Ashley Williams's foundation?"

Abrams turned his attention to tidying the papers in front of him into a pile. "I'm sorry detective, I have no idea what you're talking about. Now if you'll -"

Berlin approached the table and placed the picture of Ashley on top of his papers. "Does this help? This is the girl Charles Bryant helped Ben Rivera sexually abuse." The men at the table were trying to look at the picture without being obvious about it. "And then a very large donation was made to her parent's foundation. By you. So, what I want to know is, how much did you offer to pay when Charles was harassing the fourteen-year-old girl at his other firm? I'm assuming not as much because he didn't rape her. What's the going rate to cover up sexual harassment, Jack? Seventy thousand? A hundred? Am I close?"

Yup, that did it. Now she had their full attention. Or rather, Jack Abrams did.

Six pairs of eyes were on him as Abrams turned an unbecoming shade of red. When he picked up the picture of Ashley and moved it off his paperwork, his hands were shaking. "Gentlemen, I sincerely apologize for this interruption. Could I please ask for five minutes alone with Detective Redding? That should be all it takes to settle this matter."

They were slow getting up from their chairs, slow to murmur their comments of agreement and understanding.

Berlin kept her focus on Abrams when she said, “Don’t leave on my account, boys. I’m sure you’re just as interested in what Jack has to say as I am.” Yup, he was definitely shaking.

When the door closed behind the last lawyer, Abrams said, “I don’t know what you’re trying to accomplish, Detective, but attempting to make me look bad in my office, in front of my people is not the way to do it.”

“Fine. Next time I’ll go to the New Hampshire Bar Association and share my theory with them first. And then I’ll come and inform ‘your people’ about how much of a prick you are. Happy?”

Abrams was wearing the same sour expression that Katie had worn earlier. “What do you want, Detective?”

Berlin picked up Ashley’s picture from the table and held it up for Abrams to see. “I want to know how many more there are, Jack. How many times have you paid off a parent or a family member? How many anonymous donations have you made to keep these parasitic fucks free to ruin more lives?”

He sat back in his chair. “You don’t have anything. This is all guess-work, hoping I’ll trip up and say something.” He looked smug.

Can’t have that…

Berlin put the picture back down and drew away from the table. She began wandering toward his office area, taking in the different awards on the walls. Some from the New Hampshire Bar Association. Some from the American Bar Association. Several from the local communities and business. She moved on to the shelves but stopped almost immediately. A large, crystal orb was perched on a black stand on the third shelf. A gold plaque attached to the stand proclaimed that Jack Abrams was pivotal to the community's safety and protection.

Still staring at the crystal ball, she said, "I know Diane Long and her daughter Heather. Heather and I have been chatting quite a lot, lately." Berlin reached out for the ball. It came right off the stand. She turned and showed it to Abrams. "I think this one is my favorite." She tested the weight of the ball, lightly tossing it in the air. "Did you know Heather's going to school to advocate for harassment and assault victims?" Another toss of the ball. This time a little higher. Abrams watched, his faced slightly pinched. "I'll give you one guess who her case study is for her final thesis." Berlin smiled at him as she gave the ball another toss. She caught it and moved further into his room. It brought her next to his desk.

"Diane Long was a money grubbing nobody whose daughter tried to ruin a talented man's career. Nobody cared enough to listen to them then, and nobody cares about what they have to say now."

She turned to face him. "You're wrong, Jack. I care. I care a great deal. I also care a great deal why no one listened to Ashley Williams. And why you, Charles Bryant, Ben Rivera, and David Mitchell felt you had any right to end her life the way you did."

Abrams folded his arms across his chest. "Didn't you read the papers, Detective? She was a suicide. Nobody killed her."

Berlin's hand clenched around the glass ball. She wanted to throw it at him. "They ended her life as soon as they picked her as their next victim." Berlin looked down at the ball. She probably shouldn't throw it at him… the baseball bat on his desk caught her eye. *Be honest. Wouldn't it have felt great to smash the lieutenant's face in with a crowbar?* She looked back at Abrams. He'd lost the concerned look. "And you helped them when you made that donation to pacify her parents."

Abrams stood up. "You don't know what you're talking about. Now if you'll excuse me, I have work to do."

Berlin nodded. "You're right, Jack. I don't know everything about Ashley Williams's death yet. Or how many other victims are out there. But I will find out. And I'll make sure as many people as possible know about the part you played in it."

"You're making a mistake, Detective." He was using his firm, lawyer tone.

Guess that means I'm supposed to do as I'm told. She glanced around the room again, and then down at the baseball bat on his desk. "No, Jack, I'm not. But this could be."

In one motion, Berlin tossed the glass award high into the air with her left hand and grabbed the bat with her right. She swung the bat around and struck the glass ball, breaking it into several pieces. The largest pieced spiked across the room. It hit high on the wall, close to the ceiling and arched back down and crashed into the conference table. The chunk of glass shattered and left long cracks through the tabletop. *Well, that was anticlimactic.*

Berlin looked around for something else to smash and found Abrams ducked down beneath the table. "What's wrong, Jack? I thought you lawyer types liked to play hardball." She spied a cluster of glass pillars, all with the same engraving except for the year. Best Law Office in New England 2013, 2014, 2015… Six of them in total. Berlin lifted one up, trying to judge the weight. *Might do…*

Abrams was eyeing her from his position under the table. "You crazy bitch! I'll have your ass for this!"

She hefted the pillar into the air. It turned twice, end-over-end, giving her just enough time to position the bat. She swung and missed. The pillar fell to the floor by her feet. Berlin bent down and picked it up. A little shard off the top edge, otherwise it looked fine. "Well, damn. Glad my old softball coach didn't see that."

"Detective, that is enough! I'll have your badge, do you understand?"

Berlin flipped the glass award back in the air, higher this time, and readied the bat. When the pillar was almost eye-level, she brought the bat around. There was a satisfying thwack, and the glass went sailing across the room. It hit the far wall and shattered.

She grabbed another one off the shelf and showed it to Abrams. "These work much better than the round one did. Weird, huh?"

"Are you even listening to me?" He was red and shaking again. A very odd look considering he was still on his hands and knees.

Berlin raised her eyebrows. "Actually, I wasn't. Did you say something helpful about dear old Charlie or his pal, Ben?"

"I'll have your badge, damn it! You'll be through at the department."

"Guess not. Well, that's fine…" flip… "I'm pretty sure…" swing… "I'm done with it, anyway." Crack!

The award swung wildly and careened into one of the glass shelves. Pottery, awards, and frames went flying as three shelves crashed down.

"Oh, wow. That one was way better." She turned to Abrams. "What did you think?"

Abrams was staring at the bat, still in her hand. Berlin looked and saw the bat now had a crack running down its length. She looked back at Abrams. "That's probably not good, huh?"

"You fucking cunt!" He was almost shrieking.

If looks could kill, she'd be a dead woman standing.

Berlin lifted the bat so she could examine the crack closer. "It's really not that bad. I'm sure a little gorilla glue -"

His eyes narrowed. "Do you think this is a game? Do you know what happens if I pull my support? He'll kill you himself for losing him the election."

Berlin eyed him around the bat. "What election would that be?"

Abrams smiled, baring his teeth at her. It wasn't a sane look for him. "I don't even care. We don't want someone running this county if he can't even control his own officers. And I'll make sure he knows he has you to thank for it."

Berlin approached the table and squatted down, keeping her weight on the balls of her feet. She met Abrams's eyes. "You. David Mitchell. Ben Rivera.

Charles Bryant. And Captain Luke Phillips. The people who swore to help and protect others. Instead, you destroyed and disposed of them." She studied the bat still in her hands. Signed by the legends of New England and given to Abrams as a symbol of the power he held in the city. Berlin smiled to herself. How fitting it was now broken.

She held the bat out to Abrams. He kept his hands on the floor. "You can tell Captain Phillips that he needs to clean up his own messes from now on. I'm done with it."

The bat fell to the floor and Berlin stood up. "Tell him yourself. I'm done with both of you."

*****

It was just after seven when Berlin walked into Alex Johnson's office. Johnson was sitting behind her desk, several paper calendars in front of her. She was furiously erasing something from one of them and muttering under her breath. "You'd think in this day and age of technology, there would be an easier way to create a game schedule than to write it all down and erase it repeatedly." She threw the pencil down. It skittered across the desk and fell to the floor.

Berlin picked it up and set it back on the desk and then sat in the chair across from Johnson. "Why don't you create it on a whiteboard first?"

"Because kids think it's funny to change games around on you when you use a whiteboard. The little bastards."

Berlin raised her eyebrows. "That's a wonderful thing to say."

"Well, it's true."

"So why are you here? If you don't like the kids."

Johnson sighed. "I never said I didn't like them. I just said they can be little bastards." She finally met Berlin's eyes. "What can I do for you, Detective?"

Alex Johnson looked like she hadn't slept in days. Dark smudges sat under her eyes, and her skin held a sallow appearance. The customary braid was in place, but disheveled.

"Why did you send Albert Griffin to find me yesterday?"

Johnson's eyebrows rose. "I thought we were going to talk about Bryant."

Berlin set the folded papers she'd been carrying all day on the chair next to her. She crossed her arms over her chest, and said, "I'll wager this is all the same conversation. So why did you?"

Johnson looked down at the calendar and picked her pencil back up. She set it back down almost immediately. Then she shrugged. "I asked him to meet you because I thought he might help ease your conscious about leaving Bryant's accident alone. Give you a better understanding of the type of person Bryant was."

Berlin shook her head. "The fact that he was a complete scumbag doesn't make it okay he was killed."

"Why do you continue to insist that someone killed him? Why can't you accept it really was an accident?"

"Because there are too many details that are off. It doesn't make sense."

Johnson let out a harsh laugh. "People die all the

time and it makes no sense."

When Berlin opened her mouth to protest, Johnson held out her hand, stalling her. "If I tell someone that I hope they get hit by a bus and die, and it happens, did I kill that person?"

Where was she going with this? "Obviously not."

"So, what if someone suggested to Bryant that he put up a shelf? And he put one up, and too much weight was put on it? Does that make the person who suggested it a murderer? It was Bryant's decision, correct? It was his lack of knowledge that ultimately caused his death."

Berlin tilted her head and studied Johnson. "Is that what happened? You suggested he put it up and then just waited for something to happen? Or was it Nichole's suggestion?"

Johnson stared blankly at her.

Berlin picked up the papers, opened them up and pulled the pink sticky note off the picture of Ashley. She held it out across the desk.

Johnson looked at it but didn't take it. "What's that?"

"It's yours. I pulled it off the door yesterday. So, let's just skip the part where you pretend you don't know Nichole."

Johnson shrugged. "Fine. I know her. She works here. What does this have to do with anything?"

Berlin took the pictures of Rivera and Bryant out of her stack and put them on the desk. "I think it's interesting that you, Nichole, and Kay Bryant all know each other, and Kay's and Nichole's husbands are both dead." The picture of Ashley went down on top of them.

"And it all seems to come back to this school, and Ashley Williams."

Johnson studied the picture of Ashley and finally picked it up. She was quiet for several seconds, a sad smile on her face. Then she put it back down and looked at Berlin. "You have it partially correct, Detective. But this is bigger than just Ashley's death."

Heather's warning and Brittney Thompson's face flashed in Berlin's mind. "Why don't we start with Ashley. What happened here three years ago?"

Johnson sighed again. "You need to understand that I never met Ashley. They hired me a few months after she died. So, the information I have about what happened is hearsay. Whispers, rumors, suspicions…" She rubbed her hands over her face hard enough it made Berlin wince. Then Johnson sat back in her chair, her arms crossed over her chest. Instead of looking defensive, she just looked exhausted. "I was a recommended hire from a friend."

"Nichole." Berlin said.

Johnson nodded. "Nichole and I knew each other from college, and we kept in touch inconsistently. I was working at a school in Massachusetts, but she knew I was looking at other options and other sports programs. After Ashley's death, Nichole called me and asked if I would consider coming north. To help with some students who were having difficulties."

"There wasn't someone already at the school who could do it?"

"I asked the same thing. I thought it was weird she'd contact me out of the blue; we weren't that close. Nichole said they wanted someone from outside. I learned after that she wanted someone who hadn't been tied to this incestuous pit their entire career…"

Her voice trailed off, almost as though she didn't want to continue with that train of thought. "Most of the kids who go to school here have family legacies with the academy. Their parents went here, their grandparents. Aunts, uncles. The parents pay an insane amount of money to the school for years, calling it a donation to ensure their kids have a place here once they're of age. It's largely how the school stays in business."

Berlin shrugged. "I think it's crazy, but if parents care that much about their kids going to a particular school, what's the problem?"

"The problem is," Johnson said, sitting up, "if there are issues with any kids or staff members, no one wants to do anything about it because the school can't afford to lose public or private support."

Berlin shook her head. "Why would disciplining someone who did something wrong cause loss of support for the school?"

"For small stuff, it doesn't. But we aren't talking about small stuff like breaking curfew or missing an assignment."

"You're saying for more serious issues, no one wanted to do anything that might rock the money boat?" At Johnson's nod, Berlin asked, "So the kids would just get away with it? Because if the punishment was harsh enough, they could complain to their parents, and the school might lose that financial support."

"Yup. And the big issue with that is the kids lose protection, too. Even if they don't realize it. If everyone knows the school won't take any action that might make it look bad…"

"It becomes a free for all," Berlin finished.

"Nichole wanted someone here who would worry more about the kids than the money their families brought in. The people who work at this school would rather eat one of their own than risk losing financial backing because of a scandal." Johnson gave Berlin a tight smile. "Me, I don't care what happens to the school or the teachers and administrators in it. The whole thing could burn to the ground." She leaned forward, her thin face intent. "But I care about the students here. And I'll do whatever I can to make sure they're safe. Nichole knew that, and that's why she asked me to come."

"Safe from what?" Berlin asked. She already knew, but she wanted Johnson to confirm it.

"From the people like Bryant and Rivera. From whoever started this whole sick ring. The people who took kids who were already socially and emotionally compromised and exploited their weaknesses."

"The pictures that Albert showed me… Rivera's hand on Ashley's shoulder. He looked like he thought he owned her."

Johnson nodded. "That's what they all did. Made these kids believe they were possessions. Rivera was especially good at it. He made Ashley think she wasn't worth anything more than that."

"And Bryant helped him."

Johnson nodded again. "These assholes took turns picking a student they wanted. Usually the kid had a screwed up home life or had been through something shitty. Or the parents were just too busy to pay them any attention. This group worked together to groom their victim, convinced him or her to trust them, that they only wanted the best for them. That they loved them. There would be some type of relationship for a little while, and then the kid would be cut loose. And these poor kids are left even more devastated and fucked up in the head."

Although it was what she'd suspected, she could still feel the horror and rage building inside of her. Berlin took a deep breath and tried to calm her heart rate. "You said Ashley wasn't the first victim. How many others?"

"Honestly? I have no idea. From what I've been told, there were suspicions about this kind of thing happening years before Ashley came forward. But it wasn't until she did that anyone knew for sure. And tried to stop it."

Wait, wait, wait... pay attention, Berlin. "Who did Ashley tell?" She looked at Ashely's picture. "You weren't here, so it wasn't you." Berlin looked at Johnson. "Ashley went to Nichole. She told Nichole about what Rivera was doing to her, to the other kids. And Nichole confronted him the night he died."

Johnson kept her lips pressed firmly together, but Berlin didn't need to her say anything. She knew it was true.

"And that's also why she killed Charles Bryant."

"I told you over the phone, I'm not supposed to discuss him with you."

"Fine," Berlin said. "Then how about David Mitchell?"

Johnson opened her mouth and then shut it. She looked and Berlin, uncertainty on her face for the first time. "What?"

"Which one of you killed David Mitchell? I'm

assuming he had something to do with this."

"Dr. Mitchell is dead?" She didn't look upset. Just a little… surprised.

Berlin's eyes narrowed as she studied Johnson.

"You knew."

"I don't know what you're talking about." Johnson started tidying up her desk. "I really need to go, Detective."

Berlin slapped her hand down on the papers Johnson was gathering together. She stood up and leaned over the desk. "Where is she?"

"You don't get it, Detective. If Mitchell is dead, she's gone."

That didn't feel right. "You know that for sure?"

Johnson stared at her. Stubbornness written across her face.

"If there's someone else, you have to tell me! Nichole's on her way out, which means she'll go after them now! Before she leaves."

"I don't care!" Johnson's eyes were wild. "Those men were animals. Worse than animals. They preyed on weak, vulnerable kids, and no one lifted a finger. Not even when one of them was brave enough to come forward." She stabbed a finger at the picture of Ashley. "Ashley Williams is dead because men refused to listen to her or do anything about it, even when it was their job. They're just as guilty as the bastards who assaulted her." She was breathing like she'd just finished a mile sprint.

Berlin's thoughts raced as she processed Johnson's rant. Because of those who refused to listen. Even when it was their job. *Come on Berlin, think!*

If Nichole was going for one last strike, she'd

want it to be big.

“Fuck.” *Phillips*

CHAPTER TWENTY

Berlin raced down the hallway from Alex Johnson's office, stabbing buttons on her phone as she ran. Even knowing it was a pointless attempt, she tried Nichole's number first. An automated voice told her the number was no longer in service. She tried Phillips's number next. After four rings, it went to voicemail.

"God damn it!" She hit 2 on speed dial as she flew around the wall of the stairwell and bolted down the two flights of stairs. As she hit the side door and entered the dark courtyard, Pete's voice droned on in her ear about who to call in an emergency. Berlin was at the far edge of the yard, heading into the parking lot, when he finally told her she could leave a message.

Racing towards her car, she yelled into the phone, "Nichole is going after Phillips! I'm getting ready to leave the school, but I don't know where she is or where Phillips is! Help me -" The key in the car's lock, Berlin found herself looking in the direction of the student dorms. In her mind, she could see the gigantic oak tree in the courtyard of the buildings with the four benches spaced around it. The items of remembrance and loss placed at the base of the tree. In front of the dorms where Ashley died.

Berlin forced herself to calm down and said clearly into her phone, "I think she's here, Pete. At the school. And I think she has Phillips."

She hit the end button on the phone and put it back in her pocket. She scanned the far end of the campus, but there was still no movement. Berlin slid her pistol out from its holster inside the waistband of her jeans, checked that it was loaded, and the safety was on. She slid it back into the holster and checked her coat pocket. No clip.

"Shit!"

She had an extra loaded clip inside her car, but that meant opening the door and potentially drawing attention to herself. Even though it wasn't that late, the parking lot was strangely empty. Berlin focused on the dorm buildings again. She couldn't see anything, which probably meant anyone standing by the dorms wouldn't be able to see what was happening in the parking lot. Possibly. If there were other car doors opening and closing, she could take the chance… maybe she was wrong, and Nichole wasn't even here…

"And maybe I'll get my ass blown off just standing here like an idiot." She had to decide and move. "Okay, no clip."

The adrenaline racing through her, Berlin abandoned her car and began moving across the parking lot toward the closest building. It was similar to all the other buildings, rectangular with the red brick exterior. Small ornamental trees and bushes were sporadically placed to give the whole thing more appeal. Luckily, they also provided some cover.

Berlin paused at the far corner and studied the first dorm building. It was at least 100 feet away, made up of open ground. If she angled toward the back of the building, she increased the distance by at least another 50 feet, but she had a better shot of staying unseen. She could then make her way to the back of the second building and toward the tree.

Deciding it was her best option, Berlin took a deep breath and moved. She kept her steps quick and light, pausing briefly every so often to listen and scan the surrounding buildings. As soon as she was past the corner of the first dorm, she ran the length of the back of the building and then stopped at the next corner.

The only thing she could hear was her heart pounding in her ears. Berlin took a couple of deep breaths, holding the last one until the surrounding sounds started filtering in. An occasional shout of a student, some laughter. A car starting in the parking lot. *Sure, now you're there.* Nothing close and nothing out of the ordinary.

There was minimal light behind the buildings, so little risk of being seen. Berlin stopped stalling and dashed as quickly as she could across the open space between the buildings. Keeping up her pace, she crossed the back of the middle building and stopped just before rounding the last corner. She quieted her breathing again and stood still. Nothing.

Berlin tried to bring the front of the buildings, courtyard, and location of the tree into her mind. The tree was directly in front of the middle dorm building; maybe 100 feet from the main entrance. The benches were about 30 feet from the tree trunk. The only cover she would have was the large shrubs in front of the dorm buildings, and if Nichole was on the opposite side of the courtyard, Berlin was screwed.

Time to move, Nichole won't wait forever to kill him. Berlin pulled her pistol from its holster and stepped around the corner of the building. She stayed as close as she could to the wall, using it as cover, but careful not to press herself against the rough brick. She moved cautiously forward, scanning the area in front of her.

She was almost three-quarters of the way along the building when she heard a muffled grunt, followed by Nichole's voice. Her tone was sharp but the words inaudible.

The one time I would have been fine with being wrong. Resisting the urge to hurry, Berlin continued along the wall, stepping carefully between any of the bushes and the brick. Finally, she reached the front corner. Berlin crouched and dared a look around the corner of the building. Luck was with her.

Nichole and Phillips were on the near side of the courtyard. Phillips was hunched over on the ground, his arms bent awkwardly behind him and his hands tied. He was gagged but was doing his best to yell at Nichole through the cloth stuffed in his mouth.

Nichole was throwing something up into the tree, but from the occasional words Berlin caught, whatever she was trying to do wasn't working. It took a few times of the item falling on the ground before Berlin realized Nichole was trying to throw a rope over the lowest branch of the oak tree.

She's going to hang him. The way Ashley killed herself. Berlin took two steps back and crouched next to a bush.

She could still walk away. The thought sent chills up her spine. She wanted to. A part of her, a bigger part than she cared to admit to, agreed with what Alex Johnson had said. Phillips and the police department had played a role in Ashley's death. If Phillips had done his job, Ashley would have graduated and probably been off at college somewhere, instead of in the ground.

From what little information she'd gained from Abrams, Phillips was running a crooked race for sheriff. It wouldn't surprise her if the race was tied to what was happening at the academy. Based on the paperwork in Pete's files, Phillips had also received financial compensation for the department. It was dirty money and tainted the LRPD because of it. It left Berlin wanting to walk away and leave Phillips to his fate bad enough she could picture doing it.

But the thought of Laurel, and how proud she'd been when Berlin started taking criminal justice classes, kept Berlin from taking the first step. Instead, she silently cursed Phillips and moved back around the corner.

Nichole had the rope up over the lowest branch and secured. Phillips was standing up, his hands still tied behind his back. He balanced slightly on his toes, and it looked like his feet were also tied. Even bound the way he was, with the noose was around his neck, he was struggling against the rope

Berlin looked around the scene, confused. How the hell did Nichole expect to hang him if his feet were on the ground?

From the occasional words Berlin caught,

Nichole was talking to him, but not loud enough for Berlin to make sense of what was being said.

She needed to move closer. There was a large shrub beside the front entrance of the dorm building and another one further up along the walkway. If she could make it to the second shrub, she'd probably be close enough to hear Nichole and Phillips. The problem was it put her in a vulnerable position. She'd be on the ground, making a quick retreat or get-away nearly impossible.

Before she had a chance to decide, Berlin's phone buzzed in her back pocket. She backed away down the wall until Nichole and Phillips were no longer in view. She pulled out her phone and glanced at the screen. Pete.

As quietly as possible, Berlin said, "She has him strung up by a rope but he's still alive."

"Where the fuck are you?" Pete sounded seriously pissed.

"I told you were I am. I'm on the school campus, the common area by the dorm buildings."

"We're less than ten minutes away. Don't let her kill Phillips, Redding. And don't let her get away. Try to get any information you can. And don't hang up!"

"You don't ask for much, do you?" Berlin hissed. "Now shut up so I can hear what she's saying."

She slipped the phone into her coat pocket and the pistol back in the holster and returned to her spot beside the bushes. She had her orders. It was time to move.

Berlin progressed to the corner of the building, and then staying as low to the ground as possible, she made her way to the first shrub. The branches were too low to the ground to hide under, so she scooted around it and peered out toward the oak tree.

She could see Phillips's face. He looked like he'd gone several rounds in the ring with a guy twice his size. Whatever Nichole had hit him with, it had been effective. Even beaten and with a rope around his neck, Phillips still wore the same prickish expression on his face.

Nichole's back was toward Berlin. She had one hand on the end of what looked like a handle. She moved toward the base of the tree, her voice shrill and angry. Berlin picked up most of what she said, but not everything.

She heard, "because of you," and then Nichole pointed at the base of the tree and one of the buildings with the handled thing. Berlin finally saw what was on the other end.

What do you need a sledgehammer for, Nichole?

Keeping low to the ground, Berlin inched her way to the second shrub, hoping Phillips was smart enough to ignore her if he saw her. She didn't have to go far before she could hear everything Nichole was saying.

"… your wife… no, your daughter, think if they knew you ignored Ashley's cry for help?"

Phillips yelled into his gag, sounding slightly frantic.

"I'm sorry, Captain Phillips. What was that? Actual concern?" Nichole stepped forward and reached up toward his face. She grabbed the cloth and yanked it down, out of his mouth. "You were saying?"

"If my daughter was a whore, she'd deserve no better than the bitch who died."

Nichole shook her head, sending short curls

bouncing. "Wrong answer, Captain." The sledgehammer came up waist high and then down into Phillips's right knee. He went down with a sharp cry and a horrifying crunch of bone. The only thing that kept him off the ground was the rope around his neck.

Berlin lay still, stunned once again by Nichole's viciousness.

Nichole's face held no expression as she watched Phillips struggle to get his left leg under him. She looked at the sledgehammer. "Let's try again with another question."

Berlin finally understood Nichole's plan for hanging Phillips. "Jesus Christ. She's really going to do it." Berlin whispered.

"What? What did you say? Redding!"

Berlin grabbed for her phone as Pete shouted at her, searching for the end button. She looked over at the tree and found Nichole staring in her direction. She stopped moving, but it was too late.

"Why don't you join us, Detective Redding? I'm sure Captain Phillips would appreciate seeing a familiar face."

Keeping her eyes on Nichole, she held the phone close to her chest and whispered harshly, "Shut up, Pete. And get your ass here now! She saw me." Berlin put the phone on the ground, a little distance from the shrub, and scooted back. She got up slowly, keeping her hands where Nichole could see them and the phone just in front of the toe of her boot. And then she waited.

Nichole's threads were quickly coming unraveled. Not surprising given she'd probably killed at least one person in the last twenty-four hours. She was wearing the same outfit she'd been in the previous night and her hair stuck up in crazy curls all over her head. She looked like she hadn't slept since the last night they'd been together.

"You look like shit, Nichole. I don't think a life of crime agrees with you."

Nichole frowned. "It's mostly your fault. If you had just let this whole thing go, I wouldn't have had to rush. So, thank you for screwing things up so spectacularly, Berlin."

Berlin shrugged and took a small step, scooting the phone forward with her. "You knew this is what I did, Nichole. Which is why I'm assuming you started spending time with me?" Another partial step forward. How close did she dare get it?

When Nichole didn't argue, Berlin said, "Well, thanks for not lying about it, I guess." One more half-step was all she was willing to gamble on, and with the next step she left the phone behind. *Listen hard, Pete.*

With her hands still up, Berlin finished her approach, keeping her steps short and careful at first and then lengthening her stride.

When she was within ten feet of Nichole and Phillips, Nichole said, "That's close enough."

Berlin stopped. Trying for ballsy, she focused on her boss and let out a low whistle.

"Well, Phillips, I see you met someone else who doesn't appreciate your treatment of women."

Phillips balanced on his left leg. Every time he swayed to one side, the rope cut into his neck, forcing him to quickly correct his balance.

"Shoot her, Redding!" He was sweating profusely and heavily sucking in air, but instead of sounding scared or worried, he sounded pissed. It was almost admirable. If he wasn't such a crooked bastard.

"For what? Beating the shit out of you? I don't think that's a shooting-type offense, Captain."

"For killing David Mitchell, you stupid bitch!"

Nichole shoved Phillips off balance and watched him choke as the rope caught him. "That's not how we talk to ladies, Luke. We've already been through this."

Berlin took a quick step forward. Then, trying for nonchalant, she lied over his choking, "The report hasn't come back yet, Captain. There's no proof Nichole had anything to do with Mitchell's death." *Come on, Pete! Where are you?*

Phillips regained his balance. While he was too busy gagging and coughing to say something stupid, Berlin said to Nichole, "As of now, we don't have you for anything, Nichole. If you kill Phillips, your life is over."

Nichole laughed. "You and I both know I'm not walking away from this, Berlin."

"Okay, fine. You won't walk away from kidnapping and torture. But you're talking about the difference between a couple of years and a lifetime. Come on, Nichole. I'll put in a good word for you. We'll tell them about the abuse you received from Ben, maybe get you a lighter sentence. I can even come visit you and help you start a new life once you're out." Half a step forward.

"Shut up, Redding! She's done! We both know it, and she does, too!" Even through his hacking, Phillips was still being a pain in the ass.

Nichole shook her head. "He's right, Berlin. I've gone too far." She looked at Berlin, her expression caught between sadness and insanity "You're right, too, though. I started spending time with you so I'd know what the police knew about Charles's accident. But then I really did start to like you. I wish we'd stayed at the cabin. Or run away together. Or that you had just let this go when you had the chance!"

"What about you, Nichole?" Berlin demanded. She took another step, her heart pounding at Nichole's confession. "Why didn't you let it go? You didn't have to kill these men. Someone would have listened to you if you'd brought it up again."

"Don't you get it? I'm the one who Ashley talked to. And then, when she trusted me, I convinced her to let me file a complaint against those men. I convinced her to talk to the police. To the school. Ashley is dead because of me! I thought you of all people would understand."

Nichole turned and looked at Phillips. "He's the last one who has to pay. He knew about the assaults at the school. He's known for years what was happening to those kids. And instead of doing his job, he took bribes and payoffs, and promises of support when he ran for sheriff."

"You can't prove any of it," Phillips said.

Nichole smiled. She was looking even more unhinged. "What do you say, Berlin? Want to bet on how long it takes him to admit to it?"

Berlin inched closer. "I'm pretty sure I'd get written up for taking that bet."

"While we were getting to know each other better, Luke told me you were the least effective officer he's ever worked with."

Nichole was probably lying, but it sounded like something Phillips would say. "Well, in that case…"

Phillips snarled at her. "I'll have your badge, Redding! You're done in the department!"

Berlin eyed Phillips and closed another inch between them. "That's funny. Your pal Jack Abrams told me the same thing just before I demolished his office. He also said he was done doing your dirty work."

That at least shut him up for two seconds. "You don't have anything, Redding. And God knows you're too stupid -"

Nichole brought the sledgehammer around and struck his already shattered knee. Phillips howled this time.

Over the noise, Nichole said, "I'm tired of listening to you, Captain. The next thing out of your mouth better be admitting to your part in Ashley's death. Or, so help me, I'll beat you with this thing until you wish I'd killed you. And make sure you speak nice and loud so the police listening to Berlin's phone can hear you." Nichole prodded the knee again, evoking another howl of pain. "Say it! I want to hear you admit to it!"

It was almost impossible to make out what he said when Phillips bit out, "Yes! I did it!"

An eerie look of peace settled across Nichole's face. "Thank you, Captain Phillips. That's all I wanted." She raised the sledgehammer again.

Berlin pulled her pistol and pointed it at Nichole. "Drop it, Nichole. This is done. Now."

Nichole glared at her but lowered the sledgehammer.

"Step away from Phillips and get on the ground," Berlin said.

Nichole looked toward the flashing lights, finally racing into the parking lot, and then back at Berlin.

"On the ground, Nichole!"

That crazy smile. "I don't think so."

Nichole swung Phillips into Berlin, hard. Phillips bumped into her, and in a classic rookie move, Berlin took the bait. She put her focus on moving him out of her line of sight and before she knew what was happening, Nichole brought the sledgehammer down across Berlin's arm. Berlin dropped the pistol.

Nichole had it in her hands within seconds.

Berlin's forearm and hand were completely numb. She sucked in air at the pain and wondered how something could be numb and hurt so much at the same time.

Nichole made a disapproving sound. "I thought you were a better cop than this."

Berlin refused to look at her gun in Nichole's hands and focused on Nichole's face. "Think about what you're doing, Nichole. If you kill Phillips, you'll have to kill me, too. You know I can't let you walk away from this." There was yelling coming from the parking lot now, and car doors slamming.

A single shot rang across the courtyard, followed by a cut off scream. The bullet shattered Phillips's left leg, and with nothing left to support him, he went down. The rope stretched taunt when his full weight hit it. He started gagging and choking almost immediately, his body thrashing as it fought against the loss of air.

Berlin turned back to Nichole and found the pistol now held on her. Nichole's gaze was unwavering as Phillips choked beside her. "Let's see if you can practice what you preach, Berlin. Are you going to save Phillips? Or are you going to come after me?" Without another word, Nichole turned away from Berlin and dashed toward the back end of the dorm buildings.

Berlin took a few steps forward but Phillips gagging and choking stopped her. She watched Nichole's fleeing figure another second and then turned to Phillips.

"There's no way I'm letting you get away with this shit that easy, you dick." She reached into her boot with her good hand and pulled out her knife. Cutting with her left hand was awkward, but the rope was old. With four slashes Berlin had Phillips down and on the ground.

She turned around, searching the far end of the buildings just in time to see Nichole dash through the tree line that separated the buildings from the back parking lot. And then she was gone.

*****

They put Phillips in an ambulance and took him away. The handful of officers left on scene were finishing up taking pictures, collecting evidence, and cleaning up. A crowd of about twenty students and staff members had also gathered. The students watched the police and took selfies, joking and laughing like it was a big, impromptu party. The staff watched and chastised the students when they got too rambunctious. Alex Johnson and Albert Griffin were not among them.

Berlin observed everything from a distance, glad she wasn't required to take part in any of it.

Heavy footsteps approached her from behind, announcing Pete's arrival. He stopped next to her, eyeing the academy crowd.

Without looking away from the activity, Berlin said, "It's interesting how an hour ago the campus was a ghost town. I mean, no one was around."

Pete nodded toward the group of students and staff. "Apparently there was some re-enactment of a Harvard butter protest at the assembly building tonight. Almost everyone was there."

She looked at him, her eyebrows raised. "A butter protest? Is that some weird joke?"

"I don't know. I'm just telling you what they told me."

"Huh. Strange." Berlin said. She wanted to fidget but had nothing to fidget with. Instead, she blurted out, "How pissed are you at me?"

Pete gave a deep sigh. "Where do I even start?"

At her look, he shrugged. "I'm not real happy you acted on your own. If I'd known you would do that, I wouldn't have left the files for you. But other than that," he shrugged again. "She didn't give you much choice, Redding. You did what any of us would have done."

Berlin shook her head. "The only reason I saved Phillips was because I didn't want him seen as some sacrificial hero taken out by a madwoman. I want him to pay for what he's done."

"It doesn't matter what your motive was. You still did the right thing."

They stood quietly for a minute.

"I feel like I really messed this up. I should have known there was something wrong with Nichole. I'm a cop, goddamn it! And Nichole was responsible for at least two murders. Three, if she lied about accidentally killing Rivera." Berlin looked at Pete. "How did I not know?"

"Actually, we just have her for Mitchell's death, and that happened after she'd taken off on you. But it's looking like Bryant really was an accident."

"What?" Berlin couldn't believe it.

"Yup. Andrea Butler finally came forward and admitted she'd been sleeping with Bryant. They had sex at his house the day he died. That's why he lied to Kay about having a meeting. We still don't understand why he was in the basement storage room after work, though. Or why he put the shelf up in the first place."

Berlin sighed. She really did have it all screwed up. "Johnson hinted that either she or Nichole suggested he put the shelf up. And that too much weight was added to the shelf. Maybe by Nichole when she was visiting Kay. Maybe by Kay."

"It's not one of those things we'll ever know, Redding. So, forget it. And stop beating yourself up about missing the part about Nichole being a basket case. We all have crazies in our past."

Pete paused, and Berlin could feel him studying her. "But just so we're clear, you know we'll eventually catch her, right?"

Berlin met his gaze and nodded. "I know. And I know she needs to be caught."

She slipped her hand into her pocket and took out her badge. She looked down at it, running her thumb over the shield and her badge number. Then she looked back up and held it out to Pete. "But it won't be with my help."

Pete looked down at the offered badge. “Come on, Redding. I know you liked her -”

“It’s not about her, Pete. Like you said earlier, it’s about doing the right thing. And for me, this is the right thing. For a lot of reasons.” She stepped forward and took his hand. She turned it so his palm was facing up and then placed her badge on it and smiled at him.

“You know I’ll be around. You’re not getting rid of me that easy.” She patted his arm and started walking toward the parking lot.

CHAPTER TWENTY-ONE

December

A car door slammed shut, drawing Berlin's attention away from her wood pile. She finished stacking the pieces she was holding, brushed the bark and wood chips from her wool work shirt, and exited the woodshed. She whistled and a lanky, shaggy-haired puppy looked up from the piece of wood she'd been chewing on. The puppy tilted her head, giving Berlin a puzzled look. As always, it made Berlin laugh.

"Come on. We have a visitor. Go do your job and attack him."

The puppy stood up, shook, and trotted away on legs too long for her frame.

"What the hell is that thing?"

"Never mind, I guess the visitor found us."

Pete stopped in his tracks, staring down at the puppy who was happily sniffing his legs.

"That's a puppy, Pete. Aren't you detective

types supposed to be better at identification?"

"That's not a puppy, Redding. That's a full-sized dog."

"Not for an Irish Wolf Hound. Meara's only four-months old." Berlin bent down and stoked Meara's head. The puppy grabbed Berlin's fingers lightly, released them and then took off. "She'll be at least as tall as my hip when she's fully grown." Berlin straightened back up.

"Why would you get something like that?"

Berlin looked at the puppy, now rolling in the snow. A look of k-9 bliss across her furry face. "Because she makes me laugh." She looked at her old partner. "Why don't we go in the cabin and warm up? I've been outside for a few hours and could use a break."

"Thanks. I'll take coffee, too. If you have it."

"Sure. Why not? Maybe I can bake you a cake while I'm at it."

"Well, if you're offering…"

When they were in the cabin, Berlin took off the wool shirt and hung it near the wood stove. She pulled off her boots and slipped into leather slippers. "Shoes off. I don't want snow and water on the floor."

Pete sighed but did as he was told.

He settled himself at the little table and Berlin gave Meara a beef bone by the wood stove. Once the puppy's focus was on it, Berlin entered the kitchen. "Do you mind if the coffee is from this morning? It's still hot."

"No, that's fine."

She poured two mugs of coffee, set them on the table, and set the creamer and sugar next to them. Berlin sat down across from Pete.

He added sugar to his cup and said, "Looks like you've been busy up here."

She nodded, "There was a lot that needed to be done so I could live up here through the winter. I think we're finally ready."

He looked around. "It doesn't look like you have anyone close by. You okay up here by yourself?"

She nodded toward the puppy. "I have the rat for company. And mom's been up a couple of times. Jamie and Ellen even brought the kids up around Thanksgiving."

"You don't miss being closer to them?"

Berlin sighed, "I know that's not what you're here to talk about. And not that I haven't missed you, but what can I do for you, Pete?"

Pete studied his coffee. "I didn't get much of a chance to talk to you at Tom's funeral."

Berlin's heart tightened at the mention of her dad's death. She stirred cream into her mug until the pain eased a bit. "Yeah, well, not a great time for any of us." She put her spoon down and took a sip of her coffee.

"No. But I've talked to your mom, and she said I should come up here and see you."

Berlin just waited. Pete grinned at her. "Still remember my old tricks, huh?"

When she still said nothing, he sighed. "I wanted to be the one to tell you. Phillips is officially gone. We have a new officer in charge of the department."

Berlin studied his face. He looked tense about something. Worried… She cocked her head and gave him a crooked smile. "Congratulations, Captain Lewis.

It's well deserved."

Pete let out a whoosh of air. "Thanks, Redding. I didn't know if you'd be pissed about it."

Her brow furrowed. "Why would I be pissed?"

"Because of how the whole academy thing played out. I know you took the brunt for Nichole Kellner disappearing. And I know I set you up to run with it so I could keep my name out of it."

"Well, when you put it that way…" But she smiled at him over her mug. "When did you suspect Phillips was involved?"

"It wasn't until after you talked to the old guy at the school. I'd already found the investigation report, but I hadn't realized Phillips pencil-whipped it. After talking to you, I looked back at the report and got a bad feeling about it. It wasn't his style to be so sloppy, so I figured there had to be a reason." Pete sighed. "And then I came across the money given to the department by the school."

Berlin got up and brought the coffeepot back to the table. She divided the rest of it between them and set the empty pot on the table. "What's happening with Phillips? Will he spend any time in prison?"

Pete sat back, looking relaxed. "I hope so. I've done everything I can to make sure it happens. It's been a lot of combing through old files, talking to cops who've moved or retired." He sighed. "You know how it goes. No one wants to say anything that will make them look like a rat."

He was quiet for a moment. "We found an interesting case he signed off on, though. The heart attack of one Ben Rivera. It seems Phillips signed off on it, even though the ME commented on unusual burn marks on his chest."

"Why would Phillips have done that?"

Pete shrugged. "Either it was just part of his push to close files, or he didn't want anyone digging too far into Rivera's background."

"Because they may have found other connections between Rivera and Phillips."

"That's what I think, but I've added it to the lengthy list of things we probably won't ever know. Phillips was damn good at hiding his involvement in anything shady."

"What about any of the others from the academy?" Berlin asked, frowning.

"A few victims, some who were at the school over ten years ago, and staff members have come forward. With their statements we've been able to get a clearer picture of what roles guys like Mitchell and Bryant played." Pete looked grim. "But I gotta be honest, Redding. The active offenders are dead. So, it's a question of do we drag things up that a lot of the victims don't want to go through, or focus on making sure it doesn't happen again?" In an instant, the grim look was replaced with a smile. "Actually, Mitchell's asshole brother may end up doing some time. We found out he was involved in Mitchell's nasty little sports physical program at the school."

"At least that's something," Berlin said. "But I'd rather see Phillips behind bars."

"Me too. I just don't know if it'll happen. Either way, he'll never work in law enforcement again."

Looking disinterestedly at her coffee mug, Berlin asked, "What about Nichole? Have you heard anything on her whereabouts?"

He barked out a laugh. “You know I can’t tell you that, Redding.”

She raised her eyebrows.

“Yeah, like there’s anything to tell, anyway.” He shook his head. “She did an expert job of disappearing.” He looked closely at Berlin. “What about you? You haven’t heard from her, have you?”

Berlin held his gaze. “No, Pete. I haven’t heard anything from her. And I don’t expect to.”

He stared her down for another few seconds and then said, “Yeah, okay. I didn’t think you would.”

Berlin sat back in her chair and folder her arms over her stomach. “You know, what kills me is with everything we dug up, and with everyone hurt by this, nothing’s changed.”

“They’ve made some changes at the academy. They’re talking about limiting the number of years someone can work there. Tightening background checks. Limiting volunteer time. They think that will help.”

Berlin laughed, but there was no humor in it. “I don’t think that will do it, Pete.”

Pete tapped his spoon on the table. Meara looked up from her bone to see what the noise was. When nothing else happened, she lost interest. Pete said, “You know that’s how our system works, Redding. It’s not perfect, but it’s what we have.”

She nodded. “I know. I just forgot how frustrating it is to be on the civilian side of it.”

He nudged her leg under the table with his foot. “You can have your job back whenever you want it.”

Berlin snorted. “Thanks, Pete. I appreciate it. But I think I’m done with that.”

"Yeah, I figured that's what you'd say. But just know I'd be honored to work with you again."

"Thanks."

Pete looked around at the little cabin again. "Are you sure you won't go crazy up here? I mean, what do you do all day? There's not even a TV."

"I'm staying plenty busy. I promise."

"Have you thought about what you'll do for work?"

Berlin shrugged. "I'm not sure where I'll land. But right now, I'm free-lancing with an advocacy group. Heather Christiansen started it with some other students in her program, so I'll see if I can help them."

He nodded. "Yeah, I can see you being good at that. What are you doing for them?"

She grinned. "I'm a liaison between their group and the police departments."

Pete groaned.

Laughing, Berlin said, "I did warn you that you wouldn't be rid of me that easy."

Later, as he was putting his coat on to leave, Pete glanced at the small bulletin board hanging on the wall. There was a picture of the two of them together in uniform. Pete's arm was slung over Berlin's shoulder, a big grin on his face. She had a fake scowl on hers. "Cute picture. Good-looking guy."

"Yeah, yeah." Berlin slipped her boots on and grabbed the wool shirt, now nice and toasty warm from the fire. "I'll walk you out, and then I have more wood to stack before it gets too dark. Hey, mom said something about you coming for Christmas?" When he didn't respond she looked up from buttoning the shirt.

Pete was still staring at the board. Peeking out

from under a grocery list and a picture of Tom and Christine was a postcard. 'Greetings from Formentera, Spain!' was scrawled across a picture of a sandy beach. He studied it for a minute, lifted it away from the board just enough to see there was nothing but Berlin's address on the other side, and then looked at Berlin.

She raised her eyebrows and asked, "What?"

He shook his head, smiled, and said, "Nothing. Yeah, I'll see you at Christmas, Redding."

ABOUT THE AUTHOR

Morgan Currier spends her time writing murder mysteries, fantasy, romance, children's stories, and anything in between that her brain decides to dabble in. She currently has several short stories published in anthologies and on literary websites under the name Francis Currier.

Morgan lives on Bedlam Hollow Farm near the White Mountains with her husband and three of their five sons. She poorly balances her time between family, farming, school, Halloween plans, and writing.

Made in the USA
Middletown, DE
26 January 2021